ALSO BY CHELSEA ICHASO

Little Creeping Things

For Alyssa,

DEAD GIRLS CAN'T TELL SECRETS

So nice meeting you!

♡

Chelsea Ichaso

Chelsea Ichaso

sourcebooks
fire

Copyright © 2022 by Chelsea Ichaso
Cover and internal design © 2022 by Sourcebooks
Cover design and image by Erin Fitzsimmons
Internal design by Ashley Holstrom/Sourcebooks

Sourcebooks and the colophon are registered trademarks of Sourcebooks.

Published by Sourcebooks Fire, an imprint of Sourcebooks
P.O. Box 4410, Naperville, Illinois 60567-4410
(630) 961-3900
sourcebooks.com

Cataloging-in-Publication data is on file with the Library of Congress.

Printed and bound in Canada.
MBP 10 9 8 7 6 5

For Matias,
with love

1

"How's Piper? Any word?" A girl with long, raven-black hair swoops in front of me, blocking my way down the crowded school hall. She blinks dewy eyes and bites her bottom lip like she's about to cry. Like she's been losing sleep worrying about Piper.

I clench my teeth and consider barreling by her. Instead, I shake my head. "No, nothing."

The girl frowns, stepping out of the way. I'm nearly out of earshot when she calls after me, "I really hope she wakes up."

The words pummel my gut. Raven Girl must think it's that easy. She probably thinks going into a coma is like going into some sort of machine, like those hibernation pods in sci-fi movies. The person just lies there for days, weeks, however long it takes for their body to decide it's had enough. And then, like no time has gone by, they wake up.

That's how it used to go in my imagination too. At some point, the person always woke up.

But Piper's not in some cryogenic chamber, waiting for her brain to restart.

I know she might not wake up. Ever.

And I know it's my fault.

I try to blot the girl with the inky hair and fake tears out of my mind. None of these people care about my younger sister, who was far from well known around campus. They're probably just trying to get into my good graces.

But all they're really doing is forcing me to replay everything I did—everything I *didn't* do—to push Piper to her breaking point. I'm one well wish away from ending up a puddle on the crusty linoleum floor.

The school hall is lively and bustling as students rush to first period. It's drafty—it always is in the fall until sometime around eleven, when the sun comes out. I shrug my backpack off and rifle through it for my Grayling High Girls' Soccer jacket. But it's not here. I must've forgotten it. Annoyed, I wrap my arms around myself and trudge to class, goosebumps prickling my arms.

When I reach the end of the lockers, a memory stops me. Piper keeps an extra sweater stuffed inside her locker because she's always cold. No meat on her skinny bones.

I rub my frozen shoulders again. She wouldn't mind. We borrow each other's clothes. I mean, we *would*, if we were closer in size.

And closer in other ways.

A different kind of chill racks my body. She certainly isn't going to need that sweater today.

I head back the way I came, pushing through the herd until I'm at Piper's locker. No one's touched it since the day she fell. Everyone's acting like she's going to waltz back through the school doors any second, even my parents.

Even though they know Piper's prognosis.

My parents, for all their brilliance, are very stubborn.

My backpack slides to the floor, and I work on the lock. The numbers don't come to me right away. We aren't the kind of sisters who share locker combinations or passwords, but I've gotten her books a couple of times when she's been out sick. I dig out my phone and find the combo in my notes. Then I grasp the cold metal and twist until it clicks, falling open.

I tug on the door, and immediately, Piper's scent wafts out. Dusty old books and raspberry vanilla shampoo. My chest constricts. Piper's locker is a reflection of her room at home. The books are neatly lined up at the back. There's a

pile of spiral-bound notebooks on the left. Everything else—
her sweater included—is piled up on the right.

The tardy bell rings, startling me. I take a breath and
reach for the sweater, tugging it from beneath a pile of
ChapSticks, pens, and packs of gum. Being late doesn't worry
me. Teachers tend to make exceptions for the girl whose sister
threw herself off of the town's scenic viewpoint.

Once the sweater is free, I shut the locker door and cradle
the fabric in all of its bright yellow, cotton-blended glory.
Piper looks like a canary when she wears this, frizzy blond
hair spilling over the yellow threads. Suddenly, I don't know
why I thought borrowing the sweater was a good idea. I can't
wear this. It looks like her. Smells like her.

Then again, maybe wrapping a constant reminder around
my body is exactly what I deserve. I shake it out of its perfectly
folded state to slide an arm inside, and something slips out,
tumbling to the floor.

A note.

I bend over to retrieve it. Just an office note, telling Piper
about a change in plans for one of her millions of after-school
clubs.

*Survival Club will be holding an extra skills session after school
today at Vanderwild Point.*

—Mr. Davis

My pulse quickens. Vanderwild Point: the place where Piper tried to take her own life four weeks ago. Despite the chill in the hall, my forehead starts to sweat. In addition to being signed by the Survival Club's advisor, the note is dated.

September sixteenth. The day Piper fell.

2

After I spend all of first period wondering how Piper possibly could've had a Survival Club meeting at the exact place and time of her fall, the bell finally rings. I leap from my desk, ignoring Señora Pérez's last-minute homework instructions.

I scan the hall for my boyfriend, Grant, and spot his dark curls and athletic build through the crowd. He's coming to walk me to World Lit. Hurrying over, I take his hand and drag him to an empty corner.

I glance over my shoulder before facing him. His gorgeous brown skin is flushed pink.

"Missed me, huh?" He wraps both hands around my waist and leans in.

"Of course," I say, pulling back. "But I wanted to ask you about something." I tug the note from the pocket of my jeans and show it to him. Grant's in Survival Club too. "I found this in Piper's locker. Were you at this extra skills session the day she fell?"

His brow furrows as I hand him the note. "No," he says, examining it.

"Really?" Disappointment hits me like a soccer ball to the chest. I was really hoping he could tell me something, anything. "I just don't understand—"

"I wasn't there," he interrupts, "because there was no meeting that day. We always meet on Mondays."

A tingle courses up my spine. "Then why would Piper get a note that says otherwise?" I take the paper back, turning it over in my hand.

Grant shrugs. "Maybe Mr. Davis thought she needed extra practice."

"Just the two of them?" I ask skeptically. "And if that were true—which would be super weird, by the way—why wouldn't he have mentioned it? He would've been there, where she…" Sadness swells in my throat, but I swallow it down. "He would've seen her just hours, maybe minutes, before it happened, right?"

Grant places a hand on my shoulder, peering down at me with concern in his hazel eyes. "Just ask him, Savannah. After chemistry."

"I'd rather have you there," I say.

"Then swing by our meeting after school."

Swing by our meeting. In Mr. Davis's room.

It might be the only way to find out the truth.

Two steps into room twenty-five, I want to creep out into the hall again and shut the door. But I can't.

Not until I find out if someone was really up at the Point with Piper that day.

Mr. Davis sits slouched on top of the desk, the same way he does during chemistry class. He's wearing jeans and a gray collared shirt, and he casually sips coffee from a mug that says WORLD'S MOST OKAY TEACHER. He's young, probably the youngest teacher at Grayling High.

Piper loves him. She was always talking about him. He's probably the reason she joined Survival Club. She took chemistry two years early, because Piper was—*is*—like that, and afterward, he let her become his student TA as part of some program she could put on her college applications. Not that she needed more shiny programs.

Guilt ripples through me, and I take a deep breath.

I can sense someone watching me from the other side of the room. When I glance over, I find Jacey Pritchard, Grant's ex, standing in the middle of a circle of chairs, glaring.

My stomach clenches. I'd forgotten she'd be here.

Where the hell is Grant? I pull out my phone to text him when a deep voice says, "Hi, Savannah."

A chill runs like droplets of cold water down my back, but I force myself to meet his gaze.

"Looking for Grant?" Mr. Davis's blue eyes sparkle at me as he brushes a strand of sandy blond hair off his forehead. The grin is a permanent fixture on his face. All the girls at this school find him so dreamy.

I used to think so too; now I just find Mr. Davis problematic. A possible roadblock in the way of living happily ever after with my boyfriend.

I move closer to the desk. "Actually, I was looking for you." There's a tremor in my voice. I haven't spoken to Mr. Davis directly in weeks. I wasn't planning on speaking to him directly ever again, if I could help it. Each day, I sit in the back of his fifth-period chemistry class and will myself invisible. "I need an extracurricular," I lie. "I was thinking about this club."

Mr. Davis looks surprised. "What about soccer?"

"It's preseason. My parents want me involved in something now."

"Even with things..." His eyes drop to his mug.

"I could probably use the distraction," I mumble over the noise drifting in from the hallway. "I should keep busy. And I think Piper would want me to join this club. Sort of, like, in her honor."

"I understand." His voice is warm.

The truth is, my sister would want me locked in a cell after what I did to her last month. "The only problem is that I might have a scheduling conflict."

"Well, you're here now," he says, tilting his head, "when we meet."

"I know, but Piper said you sometimes have extra skills sessions on Wednesdays."

"Extra skills sessions?"

"Yeah, like, on Mount Liberty or whatever."

He shakes his head. "We only meet on Mondays. There's a biannual backpacking trip, but that's it. Could you commit to that?"

I pause thoughtfully, even though my heartbeat accelerates with each lie. I unzip my backpack and tug out the letter I typed up in the computer lab at lunch. "I think so. Can you do me a favor and sign this? My mom is making me bring it back to prove I made an effort to get involved in something."

Mr. Davis quirks a brow as he takes the note. "Shouldn't I be signing this *after* you attend the meeting?"

"Please? I promise to at least stay long enough to find out how boring it is."

He grins, letting out a too-exhausted-to-care sigh as he grabs a pen from the desk and scribbles his name. Before releasing the note, he leans in and whispers, "We're all really pulling for your sister."

I freeze for a moment before forcing out, "Thanks."

I head to the circle of chairs. Jacey is still looking at me like I'm a bug she'd like to squash, so I plunk down into a seat as far away from her as possible. Then I pull my backpack into my lap to block Jacey's view and hold the fake note from my mom beside the one I found in Piper's locker.

My pulse throbs in my neck as I glance from one signature to the other.

They don't match.

Mr. Davis is telling the truth about not holding an extra skills session the day Piper fell.

So why would someone forge a note from him?

I glance around the circle of chairs, taking in the setup of the place Piper's been spending her Monday afternoons. When my sister told me she was joining Survival Club two weeks into the school year, I laughed. "Good one," I said. Piper does not do outdoors.

But she wasn't joking.

My gaze darts from Jacey's glare to a girl with braces and amazing curls: Alexandra Martinez, a sophomore. She's always trying to interview me for some piece or another for the school's online newspaper. Homecoming. Prom. Soccer. The articles were always about things I'd won until a couple of weeks ago, when she did a piece on the vigil the school held for my sister.

Next to Alexandra is a hand-holding couple wearing

matching hiking boots and creepy smiles. Oh, and red flannel shirts. They look like members of some sort of mountain cult. I've seen the scruffy-looking lumberjack guy around, and I know the redhead as Miss Humsalot. She's some sort of musical prodigy who sings to herself in the halls like we're all just side characters in her Disney movie.

The guy two seats to my right is dressed like Halloween incarnate, wearing black from the clunky boots on his feet to the hair on his head. Metal chains tumble from his belt loop, rattling whenever he moves. I've never seen him before, but he's the furthest thing you could find from a mountain man.

The rest of the chairs are empty. I pull out my phone to look occupied until Grant arrives, but it doesn't work. Mr. Halloween shifts closer. "Hey, I'm Tyler."

"Savannah Sullivan," I say, though everyone at this school knows who I am. He's probably going to ask me about Piper next. The thought sends an image of her lying in the hospital spiraling into my mind, and now I wish I'd sat next to the mountaineer couple.

But instead, he asks, "You're joining the club?"

"Just auditing today."

"Seems fun so far. I only joined a couple weeks ago. I go to Foothill, but they don't have an outdoor club." He leans back in his chair, arms crossed.

That explains why he doesn't know about Piper or me.

"Do you want to be a wilderness guide or something? You'd have to be pretty motivated to drive over here after school."

Tyler shrugs. "I like this kind of stuff. Being outdoors. I used to fish and camp and all that with my dad, but"—his gaze drops to his black boots—"he passed away last year."

A giant knot forms at the base of my throat. *He passed away.* Even though Piper's still alive, I hear my mom's sobs every morning when she wakes up and remembers this isn't a dream. I heard my parents' hushed conversation two nights ago after they spoke to Dr. Porter. He no longer believes Piper will recover. He recommended removing her from life support. Piper's body is hanging on, but there's a good chance that whatever makes her *her* is already gone.

My throat feels swollen, and my nose threatens to drip. I need to be excused. I start to apologize as the door squeaks open.

Grant walks in, and my heart buoys. "I'm really sorry about your dad," I say to Tyler. "And about the wilderness guide thing. I have trouble keeping my mouth shut. It's, like, a real problem."

A glimmer of a grin slides over his lips. "Don't worry about it."

I motion for Grant to take the empty seat on my left, and when he does, I cup my hand and whisper into his ear, "Mr. Davis didn't write the note. Someone else did."

Grant's head draws back. "Like a prank?"

"I don't know, but it's sketchy, right?"

"I guess, if you think whoever wrote the note was up at the Point when it happened."

"Yeah," I say, taking in the faces around us again.

Mr. Davis sits down in the circle, cutting off further discussion.

"I guess they let just anyone into this club," Jacey stage-whispers to Humsalot while looking straight at me. She crosses her legs and folds her hands, polished red fingernails on display. Jacey, a.k.a. Piper's best friend since kindergarten, has come a long way since her days of oversize science camp T-shirts paired with track pants. In the last couple of years, she's been styling her drab brown locks and dressing halfway normal. She actually looks good today in her distressed jeans and form-fitting tank top. I used to spend so much time planted in front of my vanity mirror, trying to teach Piper and Jacey how to do their hair and makeup. I even taught Jacey how to put on that eyeliner she managed to apply flawlessly today.

I don't foresee those lessons continuing.

"Careful," Jacey continues. "Keep your eyes on anything you don't want stolen."

Beside me, Grant squirms. My fists twitch, but Mr. Davis, clueless about the social dynamics of the room, just frowns. I'm about to say something I'll undoubtedly regret when the door flies open. A gust of wind riffles the posters lining the walls, and in stumbles Noah Crawford, late as usual.

He meets my gaze, and surprise lights his eyes.

"Sorry, Mr. Davis," he calls out like he's not sorry at all. He ambles over, backpack weighed down by what he calls "supplemental reading." "I had to talk to a guy about a thing, and *then* I had this momentary bout of amnesia. Couldn't find the place. There was room twenty-three and twenty-four, but room—"

"Have a seat, Mr. Crawford," Mr. Davis interrupts, shaking his head. "We were about to get started. But make sure you bring a compass this weekend."

Noah salutes him, taking the seat beside Jacey. She leans to whisper something in his ear, clearly continuing her campaign against me.

When Mr. Davis wanders back to his desk, mumbling about forgetting something, Noah grabs his backpack and moves to the empty seat on my right. My fists relax. Something about his younger brother–like presence is comforting.

"Hey." His tone is concerned. "What are you doing here?"

This is weird. My sister's boyfriend hasn't spoken to me much in ages. Not since long before Piper's fall. In fact, Noah Crawford hasn't been able to look at me or Grant without disgust written all over his face for almost a year. "Just, uh, checking out Piper's club. Trying to get close to her in whatever way I can."

The words don't sound like me, and I can see in Noah's narrowed green eyes that he knows it too. He adjusts his glasses and begins fumbling through his backpack. It takes him forever to wade through the books. Noah must be the only high school junior who carries an entire library around with him at all times.

Finally, his hand emerges with a ratty paperback. "Here." He hands it to me before running his fingers through his ash-brown hair. "It was Piper's."

An angry heat crackles in my chest. My sister's *not dead.* Not yet, anyway. Still, I say, "Thanks," and tuck the book inside my own bag. "How have you been?"

He shrugs. "I'd be better if I could visit her."

"I know," I say, placing a hand on his arm. "It's a stupid hospital policy."

There's something overwhelmingly sad in Noah's eyes. Something that makes me want to lock myself in a bathroom stall and cry. Piper has always had a crush on Noah. They were friends for years, but I always referred to him as her future husband. I just knew that one day, they'd be together.

It had finally happened. So why did she try to end everything?

With a shiver, I think of the note tucked inside my back pocket. Maybe she didn't. Maybe something else happened, and whoever wrote this note—someone who could be sitting in this very room—knows all about it.

I survey the faces again. Everyone here is connected to my sister in some way.

Guess I'm joining a new extracurricular after all.

3

Mr. Davis passes a small stack of papers around the circle. "This is a waiver your parents need to sign. If you're eighteen, you can sign the waiver yourself, but please pass along the details to your parents."

"What exactly are we signing?" I ask, not bothering to glance at the paper.

"This form pertains to this weekend's backpacking trip on Mount Liberty," Mr. Davis says. "You'll all be excused early on Friday—"

The room bursts into applause.

Mr. Davis attempts to continue over the clapping. "We'll camp Friday night, then spend Saturday at the river below the falls. After another night camping beneath the stars, we'll hike back down to school Sunday morning. Pretty basic. But we still have some ground to cover." He stands. "Part of my job as your advisor is teaching you to rely on each other. Our group is going to work as a family."

"A dysfunctional family," I whisper to Grant. No amount of skills could help me survive a weekend with Jacey Pritchard, who hasn't taken her beady eyes off me since I got here. How has Grant managed to last so long in this club?

I can't leave now, though. If I'm going to find out who gave Piper that forged note, I at least have to make it through this meeting.

"Which is why," Mr. Davis continues, "we're devoting the rest of today's meeting to team building."

A chorus of groans echoes around the circle.

Mr. Davis shuts his eyes, probably counting to ten under his breath so he doesn't murder one of us. He may look calm and collected now, but as the boys' soccer coach, the guy can definitely yell. The team has been in the spotlight since last year, when Mr. Davis miraculously took them from being the worst team in the league to regional champions.

Just like my sister and most of the other kids at this school, Grant worships the ground Mr. Davis walks on. And the feeling seems to be mutual. This year, Mr. Davis made Grant senior captain of the guys' team.

Which is perfect, since I'm captain of the girls' team. King and queen.

Not that this accolade means anything to my family. The second week of school, I told my mom that I needed money for the preseason tournament. But Piper had a debate tournament scheduled for the same weekend, and they could only afford to pay for one.

Big surprise—they chose Piper's.

It didn't matter that a scout from Mount Liberty College was going to be at my tournament. Or that I was older. Or that Piper had perfect grades and tons of other extracurriculars and one debate tournament wasn't going to make or break college acceptance for her.

My mom told me I'd have to figure out how to pay for it myself, and that was her final answer.

Final answer. I guess it would've been, if I'd let it go.

Mr. Davis opens his eyes, and there's a slow rise and fall to his chest. "All right, everyone. We're heading outside."

"We are?" asks Noah, comfortably slouched in his seat.

"Even though you're clearly all so eager for the activity"—Mr. Davis lifts a folder from his lap—"first I need to provide a quick overview on packing your backpack for a three-day hike." He stands up and walks toward the door, motioning for us to follow. "We're off to the athletics equipment locker. Everyone take a gear list."

He hands each of us a sheet of paper on our way out the door. The hall smells like the pizza they served in the cafeteria today, reminding me I skipped lunch. I wait for Grant, taking his hand as we amble after the others. When we pass by the athletics office, my chest constricts at the memory of the colossal mistake I'll never be able to take back.

Grant's fingers tighten around mine as we pass beneath the huge WE LOVE YOU, PIPER banner strung from wall to wall. It's signed by half the school, including people who never even knew her. Strangers who may be hoping for the best but believe that Piper did this to herself.

My parents are probably the only people in town who have a different theory. They like to tell themselves that what happened to Piper was a freak accident. Like she's this daring thrill-seeker who would have climbed up on top of that guardrail for the sheer rush of it. Like a gust of wind or a loss of balance caused her to plummet down the mountainside.

The truth is, I used to fantasize about life without Piper. Without the younger sister who could say more words at ten months than I could say at two years. The award-winning journalist. The debate club champ. The Future Scientist of America. The prodigy who had to take AP classes at another school because Grayling High couldn't keep up with her.

In my fantasies, there was never a concrete reason for Piper's disappearance. I didn't dream up ways to get rid of her. She was simply blotted out of existence. And the end result was always the same: I ended up the favorite by default.

Now I know that's not the way things work. You can't become the favorite child. If the favorite disappears or dies, she's just gone, and the leftover child is still the one who will never measure up. Only now, that leftover child has a new label to add to all the baggage.

Now she's the child who should have fallen instead.

I shudder to think of another possible label for me—one I've locked away. One I hope my parents never discover.

I press my fingers against the little charm dangling from my neck as we slip into the afternoon sunlight. Mr. Davis unlocks the large black athletics cabinet and starts extracting backpacks. Everyone seems to have an assigned pack. Lumberjack and Humsalot, whose actual names are Sam and Abby, grab theirs. One by one, the rest disappear, leaving only a bright red pack behind.

I pad up to it and find Piper's name scrawled on a luggage tag.

The familiar handwriting sends a swell of sadness through me, but I find my voice as the others start lugging equipment to the empty common area. "Mr. Davis, is it okay if I use my sister's pack today?"

He looks up from a cardboard box full of supplies. "Uh, sure. Go ahead."

I can't envision Piper wearing this, or even knowing how to use it. The thing has ninety-seven different pouches and snaps. I grab it by a strap and carry it over to where the others have gathered on the gum-encrusted cement and the food-smeared lunch benches. Why did my sister join this club?

Most people in Grayling's Pass fall on a spectrum of outdoor enthusiasts. It's kind of unavoidable if you grow up here, with all of the sights and activities at your fingertips. A lot of kids spend the scalding summers fishing or rafting on the icy Golden River, which starts up on Mount Liberty and snakes all the way down to the outskirts of town. When the weather's more forgiving, we have our pick of dozens of day hikes.

Piper was always the exception, though. She came back sobbing from her first and last camping trip with Jacey and her dad, something about losing her magnifying glass and not having access to her microscope. Jacey and Noah used to drag her off on hikes to get her out in the sunlight. She would do anything for those two.

Is that why she joined this club? She wanted extra time with her two besties?

I plop down beside Grant, Piper's pack between my feet as Mr. Davis begins his demonstration.

"A hiker's backpack is only effective if it's packed correctly. Please follow along on the gear list." He picks up a massive orange pack, pointing at the array of mesh pouches and commenting on their various uses.

A minute into the demonstration, Grant is immersed in his phone. He already knows all this stuff. Jacey too. But Piper? She and our science professor parents are alike in every way. Complete geniuses. Completely inept when it comes to the outdoors. Maybe that's why someone gave her that note; they realized how out of her depth she was and pranked her.

I shift the pack, noting the bulk at the base where the tent must be stored. I flip it over and unzip the first small pouch, inside which, fittingly, Piper has stuffed a pen and paper. Because those will come in super handy if you're starving or attacked by a bear out in the wild.

I zip it shut and glance up at Mr. Davis, pretending to pay attention. As I do, I catch Alexandra watching me. Resisting the urge to stick my tongue out at her like a five-year-old, I continue working my way through the bag. It's my sister's stuff, and I'll dig through it if I want to.

I shove my whole arm into the main compartment. Empty. I move on to a medium-sized pouch that runs along the front. There's a hard object inside, so I lift the flap, reach inside, and pull out a compass. At least she has one useful item. Something else seems to be tucked into the bottom of the pocket. I dig my fingertips in deeper.

But my attention whips to the flap itself. I lift it again, and my heart pushes up into my throat.

There's a message, rough and clumsy, written in thick white marker on the underside of the flap.

Quit Survival Club or ELSE.

4

Grant and I exit the double doors of the school and head toward the parking lot. I showed him the threat in Piper's pack, but we haven't had a moment alone to discuss it. Mr. Davis wrapped up the meeting by making us play some wilderness bonding game. The pack was too massive to steal, so now it's back in the equipment locker until I can return for it later.

This whole last month, I've believed my sister tried to kill herself. But maybe that's not what happened at all. My mind returns to the note tucked away in my back pocket—the one written on school stationery, sending Piper to a fake club meeting.

And now there's this message written in her pack. *Or ELSE.*

Did someone not only send her to the place she fell but follow through on that threat?

It just doesn't make sense. Everyone loved perfect Piper.

We get inside Grant's truck, and I finally blurt the question that's been battering my brain for the last hour. "Who the hell wrote that message in Piper's pack?"

Grant frowns. "The packs get reused when club members graduate. Piper could've inherited a bag that already had that in it."

"Who had that bag last year?"

"I think it was Eric's."

"Can you think of anyone who would've threatened Eric?" I ask, struggling to even remember a kid named Eric.

"Nah, but his best friend, Art, could've done it as a joke. He graduated last year too."

I consider this. "I guess it's possible, but unlikely when you put it together with this mystery note Piper got, telling her about a fake meeting at Vanderwild Point." I flip down the mirror and start to reapply my signature lipstick shade, Roses Are Pink.

Grant nods, eyes focused on the road. "Jacey could've threatened your sister."

"What?" My lipstick tube halts in midair. "I thought everything was perfect between those two ever since the carnival."

"Jacey didn't seem too happy when Piper joined the club. She yelled at her."

No way. Could *Jacey* really have threatened Piper? I know Jacey hates *me*, but I thought she and Piper were thick as thieves. Sure, they had a falling-out a while back, but this year, they were back to being attached at the hip.

At least, I think they were. I've been a bit preoccupied with my own problems these days.

"What did Jacey yell?" I ask.

Grant shrugs. "I don't remember. Girl stuff."

"Super helpful. Thank you, Grant."

"Sorry if I try not to get too involved in Jacey's affairs."

Point taken.

"Should I drive you home?" he asks, clearly done with this conversation.

"No." My house has been quieter than a tomb since Piper's "accident." I'm not sure what will happen if my sister never wakes up. My parents may disintegrate. They lived for her debate tournaments and science experiments. Everything has always been about Piper, their little clone, even though she's a year younger than me.

The proudest my parents have ever been of me was when I got an A on a biology report freshman year. I still have that report stuffed beneath all the papers at the bottom of my desk. Sure, Piper stayed up all night doing the research for me, but my parents didn't know that.

Maybe things would be different if I got better grades. If I could go to a prestigious college and major in bio.

Too bad I hate bio.

Grant fiddles with his iPhone, and the pop playlist he made for me starts pumping through the speakers. But I don't hum along like I usually would. I don't hear the beats. My mind is on last night's dinner. On the grating sound the forks made, that unnerving screeching, scraping sound of a knife on a plate. The clink of a glass against the table. The crunch of lettuce between teeth.

I'd never been so aware of these sounds before. It took sitting through a dinner with my parents in utter silence for me to notice just how noisy eating really is.

It took sitting through dinner without Piper across the table to realize just how invisible I am.

Most days, I feel like taking both of my parents by the shoulders and shaking them. I want to scream at them until they wake up and see that I'm the one who fits in. The one thriving in high school. The soccer star. The homecoming queen. The one any girl at school would kill to be.

But to my parents, none of that matters. At my house, I'm a freak.

They're not the only reason I can't go home, though. I can't go home because someone threatened my sister, and I have to find out if it was Jacey.

"Let's go to Bonnie's. We can study there." I'm willing to bet I'll find Jacey at the diner. The three amigos—Jacey, Piper, and Noah—practically lived at that place before Piper's fall.

Grant cocks a brow at me. It's unlike me to want to study.

"Colleges look at first-semester transcripts senior year," I explain. "Even if I get a soccer scholarship, I need to keep my grades up."

"You'll get one. I know it."

My stomach roils. I'd better, hadn't I? My gaze drifts to the window, away from Grant, to watch the bony trees fly by. I press my fingers against the little charm dangling from my neck, blink back tears. It would be a shame to flunk chemistry and ruin my chances at MLC now after everything I've done to get in.

"We'll both get into MLC, and it will be amazing," Grant says. "Now, can we talk about the club? You're not really coming on this weekend's hike, are you?"

"Of course not. I'm just trying to find out what happened to my sister."

Grant shifts in his seat, his silence saying it all. *We already know what happened to your sister.*

An image of Piper that day sneaks into my mind: blond hair wild, cheeks aflame, eyes stormy. A shiver passes through me.

Maybe he's right. Maybe I'm on a desperate mission to clear my conscience. A mission that will only lead back to the moment I can't bear to face.

Grant pulls up in front of Bonnie's Diner, and I scan the parking lot for Jacey's clunker.

Bingo. She's inside.

I check my makeup in the mirror and then gather my things.

The place is empty save an old lady sipping tea at the counter and Jacey and Noah at the front. They spot me and begin to whisper. Ignoring them, I make my way through the shiny red tables until I reach the back corner booth. "Can you get me a Diet Coke?" I ask Grant, dropping my backpack onto the shiny red seat cushion. "I have to use the restroom."

"Sure, babe." He tosses his backpack on the seat across from me and plops down.

I traipse past the black-and-white photos from the fifties lining the corridor to the restrooms. In one, a woman holds a milkshake at the counter, and the same giant BONNIE'S sign adorns the wall behind the waitress. You would think Bonnie's had actually been around since the fifties, based on the water-stained walls and tears in the seat cushions where cottony stuffing pokes out. In reality, these photos are a sham; Bonnie's has only been around since the nineties. Mom grew up in Grayling's Pass, and she says there was an old diner here that went out of business. Bonnie moved in years later.

Bonnie is as big a liar as I am.

I emerge from the restroom, stealing a peek at Jacey. Sipping her drink. Laughing with Noah. My sister completely erased from her mind.

Jacey Pritchard knows something.

I start down the aisle, passing by Grant at my table. I don't stop until I'm right in front of her.

She glances up at me. "Something you need, Savannah? Another boyfriend to steal, maybe?"

"Did you threaten my sister?" I snap.

Her head whips back. "What are you talking about?"

Noah lifts a hand in a calming gesture. "Can we just lower—"

"I'm talking about a message I found today in Piper's pack." I drop my voice. "*Quit Survival Club or ELSE.*"

Jacey frowns. Shakes her head. "No, of course not."

"Don't lie to me, Pritchard. Grant said you were arguing with Piper about joining the club."

"Oh, you mean *that* guy?" She pitches a thumb back toward where Grant is sitting, watching the show. "Super trustworthy Grant Costa?"

"That's not an answer."

She sighs and starts tearing off the edge of her napkin. "I didn't write anything in Piper's pack. I wouldn't do that." She loops the strip of paper, tying it in a knot.

I'm not sure I believe her. "Everyone knows you two have had *issues* over the last year."

"Issues caused by you." She flicks the little paper knot, which bounces across the table.

My insides go taut. She's referring to last spring. Grant was technically still with Jacey but was seeing me in secret. He took Jacey to the Spring Fling and kissed me in a dark corner while the three amigos were out on the dance floor.

He was going to break up with her—neither of us wanted to hurt Jacey. But he didn't get the chance before she found out.

The dark corner apparently wasn't as dark as we thought, because the *Grayling High Gazette* published a photo of Grant kissing me as part of an article titled GRAYLING HIGH SPRING FLING A SUCCESS!

Boy, was it a success.

Jacey was obviously furious with Grant and me. But she was just as furious with Piper, who was junior editor of the paper. Jacey accused her of knowing about the picture before it ran. They stopped speaking for months. It strained my relationship with Piper too. She hadn't had anything to do with that photo, but she *had* known about Grant and me. She'd struggled with what to do with the information all the way up until the moment it exploded in her face. My actions nearly ruined her oldest friendship. She and Jacey didn't mend things until the back-to-school carnival, when Noah convinced them to bury the hatchet.

Maybe the hatchet was never really buried.

I ignore her, turning to Noah. "Did Jacey fight with Piper about joining Survival Club or not?"

Noah blinks and adjusts his glasses. "I-I mean, I don't—"

"Come on, Noah!" I slap a palm down on the sticky table, and Noah lunges for his milkshake to keep it from toppling.

From the counter, the old lady shushes me.

"Sorry, ma'am," Noah says, throwing me a look as he wraps two protective hands around his plastic cup.

"Just tell me the truth. Did Jacey have an issue with my sister joining your idiotic club?"

"She was surprised that Piper would want to join," he admits. "We all were. But she never threatened Piper. She wouldn't do that."

My gaze swings back to Jacey. I grit my teeth, managing to keep my mouth shut for the first time in my life.

I don't believe her. Someone threatened Piper. Someone gave her specific instructions to go to the Point, where they would be alone.

And my sister never returned from that trip. Instead, she wound up unconscious on the side of the mountain.

If Piper didn't fall on purpose, then it's not my fault.

And if Jacey had something to do with it, I'm going to find proof.

5

My parents nearly murdered the hospital staff when they discovered that Piper's phone was missing from the plastic bag with the rest of her belongings.

They didn't know that the hospital staff had nothing to do with it.

I took Piper's phone. I couldn't let my parents see the last text I'd sent her. I couldn't let them realize that I may have been responsible for what had happened.

But right now, I want to see what else is on her phone. Maybe Jacey—or whoever did this—didn't stop at threats in my sister's bag. Maybe the proof that someone was harassing her is on that phone.

As soon as my parents leave for the hospital after dinner, I head to my closet and dig the phone out from where I buried it at the bottom of a box of old soccer gear.

A sick feeling rises in my stomach as I pull it free. The screen is cracked and still coated in a fine layer of dirt. I connect it to a charger, shutting my eyes and hoping it still works.

When I open my eyes, the phone is lit. I exhale in relief, but then a realization hits me: Piper's phone is password protected, and we haven't shared passwords in years.

Knowing my sister, her password is something too obscure for the CIA to crack. This is where one of my parents' normally annoying family rules suddenly becomes *not* annoying. We have to share our passwords with them.

I head to my parents' room and snoop around in Mom's top dresser drawer until my fingers brush a note card containing every password for every device my family has owned in the last ten years.

Back in my room, I unlock Piper's phone using the series of letters and numbers that I'm guessing make up some chemical formula. My fingers shake as I navigate the texts, finding nothing new after mine, which I delete. I move on to the calls, scrolling past the six missed ones from Mom when dinnertime came around and Piper was nowhere to be seen. It was thanks to Mom's calls that Piper was discovered. Some hikers heard the phone ringing while they were taking in the sunset. They realized someone had fallen and called 911.

Before those calls, though, things get weird.

On the day Piper fell, she received three calls from someone named Alex. Two answered, one missed.

Alex? I rack my brain, but can't think of a single person named Alex in my grade or Piper's. But then a thought nails me in the gut, and I nearly drop Piper's already-damaged phone.

I do know an *Alexandra.* And she's in Survival Club.

Does Alexandra go by Alex? If she does—and if she's the person in Piper's contacts—then she might've been the last person to talk to my sister before her fall. Alex, whoever she is, was certainly the last person to speak to Piper over the phone. Had she known what my sister was planning? Had Piper given any indication?

My finger hovers over her name. Before I can talk myself out of it, I hold my breath and press call. Then I wait.

It rings twice before someone picks up. No answer. Only breathing.

My heart jerks. I'm not sure what I was expecting, but I have no prepared speech to get this person to talk to me. "H-hello. This is Savannah Sulli—"

Three beeps sound in my ear, jostling me like an explosion. Then nothing but silence.

I should take Piper's phone to the cops. Someone knows more than they're saying. Alex was the last person to speak to my sister before she fell. She might be able to tell us something about Piper's state of mind that day. About what happened.

But the cops will see my text. Sure, I deleted it, but they have ways of recovering it. Don't they?

What if they start to think *I* had something to do with Piper's fall? Or what if they just write me off? After all, the cops never even came around to ask questions. My parents can keep telling themselves that what happened to Piper was an accident, but everyone else—the cops included—see Piper's fall as something else. That spot is known as Suicide Point. My sister wasn't the first person to have that kind of "accident" there.

No, if I want the cops to listen, I'm going to have to get Piper's bag from the equipment locker and show it to them. Then I'm going to have to figure out how Alex plays into things. If I can prove she was there with Piper or spoke to her, maybe the cops will take Piper's file and stick a new label on it.

There's a tug in my chest as my mind wanders back to a different kind of file, one lying open on Piper's desk. She was typing away, mostly ignoring me. It was Saturday, two weeks into the school year. Late afternoon, but I was still in my pajamas, sprawled out on her bed.

"You know we should split the money, right?" I gazed at the debate trophies lining the mantel, outshined only by the journalism awards plastered all over the wall. When she'd joined the paper, Dad got so excited that he went out and bought her one of those old-fashioned pocket recorders. She started bringing it with her everywhere, even though she could've just used the app on her phone, pausing in the school halls to babble into it like a private eye.

When I told Dad I'd made varsity soccer as a freshman, he only squinted and told me to keep my options open.

"That's the fair thing to do," I continued, picking at the embroidery on the quilt Grandma had made when Piper was born. "If I have to earn the money to go to my tournament, you should have to earn some too."

"But you heard Mom," Piper answered, never breaking momentum on the keyboard. "I don't have time." Of course she was just parroting Mom. I bit back a retort; I had to play nice if I was going to make her see reason. Plus, it was hard to fight her on this point in my pajama-clad state.

"We still have a couple of months. We could earn the money together." I poked a decorative pillow on her bed, and dust motes spun up into the air.

"Doing what?" She punched a few more keys and then started flipping through a textbook.

"Lemonade stand?" I offered.

"Funny, Vanna." Piper's the only person who's ever called me that. She gave me the nickname when she was two years old, not because she couldn't pronounce my full name but because *Wheel of Fortune* was on TV and she realized my name and Vanna White's name had some syllables in common. I pretend to hate it, but I don't.

"I'm still thinking." I flipped onto my stomach and examined the chipped pink paint on my nails. "Got any nail polish?"

Piper stopped reading to tilt her head at me.

"Kidding. I don't have time to paint my nails either. Because I'm thinking of a way for us to make money. Lots and lots of it. What are you working on, anyway?"

"AP World Literature. But these," she said, pointing to a file folder stuffed with papers, "are last week's chemistry tests, which I have to grade this weekend for Mr. Davis."

"Wow, I thought being a TA meant getting out of class to make copies in the teacher's lounge. Why can't he grade the tests himself?"

"I offered. It's just multiple choice. But I didn't realize Mrs. Sanderson was going to give us a ten-page essay over the weekend or that my physics group was going to have to meet all day Sunday for a project." She sighed, and the sunlight from the window caught on some loose strands of frizzy, white-blond hair, casting her in an ethereal glow. Perfectly fitting: Piper the angel.

"Well, maybe I can grade the tests. I help you, we split the money?" I winked obnoxiously. "There's an answer key, right?"

Piper looked at me, considering it. She glanced back at

the stack of tests. "I don't know, Savannah. That might be a conflict of interest."

"You really think I'm going to change my answers? You grade my test, then."

"No, it's just that Mr. Davis is trusting me with this. If there are mistakes in the grades..."

"I won't make any mistakes. I'll even log them for you."

She shook her head. Another wave came loose from her ponytail. "You can't. I had to get his password to access the grading program. There's no way I can share it with anyone."

"Okay, fine. Don't give me the special password. But let me help with the grading, and I'll think of a way for us to make the money. And we'll all live happily ever after."

Piper eyed the file folder again, her chest rising slowly.

Now, I take a shuddering breath, suffocated by the memory.

Nothing I find is going to change what happened on September sixteenth. It won't fix what I did. It won't make my parents snap out of their depression.

But I have to know if Piper did it because of me or if something else happened to her. And I'm going to start with Alex.

6

Before school, I find Coach Lennon in her office and ask for the key to the equipment locker. "I want to get an early start on ordering uniforms," I explain. "I'll grab an old one just to make sure I get the colors right."

Coach rolls her eyes. "You should stop worrying about what we're going to wear and pray our team is good enough to win some games." The subtext is clear: unlike the boys' team, we haven't had a miraculous turnaround. We're going to have to work extra hard this year.

I smile, used to her snippy remarks. When she's not yelling at me to stop messing with my hair during a game, she's mocking me for wearing lipstick to practice. But you get to brush all that off when you're the best player on the team. You also get pretty much everything you ask for, which is why she hands over the key before waving me away.

I shut the door to the equipment locker behind me, using my phone's light to guide me. I grab one of our old uniforms from the team bag and toss it beside the door so I don't forget about my excuse. It's difficult in the dark, but I locate the bins with all the Survival Club gear.

I dig through the bin full of backpacks, removing the ones on top, trying to find the one from yesterday. I spot a pop of red and reach for it, my heart soaring. But the tag on the pack says SAM.

There are only three packs left at the bottom of the bin, none of them red.

Holding in a scream, I return everything to the bin and shove it back into place. I stand and examine the rest of the room, shining my phone's light in a slow circle. Piper's pack must've gotten misplaced. I scan the shelves up high and then scrounge through the athletics teams' bins.

The pack isn't here. Which means I have nothing.

I slam my palm into the aluminum wall, biting back a thousand curses. Whoever wrote that threat must've seen me reading it during the meeting. And now this person has covered their tracks.

I sling the stupid uniform over my shoulder and lock up. But my thoughts go to yesterday, when Mr. Davis was yammering and I was looking through Piper's pack.

Someone was watching me: Alex. Now I just need to prove she's hiding information about Piper's fall.

The bell has already rung by the time I stash the useless uniforms in my car. I rush back to the main hall and find Alexandra at her locker, talking to this other sophomore girl whose name might be Deb or Diana. I think of her as Country Club because she wears tennis skirts and looks like the kind of person who'd spend summer days lounging at the club pool while *Daddy* golfs.

I wander closer, leaning against the lockers beside them, pretending to scroll through my phone. I listen in, hoping Country Club will provide me with the smoking gun by calling Alexandra "Alex." Instead, the two simply swap out their books and chatter inanely.

Time for a new plan. I pull out my phone, where I've stored Alex's number, and dial it.

I stop breathing when the call goes through. I wait for Alexandra's phone to ring from inside her backpack or her locker.

But the seconds go by, and the only sound is the slamming of lockers and the two girls' giggling.

Okay, fine. Her phone didn't ring. That doesn't mean she's not Alex. A "good girl" like Alexandra would probably keep her phone on silent during school hours, as per Grayling High's policy. Or she could've forgotten it today.

Then again, I may have this completely wrong.

I head to Spanish. When I reach the door, my phone buzzes in my pocket. I freeze, and Señora Pérez tosses a vicious look at me through the doorway.

I back up, mouthing an apology to Señora Pérez. My throat closes up as I read the words on the screen.

Don't call this number again

I drop my books in the middle of the hall and race back to the lockers, my heart pounding as I search for Alexandra.

But the hall is empty. Everyone is tucked away in their classrooms.

And I'm alone.

Instead of meeting Grant at his car to get lunch off campus, I'm pacing the hall outside the cafeteria.

Alex spoke to Piper the day she fell. Twice. And now she wants to disappear.

I'm not going to let her. Something happened that day. Something this person wants to erase. My bet is still on Alexandra, but I have nothing other than a name and a school club to go on. The cops will need more than that, especially now that Piper's pack with the threat is gone.

"Savannah?"

I look up, irritated someone is interrupting my thoughts. Jessica McKay is standing by a trash can, watching me with concern. She tucks her flat-ironed chestnut hair behind an ear, revealing one of the silver studs I gave her for her last birthday.

"You okay?" She wanders closer, touching my arm delicately. Jessica has been my best friend since second grade, though we haven't spoken much since Piper's accident. Our friendship has always been loud parties, quiet gossip, and stolen sips of whiskey from her parents' cabinet, starting at the tender age of twelve; lately, I haven't exactly been the poster child for fun times.

"Oh, yeah. I was just going to grab something quick because I have a makeup test for chem."

"With Mr. Davis?"

I nod, and Jessica's eyes drift to the cafeteria doors. She makes a face. We haven't eaten in there since sophomore year.

"Well, it's good that you're eating again, at least."

"Yeah." *Sorry if I lost my appetite when my sister went into a coma.* "I'd better move if I'm going to finish my test." *You know, the one that doesn't exist.* "Call you later, 'kay?"

She smiles, pity practically dripping from her lips, and I steal through the cafeteria doors.

Inside, the stale scent wrenches me back to a time when life was a little simpler. Sure, I was still the stupid daughter. Sure, I still had failing grades while my younger sister passed me by. But at least she was here, not in some hospital bed.

My eyes comb the tables until I spot Country Club sitting with all her little sophomore friends, Alexandra included.

I take a breath and meander past her table. I have to talk to Alexandra's friends. But if she really is Alex—if she sent that text—I can't let her guess that I'm onto her. She's already getting rid of evidence. I don't want to spook her even more.

I get in line, ignoring the group of freshmen boys ogling me. I glance back at Country Club's table, hoping to catch her on her way out, but she's munching on an apple like we have all the time in the world.

Unwittingly, I growl, and the girl in front of me whips around. Her eyes grow wide with terror. "You can go ahead of me," she says in a squeaky voice.

"Oh, no—I'm not in a hurry. Just broke a nail." I shrug, and the girl smiles in relief.

"I hate that." Her shoulders relax.

My phone dings in my hand, and I jump, still shaky after that text from Alex.

It's Grant. Where R U?

Sorry, doing research. Go w/out me

I tuck my phone away in my pocket. It isn't a lie, exactly. Unfortunately, I can't confide in Grant about Piper anymore; when I told him about Alex on the way to school, he gave me that look again. That same look of pity Jessica gave me a minute ago. *Poor Savannah.*

It's the look the cops will give me if I go there with nothing but a name and a note telling Piper about a club meeting.

I doubt Grant would approve of me spending time

investigating a fall he and everyone else believes was a suicide attempt. Not when I should be focusing on my studies, so we can attend MLU together. I don't want to let him down. He's always been great, but after Piper's accident, he really stepped up. He spent countless hours sitting in the cab of his truck with me, gazing out at Vista Point until the sun was long past down and there was nothing left to see. Some days, I couldn't even speak, but he stayed. Held me. Let me call him in the middle of the night when Mom's crying woke me up. No one else would do that for me. Not Jessica, who hardly speaks to me now, too worried she'll say the wrong thing or that my grief will kill her fun. Certainly not my parents, who barely remember that I'm part of the family. That I'm hurting too.

And if I make it known that I'm searching for the truth about September sixteenth, Grant and everyone else will assume I'm just a grief-stricken sister looking for someone to blame.

Which isn't true.

A sudden burst of panic cracks my thoughts, and I glance back at Alexandra's table. Did I miss Country Club? But she's still working on that apple.

Then it hits me: Alexandra's gone.

I ease out of line, hurrying through the tables and trying not to slip on anyone's spilled lunch. When I get to Country Club's table, the apple core is on her tray. She's checking her makeup with her phone camera, glazing her fingers over her short brown hair. There are still a couple of other girls with her. I slide onto the bench beside her, smiling like I do this all the time.

"Hey, Deb, right?"

Country Club frowns, but then she takes me in as she lowers her phone to her lap. It's like her vision has suddenly cleared, and she straightens up in her seat. Tucks some hair behind her ear. Across the table, the other sophomores stare.

"Diana," she corrects, smiling shyly.

Damn it. I knew it was one of the two.

"Right," I say, tapping myself on the forehead like the idiot I am. "I'm Piper Sullivan's sister, Sav—"

"Savannah." She laughs, and the other sophomores join her. "Yeah, we know."

"Right," I repeat. "I was wondering if I could ask you a couple things about my sister." I glance around the table. "In private."

The other two sophomores stiffen. Before I can suggest that Diana and I move into the hall, the others stand. "We were just leaving anyway," one of them says, a girl with a smattering of freckles and long auburn hair.

"Yeah, see you later, Di," the other one says. "We're all praying for Piper," she adds solemnly before shuffling off with her tray.

"Thanks," I mumble, sudden oxygen deprivation clouding my thoughts. Why am I here? Oh, right. I turn to Country

Club, trying to find something to compliment her on before we proceed. I learned that from a book, or TV, maybe. People are more willing to do stuff for you after you pay them a compliment.

But it's tough in this case, to be perfectly honest. Finally, I settle on, "That's a really great cardigan." It's not. The green is all wrong for Country Club's complexion. But her whole face lights up, and I know it's a lie for the greater good. "Where'd you get it?"

She touches the cashmere, her fingers dropping to a little pearl button. "It was a gift from Daddy."

I do my best to hold in my laughter. I should be a freaking detective. "Well, your father has excellent taste." I grin, giving it a good pause. "So, you and Piper are friends, right?"

Instantly, her smile falters. She fidgets. I've caught her off guard, which means she isn't friends with my sister. "Oh, well, we were friendly. Everyone loves Piper. She's just so nice. And *wow*, is she smart."

"She certainly is," I say, because no one has ever rubbed *that* in my face before. "I'm just trying to find someone who was close to her. It's about this special ceremony I'm planning."

"Well, Jacey Pritchard and Noah—"

"I've already filled them in on the details," I say, hoping I don't sound as annoyed as I feel. "I'm just looking for a couple more contributors. People who are really close to Piper."

"I'm only a sophomore. You might want to talk to more juniors."

"So, not Alexandra Martinez, then?"

Country Club's brow furrows.

"I remember Piper talking about someone named Alex a month or so back. I just assumed it was Alexandra, since they were in journalism and Survival Club together. She does go by Alex sometimes, doesn't she?" I'm going out on a limb with this one.

"Well, yeah, to her friends. But I wouldn't consider Piper and Alex friends, really. I mean, especially not after what happened earlier this year."

All the heat rushes from my body as ice water trickles in. "What happened earlier this year?"

7

Country Club purses her lips, like she wishes she hadn't said anything. Like she's trying to keep herself from spilling another drop of gossip.

"What happened earlier this year?" I repeat, aiming for vaguely interested as I pick at my nails.

And just like that, she has to win my attention back. "Well," she says, glancing over her shoulder, "I guess it actually started last year. Of course, this is just what I've heard. But Piper and Alexandra were both up for the Peterson." When I stare blankly, she adds, "It's an award only journalism kids care about. Named after some alumnus." She rolls her eyes, trying to show me she's above all that. "So, Alex came up with this story she was sure would win her the award, about department budget cuts and who was getting screwed, and she pitched it to Mr. James in one of their meetings—this is how she tells the story, anyway. Apparently, Mr. James raved about the idea and then proceeded to hand it right over to Piper. Like the story was too big to give to a freshman, even if the idea *came* from one. Alex asked Piper if she could at least help, but Piper said she worked better alone, and then"—she makes a furling motion—"went on to win the Peterson.

"Not that I believe Piper would do that," Country Club adds, shaking her head.

I listen, unsure what to think, because I don't remember that story coming out, much less Piper winning some award for it. Seems like the type of thing my parents would've loved to parade around.

"Who knows why Alex thought she had a shot at the Peterson or why she got so worked up about it. Because, I mean, Piper is Piper. And she was a sophomore, while Alex was only a freshman. Anyway, Alex had her heart set on the stupid thing and then she lost, *obviously.*"

"What happened with them this year?" I ask, unable to swallow as I hang on to every one of her words.

"Alex had the nerve to go up against Piper for assistant editor, even though they almost always give it to a junior. And she lost, again, ob—"

"Obviously," I chime in, giving her an *aren't we in sync* grin.

She smiles back. "Alex was super pouty about it for the next..." Her eyes widen, and the smile disappears. "Well, until your sister's accident, I guess. While Piper's in the hospital, Mr. James asked Alex to take over as assistant editor."

So, with Piper out of the picture, Alex suddenly has what she wants. Interesting. Maybe assistant editor wasn't the only thing she wanted. Maybe she also wanted revenge for Piper taking her award-winning story last year.

"Well," I say with a shrug, "I guess Alexandra wouldn't exactly be a fit for my ceremony."

Country Club checks her surroundings one more time. "Look, I love Alex—I do. She's one of my best friends. But she wasn't one of Piper's. Like I said, Piper is a sweetie—at least, she seems like she is. I'm sure she has plenty of other friends in her grade you could talk to. Sorry I couldn't be more help."

"Oh, it's totally fine. You're right. I should be talking to other juniors."

I get up from the bench, checking my jeans for smashed bits of food, and bid adieu to Country Club, whose real name I've legitimately forgotten.

Country Club, who has helped far more than she'll ever know.

———

Piper always had journalism on Tuesday afternoons, so I head to Mr. James's room after school to talk to Alexandra. I want to gauge her reaction when I ask if she spoke to Piper that day. And I want to know why someone who wasn't even friends with my sister would call her three times right before she fell.

I walk into the room like I own the place—this has worked countless times in the past—only to find that no one even notices me.

There's a group huddled around a computer in one corner, arguing about something. Up at Mr. James's desk, I spot Alexandra. She's pointing to her notebook and gesturing animatedly.

Girl's got big plans, apparently. Now that my sister's out of the way.

I'm about to interrupt their conversation when I notice the backpacks and sweaters dumped along the wall beside the door. And the messenger bag with the initials *AM* embroidered on the outside pocket.

My skin prickles with nervous excitement. Alexandra's phone could be in there. The one that's going to prove she called Piper the day she fell. My eyes whip to her again. She's still focused on Mr. James, and I don't see a phone in her hand or back pocket.

I hover in the doorway on my toes, like the whistle is about to start the game.

Then I dive for the bag. In one quick, fluid motion, I lunge, grab, and I'm out the door, hopefully before anyone noticed me. My heart hammers in time with my steps as I hustle down the hall, messenger bag clutched in front of me. *Where do I go, where do I go?*

I turn the corner, and the library door comes into focus ahead. The light is on—after-school hours. Checking behind me, I duck inside.

A few students are scattered about, heads in books. The librarian looks up from her computer and eyes me, like I'm out of place in my own school library. Which I am. At a long table to the right, a couple giggles softly with their faces squished together. I sling the bag over my shoulder and weave through the tables. Pressing on through the aisles of books, I find a hidden corner and slump down to the floor.

I unbuckle the flap and start digging, but it's a mess inside. Impatient, I dump the entire bag over and out spills all sorts of junk. Books, pens, a sweater, little folded-up notes. No phone. But the bag still feels heavy. I bunch it up in my hands until I find something substantial tucked into that embroidered pocket. I unzip it and stick my hand inside.

An electric jolt zips up my spine. *This is it.* Her phone.

I switch it to silent and grab my own phone, my finger hovering over Alex's name. But I pause. This person might get really angry if I call again. If they had something to do with Piper's fall, what might they do to me?

I take a breath, let it out. One phone in each hand. Fingers sweaty against both. But I have to do this. I have to find out what happened to my sister.

This person said not to call again. Fine—I won't call. I set Alexandra's phone down on the disgusting carpet and type out a text.

Why don't you want to talk to me?

My chest tightens as I hit send.

Then I wait for Alexandra's screen to light up with a new text.

One second. Heartbeat. Two seconds. Heartbeat. Three. Nothing.

I slam my fist down on the carpet, sending all of Alexandra's stuff bouncing. With a flush, I remember I'm supposed to be quiet in here. Pain spreads through my jaw. I've had my teeth clenched so tightly, I'm lucky nothing's cracked.

Does this mean Alexandra isn't Alex? I don't know. She could have another phone. One she keeps hidden.

That still leaves me with zero proof that it's her.

A little spider-crawl of doubt runs through my brain. Maybe there's nothing to my suspicions. Maybe the only person to blame is the one whose face is reflected back in this stolen phone screen.

Shoving everything aside, I lean against the wall and let my head drop into my hands. I have to return this stupid bag somehow. But I can barely lift a finger to clean up this mess.

"Savannah?"

Panic tears through my chest. I'm caught. I glance up to

find Noah Crawford standing over me, stack of books in hand. "Are you okay?"

"Yeah." I straighten, gathering the items back into the bag.

"Let me help you." He sets his books down on the carpet.

"No, you really don't—"

But he's already crouched beside me, reaching for Alexandra's phone. He stops, registering the phone in my hand. His eyes flick up to mine, and a wariness I've never seen in Noah's green eyes stings me to the core. He takes everything in—the pile, the bag. "What is all this stuff?"

A text pings on my phone. One I definitely can't read in front of Noah. Not if it's an answer from Alex. Sweat beads on my forehead. I cover the screen and tuck the phone into my back pocket as I shift onto my knees. "Noah, please. I can explain."

His expression now is familiar. It's the one where his eyes bleed disappointment. I've seen it plenty on Piper, too, ever since she found out what I did to Jacey.

"I found this bag here," I lie. "I was trying to figure out who it belongs to."

"Oh," Noah says, an edge of uncertainty to his voice. He grabs the large three-ring binder and flips it open. Then he points to a sheet of half-filled-out graph paper tucked inside the front pocket. "Says it's Alexandra Martinez's."

"You're a true detective," I quip, shoving the rest of the stuff inside the bag.

"She's not in here?" He glances around.

"I don't think so." I pretend to sweep the room too. "Oh, you know what? I think she's in journalism with Piper on Tuesdays."

"Well, I can return it to her," Noah says, standing. "I'm on my way out."

"No," I blurt in what's definitely not a library voice. "Sorry, I just…I need to talk to Mr. James anyway. He's been badgering me about helping with a piece on Piper and how wonderful she is." This isn't a lie. "I really should've dropped in by now and helped." My eyes well with tears I'm not faking. "It's just hard, you know?" That crack in my voice is real too.

"Hey," Noah says, kneeling again. He puts a hand on my shoulder, and when I look up at him, any trace of disappointment is gone. "You have to do these things in your own time. Don't let people make you feel bad."

I nod, even though it isn't other people who are making me feel bad.

"Sure you don't want me to drop off the bag?"

"I'm sure. Thanks."

I sling the bag over my shoulder and make my way back through the library. In the hall, I tug my phone from my pocket, adrenaline pumping. Was that text from Alex?

I read it, and my nerves fizzle. It's only Grant, echoing the common theme of the week: Where RU?

Seems I'm completely lost.

I forgot he was waiting for me in the parking lot. We were

supposed to study together at his house. I know he's nervous for me. For *us*. If I can't get into Mount Liberty College, who knows where I'll end up? And long-distance relationships don't exactly have a great track record. Be there in 10, I text back as I trudge toward Mr. James's room.

First, I have to return this bag without anyone noticing.

I tiptoe up to the door, holding the bag behind my back. Peeking inside, I search for Alexandra, who's no longer at Mr. James's desk. Instead, she and the rest of the journalists are messing around by the whiteboard, taking selfies.

I drop the bag right beside the door frame, relief thawing my rigid muscles. Then I slide back into the hall, my gaze taking one last turn about the room.

And smacking right into Alexandra's glare.

I freeze, and her eyes stay glued to me.

I force myself to turn and flee, my shoes squeaking on the linoleum. She didn't see me with the bag. She was taking a selfie.

So why did she look at me like that? I keep going, stopping briefly at my locker to grab the books I'm supposed to bring to Grant's house, and then make a beeline for the parking lot.

When I'm out in the hazy afternoon sun, my phone dings in my pocket, startling me. *Patience, Grant, damn it.* I pull out my phone, ready to text him as much, but it isn't his name on the screen.

It's Alex's.

I think we both know the answer to that.

8

Friday morning, I hop into Grant's truck carrying a full duffel bag.

"Um, what is that?" he asks when I heft it over the passenger seat and into the back alongside his own bag.

"My stuff for the weekend."

"The weekend?" He stares blankly.

"The backpacking trip," I say like it's obvious as I lean over to kiss him.

"You're not going on the backpacking trip." His voice is muffled against my lips.

"I changed my mind." I shrug and mess up his curls with my fingers. He's wearing my favorite shirt of his, a teal button-down we picked out at the mall together. "Thought it might be more fun than hanging around at home while you're out fighting bears." I press closer and whisper in his ear, "Don't you want me to come?"

Grant's eyes fall shut and he nods, smiling faintly. "This might be the best idea you've ever had."

"Hey," I say, heat rushing through me at the thought of spending a weekend in front of a crackling fire, cuddled up in Grant's arms. It's quickly followed by a memory of the two of us that first night—the one that had to stay hidden from everyone, the one where the idea of wrong slid into the recesses of our minds, replaced by the feelings of his hands in my hair and my mouth covering his. The night that was danger and excitement and falling faster and further than I'd ever fallen.

I slap him on the shoulder. "I'm full of good ideas." Then I pull down the mirror and begin to apply Roses Are Pink.

"You are," he agrees, turning the key in the ignition. The truck rumbles to a start, and we lumber off down the road. "Which is why I'm hoping this plan doesn't have anything to do with Piper."

He glances over at me, and there it is again. The look.

I slump back in my seat. "Of course not. You were totally right about all of that. I was just searching for someone to blame."

Guilt presses down on me like a weighted blanket. The truth is so heavy I can barely breathe. Someone was always to blame. And if I'm wrong about all of this—about Alex—there's only one person left.

My thoughts flash to that day. To the last time I saw Piper without a million wires attached to her body. The last time I saw her turquoise eyes open.

They were filled with tears. And if she never wakes up, that's how I'll always have to remember her.

Add that to the list of things I'll never be able to tell my boyfriend.

"I'm surprised your parents signed the waiver," Grant says as the truck turns onto our school's maple-tree-lined street.

Another brick of guilt drops onto my shoulders. "They took some convincing. But you know my parents." I let my head fall against the window so I don't have to keep looking at him as I spew lies. "Just happy to see me getting involved in something that's not a contact sport."

"Could be good for you," Grant offers.

"That's what I told them."

The truth is that I debated getting that signature for two days. Last night, I had the perfect opportunity when my parents came home from the hospital for a few hours to eat and shower.

But dinner was so quiet. I tried to warm them up with my anecdote about dropping by the journalism room and how everyone missed Piper. I may have slightly embellished the experience. But Mom just looked up at me in that vacant way she's been doing everything lately and mumbled, "That's nice, honey." Then she went back to picking at her rice.

They never would've agreed to sign that waiver. They think I'm supposed to be like them, putting my life completely on hold while Piper's in the hospital.

But it's been a month. I can either shrivel up and stop living, like Mom and Dad, or I can prove to them that they were right this whole time: Piper didn't try to kill herself.

I can do that for my parents, but it means I have to deceive them and everyone else in this club. That's why I forged Mom's signature on Mr. Davis's waiver.

All my parents have to do is exactly what they've been doing—spending their weekends at the hospital and forgetting I exist. I'll text Mom that I'm staying at Jessica's house all weekend.

Simple.

Grant and I get lunch off campus, even though Mr. Davis said to meet him in the gym at lunch to pack equipment. I can't very well go out into the wild for three days on cafeteria food.

"Hey, I'm going to talk to Jess real quick," I tell Grant when we get back to school. He's carrying both of our duffel bags like the prince he is.

"All right. I'll go ahead and start stuffing our packs. You gonna use Piper's?"

I blink. I hadn't thought about the fact that we're now one hiking backpack short. "Yeah, sure." I can't admit I snooped through the equipment locker and discovered that someone had stolen Piper's incriminating pack. Hopefully, Mr. Davis has an extra.

I find Jessica in the parking lot, which is flooded with upper-classmen returning from lunch at one of the three fast food places along the nearby strip. "Hey," I call out, waving to her.

She smiles, says something to Taryn Locke, who's propped against the hood of her Mercedes, and then strides over. "I feel like I never see you anymore," she coos, making a pouty face.

"Yeah, I know. I'm sorry. It's just—I've really been hunkering down, trying to get good grades so I can get into MLC."

Jessica makes a face. "Did you just say *hunkering*?" She laughs, and then I laugh, because I did indeed say the word.

"Not sure where that came from."

"Sounds like Piper," she says through a giggle. Then she stops. "Sorry, I didn't—"

"It's fine. Piper would totally say *hunkering*." I smile. Bite my lip. "Hey, Jess, if my parents happen to call you—which they won't—but if they do, can you cover for me? I told them I'd be at your place all weekend."

Jessica's eyes widen. "Are you—"

"No," I say before she can get any ideas. "I'm just going

on this club trip. One of Piper's things. Sort of in her honor. But yes, Grant will be there too."

"I knew it." She grins conspiratorially. "Of course I'll cover for you. It's not like you've never done it for me."

"Thanks." I squeeze her hand. "You're the best."

The bell buzzes to signal the end of lunch just as I take off around the building to the side gym door, pretty positive I'm going to get an earful from Mr. Davis for showing up last-minute. Inside, the bleachers are folded up against the walls, and it smells like sweat and whatever food some of the club members are still finishing up. Unsurprisingly, Lumberjack Sam and his humming girlfriend, Abby, have their twin backpacks zipped and ready to go. Alexandra and Tyler are still working on theirs, and Grant seems to have ours under control.

Scratch that. He seems to have *his* pack under control. My duffel is still lying on the ground beside him, untouched. I hurry through the scattered equipment toward him. "Where's my stuff?"

"Oh," Grant mumbles without looking up. "Mr. Davis is looking for your pack. He must've left one behind in the locker."

"Great." I cross my arms, looking for a way to help him, but I have no idea what any of these supplies are. "Should I, uh, fill these water bottles?"

"I got it," Grant says, working his clothes into tight rolls. "Did you bring a sleeping bag?"

I wince.

Grant's eyes flick up to mine, and he smiles. Shakes his head. "There should be extras with the gear."

I make my way to where Noah and Jacey are digging through equipment in the large storage container. I hover behind them, trying to spot a sleeping bag.

"Why do we need this stuff, again?" he asks. "Pretty sure a thick jacket and snacks will do the trick for a campout."

"It's not a campout." Jacey kneels, withdrawing some sort of metal contraption and adding it to the pile behind her. "Didn't you learn anything on the last three trips? Just behave, and I'll give you sour gummies." She grabs a cord attached to a couple of cylindrical objects and something that looks like a razor blade.

"What's all that?" I ask, moving alongside her.

She glances over at me like I'm a fly and she can't fathom how I learned to speak.

"It's a ferro rod." Noah points at the cylindrical object, then the metal one. "And that's the striker. For starting fires." He sticks his tongue out at Jacey. "See, Captain Alpine? I did learn a thing or two."

"Literally two things," she mutters.

"Why don't we just bring a lighter?" I ask.

"What are you doing in this club, Savannah?" Jacey asks, going back to rifling through the box. In her gray fleece pullover, black nylon cargo pants, and hiking shoes, it's obvious she's a seasoned pro. Not like Noah and me, who are wearing Nikes and jeans.

"I came to bask in your delightful presence."

"I'm serious." She stands up; at a mere five foot five, she still towers over me. "It was bad enough that your boyfriend stuck around, but now I have to look at you too?"

"What is it with you not wanting anyone else to join your damn club?"

She flinches. "I told you, I didn't threaten Piper."

"Yeah, well, someone here did." Empty-handed, I march back toward Grant and spot Alexandra along the wall, staring at me. She wrenches her eyes away and messes with the zipper on her purple vest, but it's too late. This is the third time I've caught her watching me this week.

I haven't been able to prove she's *Alex*, not by any discreet means. Maybe it's time to be indiscreet.

"Hey, Alexandra," I say, hurrying over to her. "Can I speak to you real quick?"

She pauses, her hand still stuffed inside a pouch of her pack. Then she nods. "Sure." After zipping up the pack, she rests it against the wall.

I stride to the door, my foot tapping as I wait for her to follow. When she reaches me, confusion etched in her forehead, I check the hall before whispering, "Did you speak to my sister the day she fell?"

The creases above her brows deepen. "What?"

"You heard me. Did you call my sister the day of her 'accident'?"

Alexandra flushes. "I-I don't even have Piper's number."

"You're telling me you never called her? Or met her up at Vanderwild Point on September sixteenth?"

"What are you talking about?" She takes a step back, and I realize my fists are balled at my sides. "I don't have her number. You can check my phone." She pulls it out, thrusting it at me, but I bat her hand away.

"That's worthless to me. I know you didn't use that phone."

She frowns and lowers her phone to her side. "Savannah, what are you talking about?"

"Someone sent my sister up to the Point that day. Someone threatened her—told her to quit this club. Someone spoke to her on the phone twice that day. Someone named *Alex*. You're the only person in this club named Alex. And what I want to know is, were you up at the Point with her that day?"

Alexandra pulls out her phone, unlocks it. Starts scrolling through.

"I already told you, that thing is—"

She holds it in front of my face. "Just look at it."

I do. The calendar app is open. September sixteenth is on the screen. BEN'S GAME is listed from two p.m. to nine p.m. "What's Ben's game?"

"Ben's my brother. He plays baseball for the Liberty U."

Alexandra brushes a dark curl out of her eye. "My mom picked me up from school early so I could make it there in time. I was with my parents the entire afternoon and evening. We even went to dinner with Ben after the game. If you don't believe me, ask anyone in my family."

I must not be hiding my disappointment well, because she adds, "I looked up to your sister. When she joined this club, I saw at it as an opportunity to learn from her even more." She glances at the rest of the club members finishing up their packs. "But if someone really threatened Piper, we should tell Principal Winters."

"We can't," I say, suddenly regretting my tactics. "The evidence is gone. Whoever did it stole Piper's pack, which had the threat written in it."

"So what are you going to do?"

I shrug. "Go on this hike. Find out who had a reason to threaten my sister."

Alexandra looks like she might say something, but the sound of footsteps forces us apart.

Mr. Davis approaches the door, a blue pack slung over his arm by the straps. "Couldn't find Piper's, but this one will do."

I lift it, jiggle it up and down. "Shouldn't it be...heavier? Piper's had a tent."

"You don't need a tent," he says. "Someone else will share."

A few yards away, Grant catches my gaze and makes eyes at me. My cheeks blaze.

Jacey's not standing guard over the equipment anymore, so I trudge toward it in search of a sleeping bag. A wad of green nylon is nestled in the corner. I tug it out, irritation needling me; it's not neatly tucked inside its carrying sack.

Slumping to the ground, I stare down the fabric like the formidable opponent it is.

"Need any help?"

I glance up to see Tyler, clothed in black again, chains hanging from his pockets. The black boots he's wearing are a slightly more hiking-friendly version of his ones from the other day.

"Not unless you possess whatever magical powers it takes to make this thing fit in here." I motion to the wrinkled sleeping bag sprawled over me.

"As it happens, I do." He picks up an edge of crinkly fabric and plops down beside me.

"Thanks."

"No problem." As he works on my sleeping bag, I try to make small talk. "Good thing you brought chains," I offer. "You know, like, in case we need to secure a mountain lion or something."

Tyler looks up at me, amusement flickering in his dark eyes. "I keep them on hand for just such an emergency." He finishes the knot on my perfectly bundled sleeping bag.

I get up and reach for it, but he waves me off and stands. "Where's your pack?"

"Here." I lead him to it. While he attaches the sleeping bag to the bottom, I stoop to unzip my duffel so I can transfer everything. I tug out a makeup bag, a tube of toothpaste, and a travel bottle of berry-scented lotion.

"Yeah, you can't bring any of that," he says, returning my pack.

I quirk my brows at him.

"Bears love that stuff. Might as well be groceries."

I consider this for the briefest moment. "It's worth the risk."

He scratches at his jawline. "You're not afraid of bears?"

"Of course not. We have chains, remember?"

He laughs, but it falters a moment later as his gaze travels to something behind me.

"Everything good?" Grant asks, wrapping an arm around my waist.

"Mm-hmm. Tyler was trying to convince me that none of you people were planning to brush your teeth. I didn't believe him."

Grant smiles, but there's a wariness in his expression as he glances from Tyler to me. "It's called roughing it, Savannah." He rolls his eyes, pointing at some bags with cinch cords. "Anything you can't possibly leave behind goes in one of those."

Across the gym, Mr. Davis paces in circles around a mound of equipment, making marks on a pad of paper. "Savannah, I need your permission slip," he calls out.

"Oh, sure." I dig through my duffel, whip out the forged document, and bring it to him.

By the time Grant and I get the rest of my gear packed, Mr. Davis is by the door. "Come on, people. I said we needed to get out of here by one thirty, and it's almost two. We don't want to be stuck on that trail at sundown."

"No, we certainly don't," Noah says in a ghoulish voice. "That's when they come for you."

"Shut up, Noah," I say in my older-sister voice, the way I used to whenever the three amigos were annoying me. But he barely cracks a smile. I'm not that sister figure anymore.

"Okay," Mr. Davis says, making more marks on his paper. "Looks like we're—wait, where's Alexandra?" He sighs, slamming the pen against the clipboard.

"Sorry!" calls a voice from the doorway. Alexandra is out of breath and waving a water bottle. "Forgot this in my locker. But I'm all set now."

"Good," says Mr. Davis, making one final mark before placing a wide-brimmed khaki hat on his head. "Because we're leaving."

Leaving. Heading into the depths of the wilderness with a bunch of people I can't trust.

Because one of them knows what happened to my sister the day she fell.

9

Mr. Davis hurries out of the building, pausing to help a wobbly Alexandra adjust her backpack. The parking lot at the base of Mount Liberty is only big enough for two cars, so we opt to make the ten-minute walk from the school. Sam and Abby lead the way across the school lot, Jacey right behind them.

I tug on my backpack straps and check for Grant, but he motions for me to go ahead while he ties his boot.

My eyes fasten on Alexandra. I have to find out what happened that day at Vanderwild Point. This not knowing— it's a string coiled around my insides, pulling tighter by the second. Half an hour ago, I was certain Alexandra knew something about Piper. That she'd spoken to her on the phone that day, maybe even seen her.

Now, I'm just lost. All I know is that my sister was threatened by someone in this club, and then she was sent up to the Point, where she fell. And the note mentioned this club.

Alexandra claims she never spoke to Piper. And she has an alibi for that day, so she couldn't have been at the Point.

But someone else could've been. Someone else could've forged that note on school stationery and written that threat in her bag. I just need to know who sweet little Piper was having problems with.

The obvious person is Jacey. Maybe Jacey lost it, and I need to prove it.

I look ahead to where she's walking on her own beneath the brilliant orange and red maple leaves. After the Grant fiasco, there's no way she'll even talk to me. What would I even say to her? *Sorry I stole your boyfriend, but can you please return the backpack with the incriminating message so I can give it to the police?*

I throw my head back in frustration, letting out a small growl.

"That great, huh?"

I glance back at Noah, who's keeping pace behind me. He lengthens his stride to catch up, backpack clunking in time with his steps as I scan my surroundings. We're about to pass the gas station on the corner of Fifth and Wildflower, about five minutes from the base of Mount Liberty.

"It's not the hike," I say. If I can handle two forty-minute soccer halves without a substitute, I can handle a stupid hike. "Just have a lot on my mind."

"Don't suppose you have a completely rational fear of getting preyed upon by werewolves up there too?"

I roll my eyes.

"I get it," he says, suddenly solemn. "That's been happening to me a lot, too, since Piper's accident."

"No, that's not..." I lie. "I wasn't..." I shake my head, banishing the subject. "I don't think tonight's a full moon. Your fear is, in fact, *irrational*—you'd only get eaten by the regular kind of wolves."

He pretends to think about this before playfully punching me in the shoulder. And it feels nice. Like he's back to kid-brother Noah and not the disappointed-in-me version.

Maybe he's starting to forgive me the way Piper did. My thoughts tumble back to homecoming night, the Saturday before she fell. The first time I saw a true glimmer of hope for my sister and me since everything with Grant went down.

I had worked for it too. Found Piper the perfect dress. Short and blue, with layers that fluttered like the petals of the blue rain flowers that grow along the Golden River and made her turquoise eyes pop. I let her borrow my favorite clutch. I even did her makeup, painted her eyes a glimmering bronze and her lips with Roses Are Pink.

"Are you nervous?" I asked, because her hands were shaking as she examined herself in the mirror. She and Noah had only been together a few weeks, and things were still jittery-new.

"No," she said. But I could see the lump in her throat as she swallowed.

"Well, I'm excited for you." I batted my eyelashes dramatically. "You've been dreaming of Noah asking you to a dance for ages."

"Shut up," she snapped, her glossy lips pressed into a tight line. Carefully, she examined her face in the mirror. Tugged on the hem of the dress, adjusted the strap. I could tell from the way her skin glowed that she loved everything about her reflection.

Grant and I had been crowned homecoming king and queen at the game the night before. I should've been taking the customary photos with him and the other court members. Instead, I'd told him to meet me later to buy myself an extra hour with Piper.

When we arrived at school, we waited in front of the gym, Piper biting her lower lip. I swatted at her. "You're ruining your lipstick."

She stopped, only to begin picking at the black sequins on my clutch. Then she reached out to center the little gemstone on my necklace. It sparkled silver, like my dress and the clouds shifting overhead in the twinkling sky.

"You're going with a boy who loves you," I assured her. "It's going to be amazing."

Beneath the dim glow of the outdoor lights, she smiled faintly. Then she pulled her audio recorder from the clutch and pressed a button. "The walkway to homecoming was decorated with dreams," she said, transitioning effortlessly into her reporter voice while making silly faces at me. "The sparkling displays found only in realms as distant as Party City promised it would be a magical night to remember."

I clacked my fingernails together, and she tucked the recorder away. "Sorry," she said. "They assigned me the dance, if you can believe it. And I intend to do it justice." Then she removed her phone from the clutch and checked her makeup in the camera, her fingers shaking.

"You look beautiful," I said. And she did. "But I do think you need to loosen up a bit. How about a quick round of the Sullivan family road trip classic known as I Spy?"

She quirked a brow, but then started scanning the dance-goers making their way into the gym. "I spy with my little eye something you used to date in middle school."

My head whipped around, and I spotted Denny Henderson, who hadn't grown much since we "went out" for a week in eighth grade. I shoved Piper, and she wobbled in her high heels.

"Hey!" she shrieked. But I caught her by the arm, and then we were both cracking up in front of the school gymnasium.

A moment later, her smile sank. A darkness shifted into her eyes. "You know, you probably shouldn't be here when Jacey shows up."

I licked my lips, breaking my own damn rule about leaving my lipstick alone. "Right," I said, even though it felt like tiny needles were stabbing my chest. We'd made so much progress, but Piper was still embarrassed to be seen with me. Her own sister. "She just expects you to never talk to me, even though we live in the same house?"

"It's not that," she said softly. "I just want things to stay good between Jacey and me. Laughing with you isn't exactly going to help matters." She twirled a frizzy wave around her finger.

"Fine." I curled my toes, trying with everything in me not to argue because I didn't want to ruin the night for her. "I spy with my little eye...something tall and dashing and totally staring at you."

Piper turned bright red as she took a few long breaths and stuffed her phone back into the clutch. Then she full-on grinned at me, like the excitement she'd held in all day had finally burst. I gave her a discreet hand squeeze, and she spun, heels clicking down the path to meet Noah.

It was dark, but beneath the lamps, I watched him place a corsage on her wrist. His hand moved to the small of her back as they ambled up the path toward me.

"Hey, Savannah," Noah mumbled, barely making eye

contact. He'd really gone all out for their date. His tall, lean frame was clothed in a dark tux. His hair was slightly combed for once. Same glasses as usual, but somehow, he looked all grown up.

Glimpsing Jacey at the parking lot's edge, I gave Piper one last smile of encouragement and moved away from the couple, into the shadows behind the gym, to wait for Grant.

Now, I stoop to pick a dandelion as I walk at Noah's side down the last stretch of road before the parking lot. Grant said Jacey had yelled at Piper during Survival Club. Maybe that's why Piper had seemed a bit on edge homecoming night.

"Hey, Noah?"

"Yeah?"

"What did Jacey say to Piper in Survival Club the week before she fell? Why was she so upset?"

Noah is quiet for several paces. He kicks at a rock, which skips off a nearby tree and rolls into the lot. "She said, 'Why did you have to take this away from me too?'"

"What did she mean by that?"

He runs a hand through his hair. Hunches his shoulders. "Freshman year, Jacey really wanted to join journalism, and Piper tagged along for the meeting. I don't know exactly what happened, but Piper ended up staying in the club, and Jacey never went back. When I asked her about it, Jacey just muttered about Mr. James having favorites or something."

A little flash of alarm goes off in my brain. It's not the first time I've heard this accusation. Seems like Mr. James had a habit of gifting Piper everything other girls wanted.

"I guess when Piper joined Survival Club," Noah continues, "Jacey sort of freaked out. She thought Piper was going to steal it away too. Survival Club has always been Jacey's *thing*, you know? She practically grew up in the wilderness with her dad. And Piper showed up with no experience and no clue how to do anything, and suddenly, it was like she was running the show. And she didn't *mean* to—we all know Piper never means to do these things. Even Jacey knew that. So she apologized to Piper, like, the next day, and then I swear things were fine."

I look up from my dandelion to give him a grateful smile. "Thanks, Noah."

He nods, and I watch him trudge ahead to catch Jacey. That itch to find the truth is worse now, begging to be scratched.

It sounds like things between Piper and her bestie were anything but fine.

10

I wait for Grant to catch up, and we start up the mountain base, stitched with evergreens. Up at the rocky peak, the sun is blinding.

"You okay?" Grant asks, either because my eyes are watering after looking straight into the sun or because I'm never this slow.

The trail is narrow, and our group takes it in pairs. Mr. Davis is the exception, his khaki wide-brimmed hat leading the way.

"Yep." My sneakers start to slip as the terrain changes from asphalt into gravely dirt. After a rain, this path becomes sloshy mud, but now the dirt is dry and loose. The pair ahead of us kicks it up into the air.

An hour later, we reach the fork in the trail. The steeper, rockier path veers to the right: Vanderwild Trail. Slightly more treacherous, but exploding with views. Grant took me up here for a picnic on my birthday. And I was here years ago, when I followed the three amigos on one of their little adventures. I'd been home, bored after a fight with Jessica, and those three were all laughs as they put on their sneakers and headed outside. Even Piper seemed content as they sang their way up the mountain, sharing licorice and inside jokes. And I stayed hidden, playing spy, judging their clothes and song choices while part of me wished I'd been invited.

Now, I try to push past the fork, but my eyes catch on the place where the trail winds up the mountain, dropping off into a deep, lush gully on one side. A gust of wind whips through the trees, fanning my ponytail and chilling me through.

I know we're not traveling that way; you can't even get to the river by that trail. Still, my heart thuds against my rib cage. The path goes hazy. It ripples and moves like a snake in the sand. I can't catch my breath.

"Hey, hey." Grant's arms are around me. "You're pale. Sit down." I try to resist, but my pack is already off, and I'm down in the dirt. "Drink," he says, handing me my water bottle.

"I just want to keep moving," I mumble, unable to take my eyes off Vanderwild. The path that leads to the Point.

Grant follows my gaze, then places his hand on my jaw,

gently turning my face to look at him. "We're not going that way."

"I know—I'm fine."

He sighs. "This was a bad idea. I should've tried harder to get you to stay home. I'm going to run ahead and tell Mr. Davis that I'm walking you back down."

"I said I'm fine," I snap, forcing myself onto my feet. My head spins as I cap the bottle. I sway, but Grant steadies me. Up the trail, Mr. Davis takes the path on the left.

My vision starts to clear, and my lungs let air back in. The path stops moving. I find my footing again. A moment later, Vanderwild Trail disappears as we push on toward an area where the smattering of trees becomes dense forest.

Golden Trail, the path threading through the woods on this side, is named after the river. It's even narrower than Vanderwild, but there's no cliff bordering it, which makes it popular among locals.

I pause to jostle the backpack higher on my spine. But it keeps sagging, like it's trying to drag me back down the mountain. Like it doesn't want me here. Grant turns to check on me, a look of concern on his face. I take a deep breath of crisp mountain air and flick my chin for him to keep going.

We reach an unremarkable area, and Mr. Davis tells us to scout a good place to make camp. I glance around, seeing nothing but rocks and trees, the same view I've had the last two hours. I pull out my phone to check the time, then remember that I shut it off an hour back when we lost reception.

Moments later, Lumberjack Sam spots an ideal patch of land just off the trail. An old fire ring and a rusted tin can nestled in the ash are among the remnants of previous campers.

Mr. Davis instructs us to pitch our tents, and Grant asks me to start on his while he helps clear the area. I have no idea how to put a tent together, but how hard can it be? I bend over, tugging on his tent poles, but he jammed them inside the backpack so tight they won't budge. Plopping down into the dirt, I use my feet for leverage and pull. But only one stake comes loose, and the rest leave angry marks on my hands.

Cursing under my breath, I slam the whole pack into the dirt. *What were you doing in this club, Piper?* She would've hated it up here.

But she would've succeeded. She would've assembled her tent in no time and then built mine before I even asked for help. And I would've felt like an idiot for about sixty seconds—the way I always do when my little sister comes to my rescue—until she made some remark about the incompetence of the tent manufacturer and how she would've made the part I was stuck on snap together more easily. Then she would've disassembled her tent just to confirm said theory.

It's not exactly easy when your little sister passes you by in every subject in school. Still, having that massive brain around gave me a sense of comfort. I never realized how much until now. Piper has a way of swooping in and saving the day before I manage to get too worked up. She senses when she's needed. I guess some subconscious part of me has been waiting for her to take this tent from me.

At least I have Grant. "Hey, Grant," I call, scanning the area, "I tried, but you shoved this thing in—"

Grant seems to have wandered off. I abandon his pack and start poking around the grounds. A few yards from the fire ring, Mr. Davis sets a pot and a Jetboil on a large, flat rock, creating a makeshift kitchen.

I round a gray pop-up tent that's already assembled, halting when I see Jacey and Noah in the woods beyond it, both visibly upset. I back up, crouching down behind the tent and peeking through the mesh window.

"Jace, I don't want to spend another minute up here with you until we talk about it."

"I already said I was sorry," Jacey says, arms hanging limply at her sides.

Heat itches up my neck like a prickly rash. What's she sorry for? Somewhere behind me, Abby starts singing while she works, muffling their conversation.

My calves burn from the way I'm half squatting to get a view, so I lower until I'm sitting in the dirt. Mercifully, the song stops. I can hear Jacey again, but I only catch the end of her sentence. "...didn't mean to do anything to her."

I rock up onto my toes to peek at them again; Noah's head is dipped, his eyes on the ground.

"I'm sorry," Jacey pleads. "I keep saying it. I'm sorry." She wipes at her face. "Can we go now? We've got to set up."

She trudges off farther into the woods, but Noah remains there for a moment. He rubs his temple before following her.

I stand, brushing dirt off my jeans. What did Jacey do that has Noah so upset? And who's *her*?

I turn around, my pulse ready to leap out of my skin when I skirt the tent and smack straight into Tyler.

"You okay?" He squints down at me, hands in his chain-bedazzled pockets.

"Yeah," I mutter. "Sorry about that."

"No problem." Tyler grabs a pole, removing it from Grant's pack with a swift tug. He moves on to the others, spreading them out over the large polyester sheet. "It's really easy." Deftly, he secures the poles inside the little rings and motions for me to do the same on the opposite side.

"Now we just clip the tent to the poles, all the way up."

I start to clip, glancing at the focused expression on Tyler's face. The wind rustles the black hair out of his deep brown eyes. "Good. That's it. Almost done. Now we're going to put the fly on top." He waits for me to grab the other side of the fabric.

Once we finish, I admire our work. Tyler moves to stand beside me. "Nice necklace," he says, indicating the hand-painted charm strung from my neck.

My hand darts to the necklace instinctively. Protectively. I spread my fingers out, pressing the cold chain against my clavicle. "Thanks. My sister made it." My hand lowers, allowing the little silver-framed ceramic charm to rest in my open palm. "This one's supposed to be me."

"I can see that." His mouth twists into a boyish grin. "The resemblance is uncanny."

I roll my eyes. When Piper was twelve, my parents signed her up for a summer jewelry-making class. Every day when she came home, my parents asked what she was working so hard on, and every day she told them it was a secret. We all figured she was making a gift for Mom, like some clunky bracelet made of shells. But on the final day, she brought home a small, neatly wrapped present with a pink bow and placed it in my hands.

I tried so hard to squash my enthusiasm. I was the mature older sister. But as I folded back the tissue paper and uncovered the nickel-sized ceramic gem with tiny hand-painted characters, I couldn't help but smile.

It was us, side by side. She'd used special tools to paint miniature versions. But while Piper looked like herself—scrawny and plain, hair fanning around her like a halo—she'd made me into a superhero. My hair was long and shiny, painted yellow with care. I wore a pink cape and had a hand on my hip and a soccer ball nestled at my feet.

My heart burst like a firework, and I couldn't undo the clasp fast enough. Piper helped me secure the silver chain around my neck. I refused to take it off.

Eventually, I outgrew Piper's necklace. Sister-made jewelry was no longer the fashion. But I carefully placed it in its own special compartment in my jewelry box.

Over the years, the necklace moved farther and farther to the back of the box, one little velvet square at a time. Then, on the day Piper was found, I frantically rummaged for it again—the only artifact I had from a time when my sister loved me. I wanted to feel like part of her was still with me, even as her body lay in that hospital bed miles from our house. Instead, when I scooped up the silver chain, letting it dangle between my fingers, I felt like a fraud. An impostor.

I keep wearing it, though. The feel of it is comforting. I find myself checking to make sure it's there throughout the day, running my fingers over the cold ceramic. Like caring for it will somehow make up for the way I neglected its creator.

Tyler watches me, his features perked with interest, like he can read my thoughts. "Thanks for your help with the tent," I say, dropping the charm and dismissing him.

"Who are you sharing with?" he asks, not getting the hint.

"Oh, um…" I hadn't really thought about it. Guess I can't share with Alexandra after I accused her of being involved in Piper's fall, and I can't share with Jacey for obvious reasons. "Abby."

He frowns, but there's a devious glint in his eyes. "That'll be tough, since she's already sharing with Alexandra."

"She is?" I try to sound disinterested even as alarm bells blast in my brain.

"There's still Jacey," he says.

Leaves crunch behind me. "I'll take it from here, thanks." Grant stomps between us to reach the tent.

"It's done, man." Tyler lifts his hands and backs away. "I was just making sure she got it set up before dark."

"Thanks for your help." I try to catch his eye, to apologize for my boyfriend with a look.

"No problem," he says before trotting off toward the others.

"You could've asked *me* for help." Grant moves behind me, wrapping his arms around mine.

His warm breath sends chills down my spine, but I slip free, spinning to face him. "I didn't ask him for help. He just did it. He's not a bad guy."

Grant shrugs. "I'm sure he's fine. Just needs to stay away from my girl."

I blow air through my teeth. "Jealousy's not a good look on you," I say, dragging my fingertips over his chest. "I have to find Abby." And work a little magic. "There's no way I'm sharing with Jacey."

"Well, you and I could share," he says in a singsong voice.

"Sure, Mr. Davis will be totally fine with that."

"He doesn't have to know." He waggles his brows playfully, and he's just so ridiculously gorgeous that any irritation I had about his Tarzan complex starts to dull.

I shake my head and wander in the direction of the blue tent where I last spotted Abby. I'm on thin ice with Mr. Davis as it is.

Ice that Grant has no idea about. And I need to keep it that way.

"I'll come with you," Grant calls after me. "Might as well find Sam so I don't get stuck with Noah."

Noah hates Grant for what he did to Jacey. Of course, it's the Noah version of hate. Like bunny rabbit rage, basically.

When we don't spot Sam and Abby's matching camouflage jackets, we ask Mr. Davis where they are.

"I sent them to gather firewood," he replies. "If you two are done setting up, you can help."

"Great," I mumble, wandering off into the trees alongside Grant. After a few yards, he bends over to pick up a branch. "What are you doing? I thought we were looking for the lumberjacks. Once we find them, we can ask Sam to hack down a tree with his ax or something."

"Savannah, you have to play nice."

"Oh, please." Abby's at the bottom of the popularity pyramid. She's going to feel like the queen of her entire imaginary kingdom is asking to stay at her house tonight. I'm doing her a favor.

"I think they're on the other side of this stream." He points to where the trees give way to a dip in the earth. "Stay here in case they come this way."

"Sure." I scan my surroundings for somewhere to sit, but there's only a rotten stump covered in ants. After a few seconds, I tug the note I found in Piper's locker from my pocket. I've been waiting for a moment alone to reexamine it. I turn it over in my palm and rub at it like you would one of those scratch-off tickets—as if the author's mysterious identity might be hidden somewhere beneath the ink. The words send a prickly sensation up my spine.

Survival Club will be holding an extra skills session after school today at Vanderwild Point.

Whoever wrote this meant to deceive my sister.

Whoever wrote this could be dangerous.

A hum drifts through the trees, and I stuff the note back into my pocket. Sure enough, where singing is, Abby's unmistakable fire-red hair and camouflage getup will follow. She's probably made friends with the birds and the squirrels by now.

"I was just looking for you," I say, feeling almost bad that I've interrupted her Briar Rose moment.

Abby quirks a brow. "Me?" Her lips shift into a confused smile.

"Everyone's partnering up to share tents," I say, waiting for that perplexed expression to morph into a flattered one.

But her grin drops. "I sort of partnered up with Alexandra already."

"Tell her you changed your mind."

"Why would I do that?"

My face heats. "Because if you don't, I'll have to share with Jacey," I snap.

Abby takes a timid step back.

I press my hands together like I'm praying. There's got to be a way to change her mind. "You don't understand. We have a history."

Abby's forehead scrunches. "It's not exactly a secret, Savannah. You stole her boyfriend."

My neck jerks. "Excuse me?"

"The photo in the *Grayling High Gazette*." She must see the vein popping in my forehead, because her voice lowers and her face reddens, washing out her freckles. "I would think you'd want to be nice to Jacey after what you did." She makes a motherly face of disapproval. "Maybe sharing a tent would be good for you."

This doesn't happen often, but I'm speechless. I can't correct her, because she's not wrong. Still, the nerve of this flannel-covered frontierswoman, when I was trying to be nice to her. I glance helplessly at the pine trees surrounding us. At the crow squawking irritatingly, high overhead. Here in the wilderness, my social standing is about as useful as it is in the Sullivan home.

"I'm really sorry about Piper," Abby continues. "I am. But you and your sister..." Her lips twist in something like disgust.

"I wasn't aware you had such strong feelings concerning *me and my sister.*"

Abby shrugs. "You don't seem aware of much."

"What's that supposed to mean?"

"You're sort of in your own world. That's why you didn't know Piper was—" She shakes her head. "Forget it." She reaches out to touch my arm, but I step back. "My thoughts are with your sister."

"What didn't I know about Piper?" She's not changing the subject.

"It doesn't matter."

"It matters if you threatened her."

Abby's eyes narrow. "*Threatened* her?" That stupid smile reappears on her face, but it contorts unnervingly, sending a chill up my spine. "I don't know what you're talking about, Savannah."

Abby pivots and plods away, leaves crunching beneath her massive boots. Once she disappears into the trees, I flop down onto the ant stump, my legs sore from the hike, hands sore from how tightly they've been balled up.

I touch the cold silver of my necklace, pressing the charm between two fingers. Out in the middle of this forest with the wind whipping against my face, I feel exposed. Bare. I wish my bed weren't a billion miles away so I could crawl under the covers.

But the thought of my bed only conjures a memory from the day Piper fell. Raised voices. The flutter of paper. Words I can never take back.

Now, the wind sings through the trees. A woodpecker knocks, and my heart echoes the sound as it pounds in my chest.

"You didn't find her?" Grant's voice arrives before he appears through the pine boughs.

I wipe away the welling tears. "I did." I sniffle and attempt to stand.

Grant whistles in a breath and motions toward the phone in my back pocket. "Did they call about—?"

"No, nothing like that," I assure him. "I don't even have reception. I was thinking about her, that's all."

"Oh." He nods dumbly, and I can't exactly blame him; I don't get weepy often. Even when I found out about Piper, I didn't cry. He extends his arm, and I clutch it, leaning against him as we walk back to camp.

"Are you sure you don't want me to take you back

down?" His head tilts forward, a dark curl tumbling over his forehead as his eyes search mine.

"It's going to be dark soon. I can survive a couple more days with these creeps." Hopefully. "What did Lumberjack say?"

"He's cool. Abby?"

I bite my lip, trying to force new tears back into my eye sockets. "Apparently, she and Alexandra already paired up, so…"

Grant stops dead in his tracks. "Oh, no, babe."

I kick a branch so hard pain shoots from my toes up to my shoulders. A metallic taste seeps over my tongue; my teeth have broken through the soft inside flesh of my lower lip. "Look, whatever. I don't have to speak to her. We'll just be sleeping."

Grant picks up the pace again, probably relieved that the only thing I'm kicking is a stick.

As the sun hugs the top of the mountains, we round a familiar boulder. A smattering of brightly colored tents pops into view. I take a deep breath.

We enter the camp to find most of the group sprawled out in the dirt, inspecting the little packets of instant camp food. A fire blazes in the old steel ring. Sam and Abby are crouched on either side, tossing sticks onto it.

Taking a seat on a log at the edge of camp, I pretend to dig a splinter out of my palm. But I'm watching Abby, because she knows more than she's saying about Piper.

And it could lead to the truth about that day.

11

Daylight dims as Grant dangles a packet of savory stroganoff between two fingers. He squints up at it. "Freeze-dried heaven."

I make a face and dig through the packets while he pours bottled water into his Jetboil. Snatching the one that says CREAMY PASTA, I study the way Grant makes food appear from virtually nothing.

When I finish stirring my mush, I take a seat with the others around the campfire. The sun has vanished behind the mountains, its hazy glow trickling through the trees to make shadows of everyone's faces.

I steal a glance at Grant, eating beside me in the dirt, perfectly in his element. Guilt rubs at an already-raw spot.

When we got together, I tried so hard to get him to quit this club. In my head, he couldn't love me and go to meetings with his ex. I see it now, though—the way this stuff makes him come alive. His features darken as the light fades, but I can just make out a grin as he catches me staring.

I take a bite of pasta, which tastes bland and has gone cold, and set the container down. Everyone but me seems prepared with an extra coat. I shiver and cross my arms over my chest.

Finished eating, Grant scoots over to wrap an arm around me. "Cold?" he asks, pulling me in closer.

"Not anymore." I snuggle into the crook of his arm, watching the firelight dance on the tents and the figures huddled around it.

"So, is this the part where we tell ghost stories?" Noah's voice crashes through the mixture of gentle whispers and crackling from the campfire. "Mr. Davis, you brought the marshmallows and chocolate, right?"

"Sorry, Mr. Crawford. They didn't fit in my pack."

Noah exhales an exaggerated sigh. "That's okay. We can still tell stories and roast *something* over the fire. Sam, what did you catch out there?"

From the other side of the fire, Sam's brow furrows.

"You know," Noah continues, "when you were out there hunting while the rest of us were building tents. You're not pulling your weight around here. When we vote someone out of the camp tonight, I might have to toss your name into the basket."

Sam grunts, his expression bored.

Jacey swats Noah, but he's obviously determined to make himself tonight's entertainment. "Ooh!" he shouts. "Ghost story tag! I'll start."

I should let my head slump back in a show of disinterest, but someone claps, and an excited buzz builds around the fire.

"Think I might go to bed," Grant whispers in my ear.

"Don't be such an old man."

"Forgive me if I don't want to participate in Crawford's drama club story hour."

"This is going to be so much worse than that," I say like an archvillain. "Promise." I tug on his arm, but he stands anyway.

"You have fun." It's obviously too dark for him to get the full effect of my pouty face. He leans over to kiss me, then walks off in the direction of his tent.

"'Night," I say, feeling hurt but also feeling ridiculous that I'm hurt. A few feet away, Tyler is watching me like I'm his favorite Netflix show.

"Are you eavesdropping?" I ask.

He stands, the hood of his black sweatshirt falling back to reveal messy black hair, and shuffles over, taking a seat in the dirt beside me. "Sorry, couldn't help it. I'm a fixer by nature, and you look upset."

My face heats. "I-I'm not upset," I stammer as the rest of the group bursts into laughter. "Now, can you pipe down? We're missing the story. How are we supposed to kill off whatever characters they've created if we don't even know *who* they've created?"

Tyler smirks. "Fair enough." But he adds, "Sure you're okay?"

"Well, now that you mention it *again...*" I shake my head. "I'm not talking to you."

He crosses his arms, head tilted thoughtfully. "You're not a talks-about-feelings kind of gal, I gather."

"You're not a super quick gatherer, I gather."

He glances around like he's searching for something in the dirt. "It's fine. I have time. I just need the notebook where I pretend to write insights about my patients when I'm actually drawing what I think they'd look like as a cat."

I restrain my smile. "How about you invest all that energy into setting someone's things on fire? I have the perfect target. First syllable *j*, second syllable *c*."

"Ah," he says, looking pleased with himself. "Now we're getting somewhere. You don't like Jacey."

"I'm not doing this with you, stranger."

He rests his chin on a fist. "Tell me more about that."

"Stranger danger."

"I'm sensing an age-old grudge. Likely involving a feud over property, perhaps oil." His brows lift in mock hope.

"You have the gift."

He grins.

"Let's just say I'd rather stay up all night and tell myself ghost stories than get in a tent with her."

He sobers slightly. "She did something pretty terrible to you, huh?"

My insides twist, that sliver of amusement I'd felt a moment ago shredded. If only I felt this way about Jacey because of something *she'd* done to *me*.

"Changed my mind," I say, turning away. "I'd rather brave the tent than stay here with Mr. Chatty Pants."

"Hey, I didn't—"

But I'm already yards away, grabbing my pack off the ground beside Grant's tent.

I lug it over to Jacey's tent and unzip the door. Inside, I aim my flashlight at the ground, where her things are spread over the entire floor.

I shove them all to one side and start to pull out my sleeping bag.

"Hey!" comes a shrill voice from behind me. When I turn, a light shines straight into my eyes. "What are you doing?"

I bat the beam of light like it's a fly. "The better question is, why the hell didn't you leave me any space?"

"Because I never thought you'd come in here."

"Where was I supposed to sleep? The fire ring?" I blink until the blurriness fades.

"I mean, I just figured you'd—"

"Defy school policy and sleep in my boyfriend's tent?"

At the word *boyfriend*, she flinches.

"Believe me, I would, but I can't afford to get in trouble right now. My parents wouldn't be able to handle it."

Jacey's head sinks. "Yeah." She kneels down to straighten her sleeping bag and then slips inside it. "I tried to make other arrangements, you know. With the tents. But Abby hates me."

"Why?" The word is out before I can help it.

"Just—I don't know."

I get my things situated and zip up my sleeping bag around me. "I heard you and Noah in the woods earlier," I say, because once my mouth is on a roll, there's no stopping it.

"What?"

"You apologized for something. Was it about Piper?"

Jacey's inhale is like thunder inside the tiny tent. "You're a real piece of work, Savannah."

"Look, if you know what happened to her that day, just tell me. Please."

"We weren't talking about that. I never even saw Piper that day. That's the truth. Yes, we had a little...*thing* when she joined Survival Club. I was just in a bad place, and I blew up at her. But that was it. You know she's my best friend." The last word breaks off like a weak branch in the wind.

My chest tightens. It wasn't her. Which means my search isn't over.

Or maybe Grant has been right this entire time. Maybe I'm just trying to put the blame on someone else because I can't face what I did. And I'm so desperate that I nearly dragged Jacey into this. As if I haven't hurt her enough already.

"I'm sorry."

"No, I get why you...our relationship hasn't exactly been perfect the past few years. But I love Piper."

I meant that I'm sorry about *everything*. About Grant. But as usual, I'm too chicken to say it. The sound of the others' voices mixed with the chirping of crickets drifts in as the two of us lie side by side in the dark.

"I should've known you had nothing to do with it," I say. "I mean, I did know, after I saw the calls from somebody named Alex. Obviously, if you'd called her, the phone would've said your name."

Jacey props herself up on an elbow. "Someone named Alex called her?"

I nod, even though she can't see me in the dark, my chin rustling the nylon bag. "Three times. Her last calls before my mom's. And I don't think they were from Alexandra."

More silence, broken only by the crickets and the occasional giggle. "So, then," Jacey says, voice barely above a whisper, "you really think someone did something to her. Who would have a reason to hurt Piper?"

I shut my eyes, trying to breathe, slow and steady. But the

frustration rises until I can feel it in my jaw. "You think I'm being stupid, like Grant does. Piper fell from Suicide Point, so I should just shut up about all this stuff."

Maybe I'm frustrated because they could be right.

"I didn't say that."

I wait for her to elaborate, but she doesn't say anything else. Doesn't even move for a moment that stretches for ages.

"I just can't think of anyone in the club who wasn't crazy about Piper," Jacey finally says. "Everyone pretty much thought she was God's gift to wilderness survival."

The tension shoots pain through my shoulders and neck. Of course Jacey doesn't believe me. It isn't her fault. You can't just erase months of heartbreak and distrust.

And she's right. I haven't found a single motive for anyone in this club. I turn over onto my side.

There's a rustle, then a muffled noise. Is she crying?

"This reminds me of the time we camped out in your backyard and Piper thought she heard a cougar."

She's laughing.

My lips curl at the memory. Piper and I were close enough in age that we used to have joint sleepovers with Jessica and Jacey. My parents had never—*have* never—camped, but they bought a tent and told us to have fun in the comfort and safety of our own gated yard. One night, I had to go inside to use the bathroom, and when I returned, Piper heard my footsteps and practically peed her pants, she was so scared.

For all her brains, she actually thought a cougar might be prowling around in our grass.

Slowly, the tension between us begins to deflate. It's not the affirmation I was hoping for. But Jacey doesn't owe me anything. And this—it's something.

"I want to help," she says, wrenching me from the nostalgic moment and reminding me why I came here. "If someone was really up there with Piper at the Point—if someone in this club threatened her—we'll figure out who it was."

Unease slithers up the back of my brain. I don't trust her. We may never be able to trust each other fully again.

But Jacey's been in Survival Club since her freshman year. She knows these people. If I'm going to find out what really happened to my sister, I may have to put my faith in my least likely ally.

12

The camp is quiet now, everyone off to bed. My eyelids are heavy, but my heart keeps thumping to the rhythm of the crickets. Jacey's sleeping bag crinkles, and she whispers, "Have you told anyone?"

For a second, I think she knows, and my panic spikes. I haven't told a soul about what I did to my sister. Not after how horribly wrong things turned out.

Piper was so stressed over schoolwork that she finally caved and let me grade Mr. Davis's tests. I sat with red pen in hand, trying to do my best impersonation of Piper's handwriting. Sixty-two for Gary Burgess, who probably should've studied harder. Seventy-five for Dana Casillas, which sounded about right. I picked up the next test—mine—and a nervous flutter ran through my stomach.

I was nearly done. I just had to grade this one and—I lifted the rest of the stack—five more, then figure out a way to make a few hundred bucks.

I started to drop the tests back into the manila folder when a slip of paper snagged my eye. Something attached to the back inside cover. A number.

No, a *password*.

Piper's password for logging scores into Mr. Davis's grading program.

An idea danced its way into my head. Light steps that quickened.

How much would Gary Burgess pay to have that sixty-two bumped up to a seventy-five? And Lacy Santana... She was shooting for the Ivies. Was an eighty really going to cut it? A ninety would look a lot better.

I tried to knock the idea down, but it got up again. It kept dancing, twirling, flinging itself around my head.

"The real reason you're on this trip," Jacey says now. "Have you told anyone else?" My muscles relax.

An owl hoots in the distance, and I tug my sleeping bag higher. "Just Alexandra. I sort of had to tell her after I accosted her over the phone thing."

"Well, what's your plan?"

"Guess I don't have one. I was going to take Piper's pack with the threat written in it to the police. But then it disappeared."

"What about Piper's phone? You said you have the calls from Alex on there. Maybe the cops can figure out who it is."

A frenzied jolt hits me. "No," I say too fast.

There's a shush from somewhere in the camp—probably Mr. Davis. "Some phone calls won't cut it," I whisper. "The cops will laugh in our faces. Piper fell from *Suicide Point*. We need something more concrete."

And something that doesn't involve the cops digging through Piper's phone. It won't be just my parents shunning me if what I did to my own sister that day comes to light.

It'll be Grayling High.

It'll be Mount Liberty College.

It'll be Grant.

"Did you hear that?" Jacey whispers suddenly, swatting my feet.

"Hear what?" I mumble, picking a stowaway pine needle out of my sleeping bag.

"Something is right outside our tent."

I listen, and sure enough, I hear a scratching sound. It's close. "Probably just a man-eating grizzly," I whisper, burying myself in the sleeping bag.

"It's not a grizzly," she hisses. "It's a person, and they're listening to everything we say."

"Not really worth verifying, though, is it? If it is a man-eating grizzly, you'll never get the chance to say anything ever again. Because of the missing head and all." A new sound makes its way in, like air blowing hard and fast against the side of the tent. The next joke dies on my tongue.

Jacey sucks in a breath and sits upright. Before I can find my flashlight to figure out what's going on, she's unzipping the tent. "Jacey—"

But she disappears into the dark.

There's a scuffle. My body goes rigid with fear. I breathe. In and out. Listen.

Nothing. My heartbeat pounds in my eardrums as I shimmy out of the bag. Finding the flashlight, I duck through the opening.

"Savannah." The voice pierces through the night, through my chest. I jump and shine the light toward the sound.

Jacey comes into view behind the tent, her pale face hazy in the wash of light. Her hand is raised, index finger pointed at the tent.

I guide my flashlight in the direction of her gaze until its glow illuminates the nylon...and the words that are now written there.

My hand shakes. Panic screeches inside my head, shattering my eardrums.

White paint. Letters splintered like tree bark. The same writing I found in Piper's pack.

But the message is new.

Leave it alone.

13

The flashlight drops to my side, and I swallow—once, twice—
until my voice comes back. "Did you do this?" I ask Jacey,
the words hoarse.

"What? Are you crazy? You heard someone out here too!"

"Yeah, well, there's no one here now."

"Savannah, listen to me. I saw someone—probably
whoever did this. But they ran off."

I don't know what to do. She could be lying. But if she's
not, I might be able to catch this person. "Which way did
they run?"

"That way," she says, pointing toward the dark woods.
"Let's go find Mr. Davis." She reaches for my hand, but I
wrench my arm back.

"I'm going after them."

"Savannah," she hisses. "They could be dangerous."

"That's why I can't let them get away." She tries to grab my arm again, but I bat her off. Training the light in the direction she pointed, I start to sprint. The trees span out ahead of me, all claws. I let my light bounce from forest floor to eye level, trying not to trip.

I make it through the first line of trees and continue, listening for movement. But the forest is an endless void before me. I'm going to be lost out here all night. I strain my ears, but the only sound is twigs snapping beneath my feet. Just when I'm about to give up, my light lands on a person crouched in the grass.

Noah Crawford stands, the moonlight and the dim yellow circle from my flashlight illuminating his face. He glances around like a trapped animal.

I step closer, my light flicking down to the object at his feet, half buried in the grass.

A can of spray paint.

I gape at him, horror trickling from my scalp down through my body.

"Savannah?" His eyes are like two wide-open goals.

Because he's caught. White-freaking-handed.

I turn around, crunching leaves as I try to find my way out of the trees. "Savannah!" Noah calls after me. I ignore him, gaining speed until my foot snags on a root and I go flying.

The world is a jumble of black and branches. A sharp twig slams my face. My head smacks against the ground. I groan, trying to get to my feet.

Footsteps pound behind me. I scramble, but Noah's on me too fast. "Here," he says, huffing. "Let me—"

"Get off me!" I yell, grabbing for my flashlight and pointing it into his eyes.

He draws back, blinking. When I lower the light, a stunned look crosses his face. "What's going on?" he asks, still hovering, but watching me like I might try to lunge at him.

I might. I can't believe he'd threaten us. That he'd threaten Piper.

"Stop acting like you don't know about the writing on our tent."

His green eyes are slivers in the moonlight as he squints down at me.

"You have the paint, Noah. If I hadn't come after you, you'd have stashed it in the forest and no one would be the wiser." I finally push onto my feet, brushing leaves off of me. I tug a twig out of my hair, rubbing two fingers over the place my head hit the earth. Just a bump.

"I don't know what you're talking about," he says. "I came because I heard a commotion and wanted to check on you two. When I got to your tent, someone was hiding behind it. Whoever it was saw me and ran off into the woods, so I followed them."

"Right. And you just happened to have stumbled upon the can."

Noah glances down, like he's just remembering. "Yeah. The person dropped it."

"You're unbelievable." I spin back toward the tent, and he follows me.

"Why aren't you listening?" he asks, his long legs moving twice as fast as mine.

I reach the tent, were Jacey is standing with her flashlight like a helpless child.

"Wait," Noah says, his footsteps finally slowing as he takes in the painted words. "*That's* what you think I did?"

I grab Jacey by the arm to tug her into the tent, but she struggles, pulling away. "What happened?" she asks, racing toward Noah.

"I don't know." He moves closer to the tent, shining his flashlight over the message.

"Noah, I swear," I say, my breath ragged, "you need to stay away from me. Stay away from our tent. If you come anywhere near us, I'll tell Mr. Davis about this."

"I didn't write it," he says. "What does that even mean, *Leave it alone?*"

"He was listening," I tell Jacey, motioning for her to come back inside. "He heard what we said about Piper. And this is his way of trying to get us to stop investigating."

Jacey turns to look at Noah. After a moment, she laughs. "That's ridiculous."

"I found him trying to hide the paint can."

"That's not what you saw," Noah says, rubbing a hand over his face.

Jacey's smile falls. "You had the paint?"

"I caught him with it in the woods." I turn back to Noah. "You wrote a threat to Piper, too, didn't you? The writing—it matches. But why did you do it?"

"Savannah," he whisper-yells, fingers clawing through his hair, "I'm trying to tell you I don't know what you're talking about, but you're not listening."

"I've heard enough. We've both heard enough. Haven't we, Jacey?"

She doesn't answer, only stands there, brown eyes glinting.

"Come on, Jace," Noah pleads. "You can't honestly think I would threaten anyone."

For a moment, she looks up at him with an expression that starts as a question but morphs into stunned anguish. Then she strides toward me, ducking through the tent opening.

I exhale, throwing Noah one last warning look before following her inside.

I zip the door shut, turning to find Jacey sitting in the corner, knees pulled up to her chest. "He didn't do this," she says, but she isn't looking at me.

"The evidence says otherwise."

"I shouldn't have just left him like that. He wouldn't do this. I know him—*we* know him, Savannah."

I wish I could agree with her. But if I'm any indication, you never really know people the way you think you do.

At this thought, a horrible sensation grabs hold of me. It's like the tent walls have blown down, leaving me exposed to the elements. Like there's no ground beneath me. I'm just floating out here on my own.

I reach for my sleeping bag to try to cover myself, but my mind slips back to my bedroom.

To that day.

I'd locked my bedroom door behind me, tugged on my headphones, turned on music, and buried myself beneath the covers. But even in my own private space, an exposed feeling wrapped around me. Everyone would see through this. Through me.

Piper had been called to Mr. Davis's office. I'd heard her name crackle over the loudspeaker and watched her walk over there, confusion etched on her forehead. Then I left her. Took the car and drove home without her. I panicked. Like a criminal.

I knew that as soon as she told Mr. Davis what happened, he'd believe she had nothing to do with changing the grades. Even if he doubted her story, Piper could just tell my parents the truth. They'd never let their precious gifted one go down for it.

My eyes were wide open in the suffocating midday darkness of my room. The music pulsed, each note unnerving. I kept envisioning the disappointed looks on my parents' faces when they learned the truth. That not only was I going to be expelled, but I'd also nearly taken Piper down with me.

Excuses tumbled around in my head, but they didn't land. Just spun into oblivion.

A thump resounded over the music, and I jolted upright. More thumping. I peeled the headphones away from one ear. Someone was knocking on the door. I willed the noise to stop, for whoever it was to go away. When they didn't, I turned off the music and pried myself out of bed.

I cracked the door open enough to spot a few strands of frizzy blond hair before it swung open all the way, knocking me backward.

Piper burst into the room, her pink complexion flushed a deep crimson. "Thanks for stranding me at school!" she snarled. "I had to walk all the way here!"

"I was going to come back for you," I lied. "Why are you home early?"

"Could ask you the same thing, but I'll settle for letting you know that I'm suspended."

"What are you talking about?" I aimed for the apathetic tone I always used when Piper got too passionate about something. Then I collapsed back onto the bed and browsed through my phone.

"You know exactly what I'm talking about." She leaned over me, snatching my phone away.

"Hey!" I took a deep breath. Let it out slowly. "You can't be suspended. Tell me what happened." My stomach rioted as I patted the spot on the bed beside me.

Piper's eyes narrowed, and her lips pinched. "You're really going to pretend like you didn't have anything to do with the chemistry grades?"

I gave her my best incredulous look. "What do you mean?"

"Mr. Davis says there's an *issue* with last week's test scores." Little drops of spittle bubbled in the corners of her mouth, like she was a rabid animal. "For a handful of kids, the numbers in the grading program don't match the tests. When he asked Lucy Dawes if she knew anything about it, she started crying. She said the *TA* offered to bump her grade for a hundred bucks."

My clueless expression faltered. Something flickered in Piper's seething glare.

I'd expected her to be angry. But as she stood over me, her face wilting and her head dropping, I recognized that flicker. It was worse than the way she'd looked at age seven, when she'd found our guinea pig lying still at the bottom of the cage.

It was gutting. Despite our differences, I was her sister— her *big* sister. She'd never anticipated this level of betrayal.

Even I had never known how far I could fall.

"I triple-checked those scores after I input them," Piper said. "And I never spoke to Lucy Dawes or anyone else about doctoring numbers! Why would they say the *TA* did that, Savannah?"

Because I'd instructed them to. None of my "clients" had been willing to simply hand over the money. They'd insisted on knowing how I was planning to access the grades, so I'd told them I wasn't; the TA was handling everything.

"I'm sorry," I said, grabbing my head in both hands. "I never thought Mr. Davis would notice or check the scores. I didn't change anything drastically, just enough to bump them from a minus to a plus or whatever." Piper's gaze remained fixed on the carpet. "I was trying to get the money for the tournaments!"

"Tournament, singular. *Your* tournament. You think I would've agreed to split the money with you if I'd known you were going to earn it illegally? This was your problem, and you decided to make it mine." She leaned against my desk chair like she couldn't hold herself upright. "I couldn't tell Mr. Davis or Principal Winters I'd given you access to the tests, that I'd made the mistake of letting my idiot sister get hold of Mr. Davis's password. I told you he trusted me with those grades! I can't believe you did this to me."

"I never thought I'd get caught," I said, knowing it was the king of moronic excuses. "I thought I was helping both of us. You were so stressed, and I needed to make some quick cash. I'm really sorry, Piper."

Her eyes lifted slowly from the floor to meet mine. "So, you'll tell Mr. Davis I had nothing to do with this?"

"Piper, I..." The glimmer of hope that had drifted into her expression a moment before evaporated. Her jaw tensed. "If I do that, I'll lose my shot at MLC. You'll still get into college with one black mark on your record. You have next year. For me, this is it. If I get suspended or"—I swallowed—"expelled...it's over."

Her already-large blue eyes widened further. Then they shut, a drop escaping through her lashes to trickle down her red cheek.

Regret pressed on my chest like a bad infection, and I got up, stepping toward her. "Piper, I—"

Her thin frame began to shake, and she wiped away the tear. "You really think I'm going to take the fall for this?" Her voice screeched like rubber against pavement. She started pacing around my room, mumbling and huffing something about betrayal and dances and having nothing left. I suddenly wished she'd just cry. At least then I could try to comfort her.

Instead, she pushed past me toward the door, stopping to growl, "I'm telling Mom and Dad."

A rush of dread swept through me. "I just wanted to make sure I'd get into MLC," I pleaded. "I need that scholarship,

Piper." But with a biting edge, I added, "Your future isn't the only one that matters."

She flinched like I'd slapped her. And then, with more coolness than she'd ever displayed in her life, she said, "Up until a half hour ago, my future was the only one that existed. You can't get into college with your grades, Savannah. Your boyfriend is a loser and a cheater. Even if you get that soccer scholarship, you'll screw it up. The way you screw *everything* up."

She slammed the door in my face. I stood, stunned, as every poster on my wall, every paper on my desk fluttered and flapped. Something floated off the desk, dropping to the floor. I leaned over to pick up the leaflet with the sky-blue font that read MOUNT LIBERTY COLLEGE.

I crumpled it up and tossed it into the wastebasket, my body flooded with molten lava. My arms, my legs, my mouth—everything was fluid, out of my control. I grabbed my phone, and my fingers felt detached from my body as I texted her.

Go ahead and tell Mom and Dad. We're done, Piper. I don't care about you. No one does. As far as I'm concerned, you don't exist.

That was the last thing I told my sister before she ended up in a coma. Those are the words that have been stabbing at me constantly for the past month.

The reason I couldn't let anyone see Piper's phone.

The reason I was certain I was to blame for everything.

Now, I'm not sure what to think. All I know is that I may've just caught one of Piper's best friends—a kid I've known most of my life—threatening me. And that Piper was threatened the same way before she fell from the Point.

"He didn't do it," Jacey whispers, but I'm not even sure she's talking to me anymore.

I turn over, attempting to fluff the sweatshirt I'm using as a pillow. "Just be careful."

14

I wake up alone in the tent. Peeling back my sleeping bag, I yawn and feel around for my pack. Hushed voices float through the cold air. Soft morning light permeates the tent fabric, and I slide the zipper down a bit, letting more trickle in. I rummage through my backpack in search of my toothbrush to no avail. Within sixty seconds, the tent looks like a mini version of my bedroom, the contents of my backpack scattered over the rumpled sleeping bags and the nylon floor.

Finally, I locate the toothbrush and a little travel tube of mint toothpaste hidden within the folds of a shirt. I stuff everything else back into the pack, secure my hair into a ponytail, and check my face in a little hand mirror.

When I open the tent flap, everyone seems to be up,

mixing more of those crummy meals around the fire. I duck out and around the back of the tent, trying to figure out how I'm going to deal with last night's graffiti.

But when I get there, my heart lurches. The message is gone, only a gauzy smear of white left in its place.

What looked like paint in the black of night must've actually been spray chalk or some other washable substance. I head into the woods to search the grass where I last spotted the can, but of course it's gone. I don't know whether to be relieved that Mr. Davis isn't going to ask about the message or irritated at how well Noah keeps covering his tracks. Kicking a pine cone, I head back to my tent to do a quick teeth-brushing.

When I reach Grant, he flashes me a smile and raises his brows in a question.

"I slept fine." The lie comes out hoarse. I clear my throat. "Barely even knew she was there."

The last thing I need is for Grant to learn my suspicions about Noah. Not while we're up here. I need a plan, some way to find out what Noah knows about the day Piper fell. There's definitely something he doesn't want Jacey or me to uncover.

"Good," Grant says in a sexy-gruff morning voice. I bury my cheek in his chest. His body feels warm in the frigid mountain air, and his usual spice-tinged deodorant scent mingles with the smoke and pine smells now embedded in his sweatshirt.

"Anything from your parents?" Grant asks.

"I told you," I mumble into his shoulder, "I don't have reception."

He doesn't answer. I feel the tension in his arms as he releases me, giving me a peck on the cheek before wandering off toward the cooking gear.

My eyes sting, and I fight off tears. Grant is judging me for not staying home with my family. What would he think if he knew the rest?

"Savannah."

I look up to see him shaking a packet of oatmeal in front of me. "I asked if you want me to mix you up some of this gourmet breakfast."

I'm not hungry, but I know I should eat my instant mush. "Yeah, thanks," I say, trying to smile.

I take a seat in the dirt and wait for Grant to return with my oatmeal. Across camp, Jacey shares a fallen log with Noah. Apparently, she's chosen to ignore my warning.

I'm not sure I blame her. The Noah I grew up with never would've threatened us. Never would've threatened Piper.

Still, I found him there in the woods. Can I really believe his story about stumbling across the paint can while chasing someone else?

I scan the other side of camp, where Alexandra is chatting with Sam and Abby as they wait for their Jetboil to heat up. Tyler catches my gaze and motions me over to the fire. "I'm good," I mouth.

"You look like you could use some warming up," he calls out, patting the spot next to him.

"Funny." Like I'm going to buddy up with Tyler in front of Grant, especially after yesterday's turf war. I turn my head away, but a moment later, feet shuffle beside me. Out of the corner of my eye, I catch of glint of metal.

I groan. "Don't you have small animals to torture?"

"That wouldn't be nearly as fulfilling as torturing you." He plops down in the dirt beside me.

"Seriously, though. What's with the chains?" He shrugs, which makes me more curious. "Are they weapons? Ooh, is that the reason you're really here? Being in this club is punishment for some sort of crime, right?"

Tyler's eyes narrow, and the irony of my accusation hits me like a kick to the shin.

Grant starts making his way toward us with my breakfast, and Tyler takes it as his cue to leave. He stands, dusts off his pants, and slinks away to join the others.

"What was that about?" Grant asks, handing me a bowl.

"Nothing. No coffee?" I ask, just to change the subject.

"Sorry, the mountaintop Starbucks is fresh out."

"What's the plan for today?"

Grant looks at me delicately, like I might detonate. "We're kind of waiting on you, babe. Mr. Davis said we'll move out as soon as you get something to eat. Up to the falls."

"Fun." I blow on my oatmeal and take the slowest bite ever.

He kisses me on the head. "I'll tell him you'll be ready in five."

The sun is out as we hike up to the falls, following Sam, our honorary guide. Grant and I remove our sweatshirts and stuff them into our packs. A light breeze kicks up the pine needles and cools the sweat beading up on the back of my neck. A couple of hours in, the sound of rushing water covers our footsteps. I push through the final line of trees, and the waterfall bursts into view.

A rock wall encrusted with neon moss towers over the forest on one side of the clearing. White water froths and gushes down the rocks, its beginnings hidden up in the treetops. On either side of the falls, twisted vines cascade and shrubs spring from the cracks in the granite. Where the water crashes down in a churn of foam, a brilliant pool collects within the rocks. The sunlight streams through the fanning trees to bounce off the surface of the swimming hole, making it a mirror of everything around us.

The edge of the pool is shallow enough to stand in, but my gaze travels to the dark area near the cliff. The part that's deep and uncertain.

Some members of the group stop to take photos, while others begin to descend the slope leading to the cool waters below. Mr. Davis sits on a fallen log, unwrapping a granola bar. A few yards away, Noah makes vain attempts to get my attention.

Grant and I find a shady spot to remove our packs. I take a few sips from my water bottle and turn to him. "What are we supposed to be doing, exactly?" My voice is half drowned by the crash and gurgle of the falls.

"Whatever we want." He points down the gorge to where Sam is already seated on a rock, fiddling with a stick and some ropelike material. "We could see what he's making."

"Lumberjack? Who cares what he's making?" But Grant's already headed down, serenaded by Abby, whose singing echoes through the gorge. "This club is so weird," I grumble, carefully finding my footing on the steep hillside where the rocks begin. Grant continues to lead the way, skirting slippery boulders until he reaches the bank.

"Fishing?" He nods at Sam's pocketknife with admiration. Apparently, when Grant is in this club, he transforms into an overgrown Boy Scout.

Sam doesn't look up, only wipes the blade on his tan pants, leaving a trail of green. "This cordage isn't the best. You got anything better?"

Grant grins. "In my pack."

He races back up the ravine, leaving me alone with Lumberjack, who calls out, "And try to scrounge up some bait."

Sam still hasn't acknowledged me, so I tiptoe backward, trying not to fall.

"Gonna try your hand at fishing?" comes a low voice behind me.

My pulse accelerates. "I told you to stay away from me," I answer without looking.

Sam glances up at us for a beat, then returns to twisting and tying.

I spin around, trying to push past Noah, but he sidesteps in front of me. "Come on, Savannah. You don't really think I did that to your tent. It wasn't even funny. In all the years we've known each other, have I ever performed a prank that bad?"

"Get out of my way, Noah."

"Is everything all right?" Sam is on his feet now, eyes narrowed.

"No, everything is not all right," I say. "Can I borrow your knife, please?"

"Uh." Sam glances from me to Noah, brows furrowed.

"Just talk to me," Noah pleads. "Preferably somewhere he's not standing beside us with a knife. Also," he says to Sam, "I thought Mr. Davis told you last time not to bring that."

Sam only glares, so Noah turns back to me. "Savannah. We need to talk. There are…things you need to know. About Piper."

My heart whirs in my chest. Here it comes, and part of me suddenly isn't ready to hear it.

"Please?"

I inhale slowly, and then turn on my heel. "Fine." I trudge back up the slope to where the rocks collide with the undergrowth of the forest, and the leaves rustle as Noah follows. I press on, ducking under a branch and pushing into the trees. When we're completely out of hearing range of everyone down at the river, I stop at a black, fuzzy log.

Noah is quiet as he lowers himself onto it, but I remain standing, arms crossed. The air is brittle and tense until Noah's voice shatters it. "Savannah, I did not write that message on your tent last night."

"I thought you were here to tell me something new, not to repeat your denials."

A lock of dust-brown hair falls over his glasses, and he lets it hang there. "I am."

"I want to know," I say, even though I don't. Not if Noah had something to do with what happened to my sister.

"I hurt Piper."

My breath catches. Everything starts to spin.

"It was at homecoming," he says, staring down at the ground. "When Piper was dancing with you and your friends, I sort of went into the photo booth with Jacey, and..." His face crumples. "We..."

I get a flash: Jacey and Noah off in the woods. *I already said I'm sorry.*

Anger writhes in my throat, leaving me speechless. Jacey did this. Jacey, who's been pretending she wants to figure out what happened to Piper.

"I'm going to kill her."

"What? No, Savannah. I'm not done talking." Beneath his glasses, his eyes are pained. A tear brims on his lashes. "Jacey and I kissed. But it wasn't her fault. Not *only* her fault. I wanted it too."

My vision goes spotty, black flecks marring the greenery. "Piper was so happy that night. She loves you. How could you do this to her?"

But even as the words hang in the air, I picture Grant and me, bodies tangled up on the hot dance floor. They're no worse than me. "Did she find out?"

He doesn't answer at first, just nudges a yellow-flowered weed with his boot. Finally, he nods. "When we came out of the booth, she was holding the photos."

A tide of nausea rises in me. How did I not know about this? Piper would've been destroyed.

But I wasn't there. I went to the after-party, too caught up in being homecoming queen—too caught up in Grant—to notice. I ended up crashing at Jessica's, only making it home late Sunday night.

"And you two broke up?"

He pales, running a hand through his hair. "That would've required us to be together in the first place."

My legs go numb, and I turn to collapse onto a rotten patch of log beside him. "What are you talking about? You and Piper *were* together."

He winces. "I know Piper thought we were."

I feel so sick. I lean over, head between my useless legs.

"I know how it sounds." His voice is strained, its richness and depth gone, leaving only hollow sounds that make up hollow words. "But I felt bad for her. She's my best friend, and I couldn't tell her I didn't feel the same way she did. Things were easier when it was the three of us. Then she and Jacey went through that rough patch last year, and Piper and I ended up spending a lot of time together, just the two of us. She seemed to think we were a couple just because we were together all the time."

"And you never wanted to be with her that way."

His lips purse. "At first, I thought I might. I tried to make it work. But after a while, I realized I was only fooling us both. Especially after the dance."

"So, she was heartbroken, then." And I never knew. After all the time I'd spent convincing her homecoming was going to be amazing—that she was going with a boy who loved her—I never cared enough to ask about it.

He doesn't move an inch when he whispers, "She did it because of me."

Under the weight of his words, my body buckles. I pull in a breath, trying to keep my hands from pushing straight through the rotting corpse of a log. I want to hold Noah, to console him. Because if this is his fault, it's also my fault. Piper was already dealing with so much, and then I went and committed the ultimate act of betrayal.

"I was horrible to her," he says. "I wanted to do the right thing, to finally be straight with her. I asked to speak to her about"—he looks down—"what happened that night. At the dance."

I lick my lips, but they still feel dry. Like they might crack open and bleed all over my chin.

"I tried to talk to her on the way to sixth period the day she fell—to apologize—but she kept asking if I was in love with Jacey, and I didn't know how to answer. Then Piper's name came over the loudspeaker, telling her to go to Mr. Davis's office." His hands fidget in his lap. "She ran off crying."

Noah bites his lip. "I was a coward. I couldn't admit the truth, and she ran away." His gaze veers toward the trees as if he's watching Piper flee all over again. "And I *let her*, Savannah. I didn't call her back. Didn't check on her after school. Nothing. I just sat at home like a coward." His feet fidget as he mindlessly unravels the hem of his shirt. "And then..."

"Noah," I interrupt. "Stop." I want to tell him the truth, but I don't even know the truth anymore, only the mammoth part I played in Piper's distress. "I know you think you're responsible, but there was something else too."

He looks up, pale eyes glistening. "What do you mean?"

I swallow. "The message on our tent—it had to do with Piper. I found a threat just like it inside her pack last week, telling her to 'quit survival club or else.'"

"That's what you meant last night. When you said, 'You did this to Piper too.'"

"Whoever wrote it took the pack before I could show the cops. And there's more. Some strange calls on her phone. And a note from the office, telling her to go to the Point for a Survival Club meeting that day." My right knee bounces. "I think she went to the fake meeting, and whoever wanted her out of the club hurt her."

Noah squints. "Who would want to hurt Piper?"

"That's the question. It's the reason I'm on this trip. I'm going to find out who wanted Piper out of this club and why."

Noah turns to stare at the pine cones on the ground. He removes his glasses and cleans them on his shirt. My heart thumps as I wait for another lecture about my active imagination. But when he replaces the glasses and turns to me, his jaw is set. "Tell me everything."

15

I finish telling Noah about Alex and all of my failed attempts to identify them.

"Why not give Piper's phone to the cops?"

Guilt flutters in my stomach as my last text message to Piper types itself out in my head. "I can't explain how I got the phone. My parents think the hospital staff lost it."

Noah cocks a brow.

"I stole it from the hospital as soon as I found the threat in her pack." He doesn't need the *whole* truth.

"And Alex has been texting you?"

"Just to tell me to stop calling." It's cold in the shade beneath the pines. I draw my arms in tight, crossing them over my stomach.

Noah runs a hand over his chin. "What if this Alex person threatened Piper, and she didn't quit the club, so he blackmailed her or something? Maybe Piper saw no other way out. Those calls could be really important."

A bird swoops down through the brush, stirring the leaves. "I know. I'll turn it in." Just as soon as I'm certain the cops will take this Alex lead seriously. I'm not simply handing the phone over to my parents with a memo to look at Piper's deleted texts.

"Well, you should talk to Abby."

I squint at him. "The fairytale princess? That's your great plan?"

"She and Piper were always off in corners, whispering. Especially the last few days before the accident. I saw them in Survival Club. And then on that Tuesday or Wednesday, I saw Piper coming out of the choir room."

I give a skeptical head tilt. "Sure my sister didn't develop a new talent? Wouldn't be the first time."

"I'm just saying, if Piper was being threatened by someone, Abby might know who it is."

I think of Abby's face yesterday, her unfinished thought. *You're sort of in your own world. That's why you didn't know Piper was...*

I didn't know Piper was what? Being threatened?

"All right," I say, standing up and wiping the muck and a trail of ants off my jeans. "I'll talk to her. If she knows something, maybe she'll agree to speak to the cops."

Noah nods but doesn't get up. "Savannah," he says, voice threaded with grief. If this is an apology, I'm not sure I can listen to it. Not because what he did is unforgivable. If anyone should believe his actions are pardonable, it's me, since I did the exact same thing to Jacey.

I can't listen to it because I need forgiveness so much more...from a person who may never wake up to give it.

"I know," I whisper, my eyes stinging.

Then Noah's standing beside me. The same kid who used to toilet paper our house every Friday night. The same kid I always thought would end up with my sister one day.

Only now he's grown. And I'm grown.

And neither of us can look the other in the eye.

When we reach the gorge, voices drift toward us from below. Down at the shallow part of the river, most of the group is goofing around with their makeshift fishing poles and climbing the rocks along the edge of the embankment. Sam stands and tugs, his line taking a sharp course through the water as everyone shouts excitedly, only to have it come up empty.

The guys begin splashing Alexandra and Abby, who trot away through the shallows, giggles trailing behind them.

Noah wanders off in search of his water bottle, and I scan the river for Grant.

When I spot him, my heart swells at the smile on his face. He really is a huge wilderness nerd.

Then there's me: completely out of my element and no closer to finding out what really happened to Piper. I'm exhausted. I barely slept last night, between the cold and my shredded nerves after catching Noah with the paint can. And I'm tired of this constant weight that's been pressing down on me ever since the accident. A weight I'd do anything to remove.

Finding shade beneath a massive oak, I lie down, shutting my eyes and letting my brain go black. A ray of sunlight cuts through the leaves to beat against my face perfectly as I listen to the soothing, crashing sounds of the water.

I don't know how long I've been resting this way when something cold and wet hits my cheek. I open my eyes to find Grant above me. He's soaked, water dripping down onto me from his hair and bare chest.

"What are you doing?" he asks.

"Napping." I wipe a drop from my eye. "What does it look like?"

"The Savannah I know doesn't sit around while everyone else has all the fun."

"Romping around in a river is your idea of fun?"

"It is if I'm with you." He grins, the gold in his irises glinting like the flecks of mica in the granite-strewn hillside.

I sit up, resting on my elbows. "You expect me to go fishing?"

He pantomimes reeling in a fish, like that'll sell it.

"I have a better idea," I say, getting up and patting his chest before making my way toward the bank.

"Where are you going?" he calls out.

"To put on a show."

If someone wants to threaten me, let's see what they do when I put myself out there in a position just like the one Piper was in.

I look up at the rock wall cloaked in layers of billowing water, scanning the area for a decent pathway to the top. I trudge back up the ravine, branches and sharp rocks snagging my jeans along the way. When I reach the point where lush vegetation gives way to slippery stone, I slow. My plan didn't extend past climbing to the highest ledge I could see. But I will get to the top. And then, who knows? Maybe I'll jump. The water below the falls looks deep enough.

Laughter pinballs around the gully below. A cool wind whispers through the trees, and leaves float down, reminding me that it's autumn. Despite the end of the summer heat, despite the end of the greenery, the splashing sounds of my classmates and the rumbling of the water makes me want to dive in. My whole life could use the refreshing effects of the waters below.

When I was little, water was the answer to all my problems. Bad day at school? I went for a swim in our backyard pool. Sweltering soccer practice? I dove into the pool. Chlorine turned my shiny blond locks into sticky green straw. I probably could've gone out for the swim team with all the muscles I developed from swimming laps every afternoon. Even Piper liked the pool.

My parents hated cleaning it.

Piper and I used to play mermaids. It was one of the few things we could do for hours without fighting. Her mermaid persona was an underwater chemist who concocted potions out of pool toys. That kept her stationary for most of the game; she wasn't very skilled at swimming with her feet stuck together, anyway. She used to cheat, but I pretended not to notice.

One day, she dove in with her gangly little legs twisted together and didn't come back up.

I kept calling for her, but she stayed beneath the surface, her figure a purple blur on the pool floor. I swam down and pulled her up. She'd hit her head on the bottom and blacked out.

Dragging her over to the side, I shouted for my parents. I managed to heave her over the edge, unfazed by the way the concrete scraped her pale skin. My heart throbbed in perfect contrast to Piper's unmoving chest.

My parents arrived, shoving me aside to work on her frenetically until her eyelids fluttered open and her blue lips parted. I pushed my way past them to help her sit up, clutching her hard enough to break her as she coughed and gasped for air. Finally, her eyes focused and settled. She looked at me the way little girls are supposed to look at their big sisters.

Immediately, my parents made a decision. The next day our pool was filled with cement. A lovely fountain of a mermaid spewing water from pursed lips now sits atop a concrete patio where it used to be.

The rock wall is just ahead now. Droplets of water splash me as I climb. The next stretch will require more strength. I know there's a longer, less treacherous way up through the forest behind the waterfall, but I'm too close to chicken out now. I grab hold of a ridge and drag my body upward, shirt catching on the rocks, until I find footing in a little crevice. The slick, mossy face of the cliff paints my jeans green, but the surface beneath my grip is dry as I heft myself up the rest of the way.

When I make it to my feet, a loud voice nearly knocks me off balance. "Savannah!" It's Mr. Davis. "Come back down!" He stands alongside Abby and the others below, hands cupped around his mouth like a megaphone.

Instead of obeying, I edge myself out a little farther and peer down into the dark water.

"Savannah! Get down!" Mr. Davis's tone is more urgent this time, and it gives me a sick rush of adrenaline.

"Savannah!" Grant's voice now. I tear my gaze away from the shadowy surface of the water and look down at the group of people standing near the riverbank, heads identically cocked to watch me. Abby's hands are folded in front of her chest like she's praying. Mr. Davis wavers, taking a few large steps toward the forest but then stopping to watch me.

Voices buzz, dull and distant, and then Grant takes off up the embankment, leaving Mr. Davis below with his eyes glued to me.

The shadows beneath the water are sharp rocks, some of which pierce the glassy surface. I see that now. Someone would have to be out of their mind to jump from here. Still, I let the crowd squirm, my head hovering out over the ledge. Like I might try it.

Like Piper may have at the Point. I try to imagine her thoughts before she fell. Was there really someone on the other end of the phone line moments before she stepped off the edge?

Or was someone up there with her?

"You couldn't leave it alone, could you?" I startle at the voice, my feet kicking tiny pebbles off the cliff and into the water. I spin around to find Jacey standing behind me. "Told you it wasn't him."

I take a deep breath. Compose myself. "Yeah, well, there were some things you *didn't* tell me, weren't there?"

Jacey takes another step toward me. "Like *you* haven't kept secrets."

"I deserve that." Still, I get an uneasy feeling as she looks at me. I shuffle away from the ledge, but she sidesteps in front of me. "Gonna push me too?"

Her eyes narrow at this. "You don't actually think I did something to my best friend?"

"I don't know, Jacey. You wanted her boyfriend, didn't

you?" And the second I dangled myself out in front of her like a lure, she came running. Now she has me cornered with my back to the ledge. If she pushed me, everyone who just witnessed me toying with death a moment ago would see a grief-stricken sister simply following in Piper's footsteps.

Jacey's face contorts, like all the hate she has for me is about to come spewing out of her. But her shoulders sink. "I wish I could take it back. If what I did was the reason—I don't think I can handle it."

Something in me yields, like my insides have been doused in fabric softener. "You weren't the reason. Piper was tough. I'm sure she was upset. But we never should've believed she did it on purpose. Something else happened, and we have to figure out what. For Piper."

"It's not going to help her, though, is it?" Jacey chokes out through a sob, dropping to her knees. "She won't wake up."

The words lash at me. My feet feel numb, the blood flow suddenly cut off, and I find myself lowering down beside her. "Probably not."

"How am I going to tell her I'm sorry?" she cries, tears streaming down her cheeks.

It's the question that's been swimming through my mind on a constant loop since the second Dr. Porter recommended taking her off life support. Hearing Jacey ask it aloud cracks whatever was holding my torso upright. I crumple, letting my head fall to my knees. My skin becomes slick as the tears that I haven't let fall run harder than the waterfall crashing behind us.

Any chance at telling Piper we're sorry might be lost. As gone as those pebbles I knocked over the edge.

But I still have one chance. It's right here beside me, just as wrecked as I am.

I won't miss this chance again the way I did with Piper.

"*I'm* sorry." I look at Jacey through a web of tears. "I'm sorry for what I did to you. And I'm sorry I never apologized. I was..." I try to swallow. "I couldn't face you."

She glances up at me, her eyes red, face smeared with dirt that mingles with her tears. She doesn't speak. But it's there in the set of her lips, in the slump of her shoulders: a common shame. A week ago, I never thought Jacey and I would speak again, much less be sprawled out here in the dirt, sharing tears. But here we are, bonded by our mistakes.

Bonded by something dark.

16

"Savannah, what are you doing?" Grant pushes through the trees, shirt and curls in disarray. He stares at Jacey and me sitting a few yards from the ledge, tears streaking our faces.

I push myself up, wiping my face with the hem of my shirt like a three-year-old and leaving dirt tracks. "Nothing. Just wanted to look."

Grant's gaze travels to Jacey, who's turned away from us, knees pulled to her chest. Like she's simply gazing out at the view.

He examines me, unconvinced. "Well, come back down." Hand outstretched, he steps closer. "You practically gave Mr. Davis a heart attack."

Guilt pinches in my chest. "I'll apologize." I glance back

at Jacey, statuesque on the outcropping. "Let me catch up with you."

He gives me a skeptical look.

"I'll be down in a minute," I say, holding up an index finger. "Promise."

His head falls back in frustration, but he turns and plods back toward the woods.

When he disappears into the trees, I sink back down beside Jacey. "I have to talk to Abby."

Jacey's eyes dart to mine. "Abby? What does she have to do with any of this?"

"Noah says they were tight before Piper's fall. That they were always whispering. Maybe she knows who Alex is. Or who had an issue with Piper."

Jacey shakes her head. "Abby has no idea what was going on. If Piper never confided in me or Noah about the threats, she never would've told Abby."

"What if all of it happened *after* the dance? You and Noah weren't exactly speaking to Piper those last few days."

She inhales, and her fingers fiddle with a hole in her pants. "If you talk to Abby, she'll just make up a story. She's a drama queen."

"I mean, technically, she's an opera queen. It's a lead, Jacey. The only one we have."

"I just don't want you to waste your time." She shrugs like it's no big deal and starts to braid her hair over one shoulder.

But a wariness causes my muscles to stiffen. Why is she so against me talking to someone who could help us get to the truth?

"I'm not going to do anything this second." I stand, dusting gravel off my pants. "I have to apologize to Mr. Davis and convince Grant that I'm stable enough to stay on this trip." It might be hard to believe after the way I just flirted with death on the cliff's edge.

"I'll come with," Jacey says, letting the braid fall loose. She stays at my side as we walk through the weeds, like a friend accompanying me back.

Only it feels like I'm being monitored.

Grant must've trusted that I'd be right behind him, because he's back in the water when we make it to the bank. Sam and Abby are down there too.

Drained, I find my stuff beside Grant's by the pool's edge and plunk down onto a patch of gravel. I remove my shoes and socks and dip my feet into the cold water, leaning forward to let the mist catch my face. Nearby, Jacey and Noah sit on a slab of granite, sharing a snack. On the other side of the river, I spot Mr. Davis digging through his pack. Alexandra is over there, too, resting on an elbow and writing in a notebook splayed out on her lap.

I reach for my pack and scrounge through it for my water. As I tug it free, a shadow falls over me.

"Everything good?"

I use my hand to block the sun. Through my fingers, I catch a wink of metal. "Don't tell me you thought I was going to jump too."

"I don't really know you well enough to determine what you will and won't do."

I roll my eyes.

"Noah told me about your sister," Tyler says, running a chain through his fingertips. "I'm really sorry."

"Thanks," I mumble before moving the bottle to my lips. Of course, the one person I don't need to speak to is the friendliest. I guzzle the cool water, suddenly realizing how thirsty I am.

In front of us, the river roils, just like my mind. I'm dizzy. I have to get to Abby, the girl who didn't want to talk in the woods yesterday.

Tyler walks away, but a moment later, he drags his pack over and dumps it next to mine. "Want some trail mix?"

My stomach *is* a little rumbly. I hold out my palm, and he shakes cashews and dried fruit into it.

I cringe. "Where's the chocolate?"

"This is the true outdoorsman's version, not the child's."

"Well, it looks like squirrel food."

"Adds to the experience." He tosses back a small handful.

I try to smile, but my body feels like it just finished a triple-header. That climb up the waterfall drained every last ounce of my strength, leaving me with a bone-deep fatigue.

"Sure you're okay?"

I venture a peek at him, and his dark eyes stir up mixed feelings in me. Part of me could pour out my soul to this person, and the other part tenses like a gopher on alert. "Why are you always asking me how I'm doing? You said it yourself—we don't know each other."

"My mom said I should try to make friends."

At first I think he's serious, but his mouth curves up at one corner.

"Think you could use your magical sleeping bag stowing abilities to roll me up and tuck me away somewhere until this weekend is over?"

Tyler's head tilts, like he's considering it. "Sure, but it sounds painful."

"Time to pack up!" calls Mr. Davis, who's wading through the shallows toward us, wearing his pack.

I return my water to its storage pouch, and Tyler offers me a hand. I peek over my shoulder at Grant before accepting it, a red ember of guilt burning in my belly.

I keep trying to get Abby alone, but she and Sam have been surgically linked since the river.

Overhead, the stars sparkle through the treetops, and in front of me, the fire is waning. My phone is still off, but I'm guessing it's well after one a.m. Mr. Davis has long since gone to bed. I lift my head from Grant's chest. His eyes are distant, reflecting the flickering flames. I hate keeping this Piper stuff from him, but I can't have him dragging me back down the mountain early.

Across the fire, Sam and Abby show no signs of prying themselves apart. Near them, Jacey sits beside Noah, chatting quietly. She yawns but doesn't head off to bed.

Suddenly, Sam stands up, helping Abby to her feet. I straighten, ready to hustle over and cut her off on her way to her tent. But Sam slings an arm around her, and the two amble away together. Like he's a freaking Uber dropping her off at her doorstep.

I grind my teeth. How am I supposed to intercept her now?

New plan. "I'm off to bed," I say, leaning over to kiss Grant.

"'Night," he murmurs, breath warm against my skin. No offer to escort *me* to *my* tent. Despite the fact that a wolf could easily leap through the camp and carry me off. Probably.

Away from him, I shiver. The cold night air carries a memory of last year's soccer tournament with Grant. The one where things spiraled out of our control. The one that started with a note passed from his palm to mine on the bus, telling me to meet him at the pool at midnight. The one that ended with both of us soaked and frozen, but not caring as our lips finally met for the first time, his hands warm on my skin.

A red hot sweep of desire runs through me, and I glance back. But Grant's still facing the fire.

I take a deep breath and drop my hands, letting the cold consume me as I trek to the tent.

As soon as I'm zipped inside, I hear the door opening again. I shine my flashlight over Jacey.

"I'm so tired," she says through another yawn.

"Yeah, me too. Except I have to go back out there to talk to Abby. Just waiting for her bodyguard to go off duty."

Jacey starts to climb inside her sleeping bag. "Are you sure that's a good idea?"

"I'm sure it's the only idea we have."

"What if she was the one threatening Piper?"

I open my mouth to argue, but she cuts me off. "Just hear me out. What if that's the reason they were always whispering? Maybe Abby was the one trying to bully Piper into quitting, or even…into other things."

"I don't know, Jacey. It would be like finding out Snow White was bullying one of the dwarfs." But even as I say it, I know I have to consider the possibility. Someone in this club wanted Piper out, and there are only so many options.

"We could go together," I say. "It's safer."

"No," she says, already tucked inside her bag. "If Abby had something to do with all this, we might spook her if we both confront her. The best plan is to wait, at least until we get back down the mountain and it's broad daylight."

I sit for a moment, chewing on the inside of my mouth until I taste copper. "Fine." I slip inside my sleeping bag. No need to upset the only person who's trying to help me.

But I can't let fear keep me from finding out what happened to Piper. As soon as Jacey starts to snore, I'm talking to Abby.

I lie there, and my eyelids press down, the sound of the crickets lulling me to sleep. I could set an alarm on my phone, but it would only wake up Jacey. And if there's a message from my parents—something about Piper—I don't want to know. Instead, I battle sleep, drifting off and then waking in a panic, blinking and pinching my own cheeks as minutes turn to hours.

When Jacey's breathing finally turns slow and steady, I slink out of my bag, careful not to make a sound. I grab my flashlight, pull my hood up, and duck back outside.

I navigate around the backs of the tents to Abby and Alexandra's. The black forest hums around me as I approach the silent tent. How do I do this without scaring the hell out of them? "Knock, knock," I say, shining my light directly at the tent.

Nylon rustles, followed by whispers. Abby's groggy voice drifts out. "What is it?"

"It's Savannah. Can I talk to you outside? Just you, Abby."

There's a pause. "Yeah, let me put my shoes on."

My breath whooshes out in relief. "Thanks."

She emerges a moment later, shrugging on a puffy jacket, and I incline my head toward the trees and start walking out of hearing range of the other tents.

"What's going on?" Abby asks when I finally stop.

"When we first got up here, you said there was something I didn't know about Piper. Did it have to do with someone named Alex?"

Her head pulls back, hair rippling over her shoulders, streaks of radiant burgundy wherever the moonlight touches it. "Alex? What? No."

"Then what were you talking about? Please, I need you to tell me."

She doesn't answer right away, drawing circles in the leaves with her boot. But then she looks me straight in the eye. "Did you know Piper was devastated before she fell?"

The question punches me hard. I nod.

"Because of those two?" she adds, waving a hand in the direction of camp. A surge of relief ripples through me. "Her supposed *best friends*?"

Behind me, a critter rustles in the undergrowth. I flinch and press in closer to Abby. "Yeah, I knew. I mean, I just found out. So, that's it, then? You and Piper were talking about what Noah and Jacey did?" I get a pinprick of disappointment. "She didn't tell you anything about someone named Alex? Or someone who was bullying her?"

"No. Why would you think someone was bullying her?"

"I found some things," I say, rubbing at my forehead. "The day she fell, someone sent her a note telling her to go to the Point for a Survival Club meeting."

Abby's eyes widen.

"What is it?"

Her gaze swings toward her tent. "It's okay," I prod, forcing patience into my voice even though I want to grab her by a chunk of bright red hair. "You can tell me."

"Promise you won't say how you heard this."

"I promise. What happened?"

She licks her lips. Leans in close. "You should ask Jacey where she was the afternoon Piper fell."

Numbness starts to spread from my shoulders to my fingers. "Why?"

"I think Jacey met Piper at Suicide Point that afternoon," Abby says. "I mean, she didn't call it Suicide Point, but I knew where she meant. That spot on Vanderwild, just past the fork where it meets the Golden Trail." In the dim light, her eyes shine. "She asked me to lie for her, to tell Piper there was an extra skills session for Survival Club. When I refused, she asked me to pass Piper a note. It was sealed in an envelope, but she said it was an apology for the whole Noah thing." She grabs her temples, letting out a desperate moan. "Why did I believe her?"

My vision darkens, and I shake the flashlight, but it's not the issue. I am. Because I've forgotten to breathe.

I suck in so much air I get dizzy, and Abby grabs me by the arm before I crumple into the dirt. "I'm sorry," she whispers. "I should've said something."

This is why Jacey didn't want me to talk to Abby.

This whole time, it *has* been her.

The answer was staring me in the face at the waterfall, but I couldn't see it. I thought we were the same because we'd both hurt people. But Jacey didn't stop at kissing Noah. She must've decided Piper was too much competition.

"I won't let on that I know," I say, taking my arm from Abby. "Thanks for telling me."

Still woozy, I brush past her and stagger through the camp, not sure what I'm going to do when I get to the tent. Do I confront Jacey or wait until we get down the mountain and tell the cops?

I reach the tent, my heart thwacking against my ribs as I unzip it. Inside, I point my light at Jacey's side, and my heart tumbles down to the nylon floor.

Her sleeping bag is empty.

17

Jacey's shoes, sweatshirt, and flashlight are gone. Did she try to head back down the mountain?

I rush to Noah's tent, whispering his name as I crouch like a cougar beneath the watery moonlight.

The front flap unzips, but it's Tyler's head that pokes out. "What's going on?" he asks, rubbing sleepy eyes.

"I need Noah," I say, trying to keep the panic from my voice.

"He's not here. Left with Jacey a few minutes ago."

"He left?" I run both hands through my hair, turning in the direction of the trail and seeing only a black abyss. "Do you know where they went?"

He shakes his head, but his shoulders stiffen. "What's wrong, Savannah?"

I exhale, ruffling the loose hairs framing my face. "Nothing." My head falls back. "I don't know."

"Should I get Mr. Davis?"

"No!" The word flies out like a shot, and Tyler flinches.

"Sorry, I just—everything's fine. I'll talk to him in the morning." I walk away from his tent, barely feeling my feet against the ground.

Maybe I'm overreacting. Maybe Jacey doesn't know I'm on to her and she and Noah are simply off in the woods, reenacting what happened in that photo booth.

Or maybe she and Noah are in on this together. They could be on their way down the mountain, ready to destroy anything that could implicate them.

I kick a branch, sending it flying straight into my tent. I'm an idiot for not handing that note and Piper's phone over to the cops. Now I'm trapped up here with no phone signal.

Still, if Jacey was the one behind all of this...who is Alex?

My head is in my hands as I pace in front of my tent. I barely feel the cold as nerves buzz beneath my skin.

"They went to the Point." The voice is small and soft, but it sends every hair on my neck upright. I turn toward the sound, finding a figure silhouetted against the moonlit forest.

"How do you know that?" I ask, shining my light at Alexandra, who steps closer, a small book clutched to her chest.

She shrugs. "I'm a journalist."

"So, a spy." But relief floods my body.

"I followed you and Abby to the woods. I heard enough. And when I tried to sneak back inside my tent, I overheard Jacey and Noah whispering about taking a midnight stroll to the Point."

Heat courses from deep in my gut up to my jaw. Did the cops even examine that place? There could be something there—some small shred of evidence left behind. Something Jacey wants to keep buried. "How romantic. Why were you eavesdropping on my conversation with Abby?"

Alexandra's hands tighten around the notebook. "The same reason you're on this hike. To find out the truth about Piper."

Shock streams through me, but I cross my arms. Somewhere in the woods, an animal lets out a horrific squeal that ends in unnerving silence.

I press my lips flat. "Okay, Nancy Drew. Why don't you just go back to bed?"

"You're the one who came to me, remember? Claiming I'd called Piper the day she fell? That someone threatened her?"

"Yeah, well, I was wrong," I lie. "I've been through a lot lately."

"I don't think you're wrong," she says as the wind whips a brown coil of hair in front of her eyes.

Any trace of tiredness from the long day vanishes, replaced by adrenaline as I move closer, dropping my voice. "What do you mean?"

"Something was definitely going on with Piper before she fell. And I want you to tell me everything so I can—"

"So you can write a story about it for the school paper?" I snap. "Is that what your little notebook is about?"

I try to snatch it, but she steps back, twisting her body to protect it. "Of course not."

"Piper wasn't your friend. So why do you care?"

"Let's just get to the Point," she says. "I'll know more after we find out what Jacey and Noah are up to."

"You're not coming with me."

"It's not safe to go alone. Not if they're murderers."

"I'm not safe with *you*! All I know about you is that you stalk people. I'll bring Grant."

"And tell him what, Savannah? I've noticed he's not exactly helping with your investigation. Does he even know why you're really here? How's he going to react when he finds out you only came because you think someone tried to murder your sister?"

I let out a growl. Grant asked why I was coming on this trip, and I lied to his face. He's so worried about my mental state that if he knew about my investigation, he'd force me to go back down the mountain without learning the truth. "Fine. But we need to hurry. Before Jacey cleans up whatever evidence she left behind."

I zip up my jacket and pull my hood over my hair.

Heads down, we scurry toward the trail. "Do you know the way?" Alexandra asks.

I swallow, my throat raw from thirst and the dry mountain air. I think of Piper toppling over that guardrail. Then I think about my own encounter with the Point. I'll never admit I followed the three amigos to that cliff on one of their adventures because I was bored or curious. Or even jealous. "It's all the way down to the fork and then back up for a good thirty minutes after that. At least an hour from camp."

The Point. Shortened from Vanderwild Point by the locals. Shortened from Suicide Point by the faint of heart. Up until a few days ago, I was certain Suicide Point was the most accurate name. A spectacular view tainted by a series of tragedies.

And now, it might be the scene of an attempted murder.

An owl hoots overhead, the cold wind stings my face, and I tug the string on my hood tighter.

18

It's dark when the voices, low and muffled, slice through the wilderness.

Alexandra and I click off our lights, leaving only the moonlight to guide our steps as we tiptoe into the trees for cover.

We watch the hazy shapes until the sun peeks out from behind a distant crag to illuminate Jacey and Noah at the guardrail. Jacey's arm is stretched over the top bar, like she's pointing to something beyond the railing. Something down the face of the cliff. But we're too far away to make out her words.

I motion for Alexandra to follow me through the spindly branches to get closer. A twig snaps beneath my foot, loud as a gunshot, and Alexandra flinches. I shut my eyes, ducking my head.

When I look, Noah and Jacey are still peering down over the side of the cliff. The sun continues to rise, slowly painting greenery onto the dark canvas of the mountainside. I take a few more cautious steps until Jacey's voice reaches my ears with sudden clarity. "It could be evidence."

Evidence. Something she wants to cover up so badly, she hiked all the way out here in the middle of the night.

"Oh, I see it now," Noah says, leaning over the top rail to get a better view. "What is that?"

"I don't know, but I might be able to reach it." Jacey stretches her neck out for another moment, and then ducks beneath the bars.

"Whoa, whoa. Hold on," Noah says, clutching her wrist. "We should probably be getting back. You taking a spill down the mountainside right now wouldn't be very timely for a couple of reasons. We'll tell the cops to scour the area."

Tell the cops? So Noah doesn't know what she's up to. Jacey's dragging him along on her criminally motivated ride. He thinks she's trying to help when she's actually trying to bury whatever's down there.

"We can't rely on the cops," she says. "Grab my ankles." She inches out onto the ledge. "I think I can get to it without your help, if you're going to act so worried."

"You got me, I'm worried."

But she isn't listening. Instead, she's scooting over the sharp rocks that extend out over the slope. "Wait, Jace."

"I'll be fine, I promise." She hooks the toes of her sneakers over the bottom rail, and Noah clasps his hands around her ankles as she flattens her body and reaches.

"Please be careful." The frazzled edge to Noah's words slashes through the cold morning air.

Jacey keeps wriggling until she's dangling over the cliff. My heart thumps. Alexandra's hand clamps on to the back of my arm, her nails digging through my jacket. "Savannah," she hisses, "we should—"

I shake her off me, training my gaze on the cliff.

"Jacey," Noah begs now, "forget it. It's probably just trash some hiker tossed over the edge." But she keeps reaching.

Noah manages only a "Wai—" as her ankle slides from his grip.

19

Jacey's shriek tears through the dawn. Her body starts to plummet off the ledge. Before I can move, a dark blur flies past us, headed for the cliff.

Tyler.

Alexandra and I follow, close enough to taste the dirt his frantic footsteps kick up. When I reach the rail, Noah has the heel of Jacey's sneaker in his fingertips.

Barely.

Tyler sinks down beside Noah, attempting to get a better hold on some part of Jacey. But the ledge drops off so abruptly, he can't reach her without risking his own fall.

He takes the risk, inching forward under the railing, using only his feet to grip the rocks as he stretches. "Be careful!" I shout, slipping under the guardrail and diving for his boot. I pull just as he clutches Jacey's ankle in one hand. Alexandra grabs his other boot.

"I got her!" Tyler yells. "Noah, let go and help us up!"

Noah's entire body is shaking, but it's like he can't hear us.

"Noah!" I scream, my own hands trembling, my grip on Tyler slipping. "Let go! We have her!" But Tyler's boot skids, crushing my finger against a rock. I grunt as the sharp pain rushes through my hand.

Noah's head turns suddenly, like he's come out of a trance. He releases his minuscule grasp on Jacey's sneaker, stumbles, then pulls Tyler's other ankle. The rest of us keep tugging on Tyler until he's on secure enough ground for Noah to reach for Jacey.

They heft her up the rest of the way, her body bobbing against the rocks like a rag doll. Noah drags her to safety, and she sinks into his arms. Her face is scraped and bleeding, dirt embedded in the wounds.

Tyler, breathing heavily, glances from Noah to Jacey. "What were you doing?"

Noah's eyes slant beneath crooked frames. "She said she saw something down there."

"Yeah," I mutter, noting that Jacey's fist is balled tightly at her side. "Evidence."

I shuffle a little closer, afraid to touch the cold metal bars. Like they were responsible for what happened to Piper, like the rail somehow gave way. I hover inches behind it, peering out to where brambles and a rainbow of alpine wildflowers sprout on the face of the mountain below the rock formations. The sun is higher now, bathing the canyon in a warm pink glow.

A gust of wind whips through my ponytail, and I flinch. I back away from the railing, as if that breeze could send me tumbling down the mountainside like my sister did. Then I remember my pulsing finger. The nail is cracked beneath smeared blood.

Tyler turns his attention from Jacey to me. "Let me see," he says, picking himself up from the dirt.

"I'm fine," I say, which doesn't stop him from taking my hand in his and squinting at it like he's some sort of medical professional.

A few feet away, Noah helps Jacey sit up. He brushes some dirt off her face and then shifts, wrapping an arm around her and easing her back against his chest. The way he looks down at her, the way she snuggles into him—I don't know how I could've missed it before.

Alexandra finds the notebook she left in the dirt, and after cleaning it off on her jeans, she moves closer. "What happened?"

Jacey removes a leaf from her disheveled ponytail. "The better question is, why did everyone follow us?"

"Because we know what you're doing," I snap. Beside

me, Tyler stiffens, letting go of my hand. "We know about the day Piper fell. And we know you came out here to clean up your mess before the cops figure everything out."

Noah's brow furrows, and Jacey pales. A smothering, sickening silence falls over the group.

"That's n-not—" Jacey stammers.

"Come on," I say. "Tell us about how you were up here with my sister when she fell off this cliff."

"What?" Noah asks. "Where are you getting this?"

But Jacey doesn't answer.

"Go ahead," I prod. "Tell him how you met Piper up here that afternoon and how you're practically throwing yourself off this cliff to cover your tracks."

Jacey blinks, then stares ahead blankly like a newborn bird. "No," she says softly. "I came to look for evidence so I could find out who did this to Piper."

"*You* did this to Piper," I spit. "Abby told me you were willing to do whatever it took to get my sister to meet you. She thought she was helping reunite the two of you, but really, you were planning something. And it ended with my sister in a coma."

"No, that's not—I mean, *yes*, I wanted Piper to meet me up here. And I lied in the note to make it seem like it was a Survival Club thing so she'd come. Because I knew she'd never agree to it if it was just me."

"Because you backstabbed her."

Jacey reddens. "Yes, but I—" Her head falls. "I kissed Noah. But I was going to take full responsibility for it. To try to get Piper to forgive *him*, at the very least." Her hand is curled into a fist, and she presses it to her scraped-up forehead. "I wanted to speak to her here because of all the memories this place holds for us. I thought she might listen to me if I could just get her up here. So I asked Abby to pass along the note." She runs her knuckles up into her hair and then down again, so hard it leaves a red trail on her skin.

"But then I chickened out," she says, barely above a whisper. "I never went to meet her." Tears glisten in her eyes, and she bites her lip. "I panicked. I had no excuse for what I'd done. I thought maybe if I gave it some more time, the pain would thaw a bit, and I could try again."

"And we're just supposed to take your word for it."

Alexandra raises her hand like we're in school. "Maybe we should—"

"Quiet," I interrupt. "We're going to get a confession out of her if we have to dangle her over this cliff again."

"I never met Piper here," Jacey repeats. "I never even saw her that day. I'm here to look for evidence. That's the truth. Because you're right—it *was* my fault. I sent her here, and then I never showed up. So I have"—her voice fractures— "no idea what happened to her." Tears spill down her cheeks, but I just want to punch her in the face.

"Savannah, you said someone threatened Piper. That

someone might've been up here with her. I just thought that since I was the one who sent her up here in the first place, I should check the area for clues." She points toward the cliff and then glances down at her hand, balled so tightly her knuckles glow white.

"Prove it," I say. "Show us what you risked your life to grab off the mountainside."

Jacey hesitates, cupping her fist with her other hand. Suddenly, I'm not even sure *she* knows what's in there. Her fingers unfold one at a time, palm overturning to reveal something shiny and metallic.

I squint and take a step closer. "What is that?"

But as soon as the words are out, I know.

It's a metal link. A single piece of a chain.

PIPER

Fall, One Year Ago

The bell rings, sending a hot surge of panic through me. I'm late to my first day of AP chemistry.

I'm never late. I thought it would only take ten minutes to bike from my house to Foothill High, but it took twenty. And I don't know my way around this place. For all I know, I could be on the wrong side of campus.

I hurry through the eerily empty halls, searching for someone who can point me in the direction of room thirty-three. I should've asked that janitor I passed a couple minutes ago. Doesn't anyone at this school take zero period? There's a light on in one of the classrooms, but when I try the door, it's locked.

Why did I ever let Miss Lewis talk me into this? Since Grayling High doesn't have all the AP science classes I need, my guidance counselor suggested commuting to the high school one town over for zero period. Both schools have been really accommodating—Miss Lewis even finagled an independent study for me during first period so I'd have time to bike to Grayling and still earn school credit.

This is how I repay everyone's generosity—by showing up late on day one.

Compared to my school, this place is uniform and sterile. It smells like lemons instead of that pungent chemical scent that barely masks the mildew back at Grayling High. Here, the panel lights in the hallway aren't buzzing, and there's no graffiti on the classroom doors. When I round another identical corner, I finally spot a brunette with a pristine bob pulling books from her locker. "Excuse me," I call out. "Where's room thirty-three?"

The girl begins to point when a smooth baritone cuts her off. "I'm on my way there right now, if you want me to show you."

I swivel to face the Good Samaritan, and a vein in my temple begins to pulse. The boy is covered in black from head to toe, and chains dangle from his waist. I throw a look of desperation at the girl, but she's shoving books into her backpack.

I swallow. "Sure. Thanks."

20

The chirping of the birds blares louder than a jackhammer on a Saturday morning as realization sets in. Then there's no sound at all as everyone stares silently at that metal link resting in Jacey's palm.

I try to step forward, but the gravel slides beneath my sneaker. The others' movements are slow and distorted. Noah standing and leaning in to get a better look. Alexandra staring. Tyler backing away.

Then sound bursts back into existence. Jacey gasping. The snap of a twig beneath Tyler's boot.

My feet find solid ground again. I hurry forward, plucking the chain link from Jacey's hand and turning on Tyler, holding the metal piece out in front of him. "Why are you out here, you sick freak? Are you stalking us?"

Tyler's face is stoic. "I wasn't the only person stalking, by your definition. You followed them up here, same as me."

"Yeah, well, you're the only one whose little *ornament* was found on the mountain where my sister fell." My stomach hardens. I knew there was something off about him.

"Is it a crime to drop something?"

"It is here! You don't live in Grayling's Pass or go to Grayling High, so why were you even at this viewpoint?"

Tyler shrugs, and Noah moves closer to him, spine rigid and shoulders back.

"Tell us!" I march toward him with my fists balled, even though he's a foot taller than me, and Alexandra grabs at the back of my jacket.

"Just calm down, Savannah." Tyler steps back, prodding a spiderweb strung from the railing to a nearby branch with the toe of his boot. His calmness only makes my fury rise. "The chain link isn't mine."

"I don't have the patience for this." I hold the link up beside the chains draped from Tyler's belt loop. "Nobody but you dresses like they might have to prepare a vehicle for snowy conditions at any moment."

"Cross my heart, hope to die." He puts a hand on his chest.

I press closer, fists still clenched, sneakers squishing over a spongy bed of moss.

"It was Piper's."

My insides go cold. Tyler's grin is subtle, but it's enough to make Noah take that swing on my behalf.

Noah's fist strikes him in the jaw. Behind me, Alexandra yelps, and I straighten as Tyler tips backward. He regains his balance, brushing the red spot with his fingers as Noah rubs his knuckle. Jacey's mouth is parted in awe.

"Nice one," I mutter before turning to Tyler's hunched figure. "You don't know anything about my sister."

"That's where you're wrong." Tyler moves his jaw around, pressing his fingers to it delicately. He cuts an irritated glance at Noah, who backs up a few paces. "I know Piper—more than know her. She's been my closest friend since last year. She kept one of the chain links in her pocket." He reddens. "She likes to joke that it's our version of a friendship bracelet."

"Wait a minute." I pace, feet crushing a cluster of wild mushrooms. "First of all, that's absurd. What are you, twelve? Second of all, *how* do you know Piper? You said you were new to the club."

"She takes AP classes at Foothill. My school."

"She never mentioned you to me." I inch toward the railing, glancing at Jacey, who looks just as lost.

He's lying. There's no way Piper has a new best friend she neglected to mention to anyone in her life.

"Well, she told me all about you," Tyler says, turning to

Jacey. "About what a great friend you've been." Jacey goes crimson.

"And about you," he says, flicking his chin in my direction. "About your *close* relationship. About what you did to Jacey last year. And other things you did."

The others look at me, and my stomach falls. I shuffle backward, the gravel grinding beneath my feet until the railing jabs my spine.

Noah's gaze bounces around our huddle. "I'm lost."

"I called her, you know," Tyler says. "That day. She told me all about what you did to her."

My heart performs a sputtering beat. "*You're* Alex." I barely hear my own voice above the wind.

Tyler's hands fly up. "Guilty. Tyler's my middle name. In real life, I go by my first name: Alex."

"How—*why* did she keep you a secret?" I ask.

Tyler brushes a hand over his dark clothing. "Maybe because as far as Piper's concerned, everything the three of you touch turns to ash." His gaze drifts to the dense, dark woods.

"This guy is not Piper's friend," says Noah, who's still massaging his sore knuckles.

"Then how do I know all about you?" Tyler asks him. "How you loved to toy with her? How she kept holding out hope that all of your mixed messages would eventually lead to something? How you betrayed her."

I force my hand to my hip, force the tears back. Force the knot in my throat down. "That doesn't prove anything. You were the last person to speak to my sister before she fell off this cliff. You were obviously here." I uncurl my fingers, letting the metal flash. "And now, here you are again, trying to cover your tracks. That's why you wrote that threat on our tent, isn't it? You knew we'd figure it out and tell the cops."

"Go ahead and tell the cops whatever you want," Tyler says, his always-friendly eyes narrowing and sending a chill up my spine. "They already know about me."

"What do mean?" asks Alexandra, still hugging the pink notebook to her chest.

"I went to the cops." Tyler rubs at his stubble-strewn face. "I knew exactly where Piper was before she fell because we spoke on the phone. And then, the next morning, I find out she supposedly tried to kill herself? It didn't make any sense. So I told the cops they needed to investigate." He runs a hand through his hair. "And they didn't."

"Where was Piper before she fell?" Alexandra asks timidly.

"She went to talk to Mr. Davis."

My head feels tight. My lips, tongue, everything goes numb.

"Why?" Alexandra asks.

Tyler's gaze snaps to mine. "You want to tell them, or should I?"

"She went there to tell Mr. Davis the truth, didn't she?" I can't feel my mouth as the words come out. "About what I did."

A small, bitter laugh escapes Tyler's lips. "If that's what you really think, then you don't know your sister at all."

His words are sharp, and my breath catches. I fall back against the cold rail, letting myself slide down to the ground. My injured finger brushes the earth, and pain vibrates up my arm. Piper went there to do exactly what I asked her to do.

She went there to confess.

My lungs feel like they're about to burst. Everyone's hovering, staring at me.

"What's going on, Savannah?" Noah asks, reaching down to help me up. I try to push him off. I don't deserve his help. Not this time. Not ever. But my arm won't obey my brain.

I shut my eyes and draw in the slightest amount of air until the drowning sensation lets up. "I got Piper in trouble. Big trouble."

My breath is shallow, my vision foggy as I tell them about the tournament, the grades, the money—everything. "I heard the car, and I thought she was headed to the lab to tell my parents. But then she never came home. Late that night, we got the call from the hospital."

Even Jacey gapes at me like I'm a monster. And I am. Saying it all aloud, listening to what I was willing to do to get what I wanted, I know I deserve whatever's coming. That day, when I was too selfish to do the right thing, I let the darkness in me climb up my core, coat my throat, and wrap itself around my brain.

I wasn't a sister. I wasn't even a friend. I *was* the darkness.

"But she didn't go to the lab," Tyler says. "She didn't go to the Point right away either. I don't know why. Maybe she figured out the meeting wasn't happening, or maybe it was the last thing on her mind after being suspended for the chemistry tests. She went back to the school to talk to Mr. Davis. She was planning to take the fall for everything."

"Why would she do that?" Noah asks.

Because she's the sister I'll never be.

Tyler shakes his head. "I tried to talk her out of it. That's why I called her. But she said she needed to do it and that I had to trust her. And I did, for a while. But the way she was letting Savannah use her was too much, so I called her again. When she didn't answer, I drove to the school to see if I could get her to listen to reason. By that point, her car was already gone, and I didn't want to upset her more if it was already done. So I went home." He tugs on the strings of his hoodie, stretching them until they look like they might snap. "I should've tried harder to find her."

"So, then," Noah says, "she went to the school first and *then* to the Point? Because she was so upset?"

"That's what I'm trying to figure out" Tyler paces, boots crushing some feathery fronds. "I went to the police station and spoke to a cop. Detective Breslow. I told him something was off. Piper was upset about what Savannah did, but she wasn't suicidal. It didn't make sense. She'd called me from outside Mr. Davis's office. So how did she get from there to being unconscious on the side of a mountain?"

"What did Breslow say?" I ask.

"He basically laughed in my face. But the weird thing was *why* he laughed. It wasn't because Piper had fallen from Suicide Point. It was because I'd mentioned Mr. Davis. Breslow seemed very familiar with our favorite club advisor. He didn't find the situation the slightest bit worrisome."

"Did you try talking to Mr. Davis?" Jacey asks, grabbing on to the railing to pull herself up. Her eyes shut momentarily as she sways, pant leg brushing a fern bejeweled by dewdrops. Then she steadies herself. "Did you ask if Piper went to see him that day?"

"I didn't want to show my hand," Tyler says. "Figured I'd learn a lot more about him if he thought I was just some kid from Foothill who's really into wilderness survival."

"You're saying you infiltrated our club to spy on Mr. Davis?" Jacey flashes an incredulous look. "Mr. Davis is a great teacher. He cares about his students. Look, I really want to find out what happened to Piper, too, but Mr. Davis didn't write the threat in Piper's bag or"—she waves a hand toward the cliff—"*do* something to her. If that's what you're think-ing, you're wrong."

"Maybe he's not," Alexandra says. Sunlight casts a honey-colored glow over her dark curls as she glances up from the little pink notebook she's clutching.

Jacey turns to her, and Alexandra bites her lip. But she loosens her hold on the notebook. "I'm on the school paper with Piper. You guys all claim to know her, but every one of you is missing the most obvious thing ever. About Piper. About this club."

"So then say it already." I might snatch that notebook and fling it off the cliff.

"Why did Piper join this club?" she asks.

"Because Noah was in it," Jacey says, brushing some dirt off the front of her sweatshirt.

Alexandra shakes her head. "Maybe that was part of it. But it wasn't the only reason."

"She joined because she's Mr. Davis's pet," I offer. "She never stops talking about him."

Alexandra flicks her pen against her chin. "Not good enough. Why did she join a club involving all the things she hates? Exercise and the outdoors, for example?"

Noah rubs his temple. "She said she wanted to try something new. Piper develops new interests all the time."

"Piper wasn't pursuing a new interest," Alexandra says, looking exhausted. The wind picks up, hurling her curls into disarray and whipping the scent of wildflowers into the air. "She was pursuing a story."

Noah lifts a brow. "Like for the *Grayling High Gazette*? She wouldn't have kept that a secret."

"She might've, if the story put her in danger. Whatever Piper was investigating, she didn't even tell the other editors about it. She probably knew no one would approve."

Exhaustion has melted my brain so much that I giggle. "Piper was investigating Survival Club? Like, the case of the missing canteen?"

"Not the club itself," Alexandra corrects. "Someone *in* the club. I suspected she was working on something secret a while ago. She was always distracted during journalism meetings, jotting down notes and whispering into that recorder of hers. But she refused to tell me what it was. At first, I thought she was worried I'd steal her idea or something, like…like what she'd done to me." Her eyes darken. "Things have always been competitive between us. Well, one day, Piper tore a page out of her notepad and crumpled it up." A small animal darts through the underbrush next to the path, and Alexandra flinches. She drops her voice, like the chipmunks are listening. "After everyone went home, I dug it out of the trash. Most of the writing was scratched out and scribbled over, but a couple of things were still legible, just barely, like *SC*. So I asked myself, why would Piper have to write encrypted notes for a school story?"

"Or go undercover for a school story, for that matter," Noah adds.

"Because it wasn't some *school story*," Alexandra says, gaining momentum. "I think Piper was investigating something bigger. A story someone would've threatened her over to make sure she'd stop poking around. And when that didn't work..." Her gaze slides over to the cliff.

"This person resorted to other means," Tyler finishes.

"But what does this have to do with Mr. Davis?" Jacey asks.

Alexandra tugs a creased and crumpled scrap of paper from her back pocket. "When Savannah came to me in the gym, talking about Piper being threatened, the wheels in my head started spinning. I ran back to my locker to grab that note I'd dug out of the trash so I could try and figure out what Piper was working on. And I'm almost positive I've pieced together one thing." She thrusts the scrap at me, and the others gather around me to peek at it.

Letters strung together like an equation are circled in pencil among all the scribbles: *BS = danger*.

Noah slings Jacey a wry glance. "BS is definitely concerning."

Alexandra frowns. "Before this weekend, I thought these initials belonged to a person. And no one in the club fit. Sam's last name is Eldridge, so even reversed, it wasn't a match. But yesterday, I realized something about the advisor and one of the members. About their lives outside the club. Remember those rumors going around last winter? That one of our athletics teams had suddenly gone from last place in their division to champs, and it wasn't because they'd recruited a new star player or doubled up on training sessions?"

"Boys' soccer," I mutter, kicking a pine cone. Though the school treated Mr. Davis like a god after that achievement, the league gave him a hard time. The accusations ranged from bribing refs to paying other coaches to throw games, but nothing was ever proven.

"Exactly." Alexandra grins like a proud parent. "Last year, Piper asked the journalism advisor if she could write a story about it, but he said that kind of piece had no place in a student-run paper." She lets this thought simmer for a beat. "So what if Piper decided to go rogue and do it anyway? What better place to find answers about a possible scandal involving boys' soccer than Survival Club? You've got the senior team captain and the coach in one place."

The words tumble through my brain, getting stuck before I can fully process them, like a squirrel trying to make it through a cluster of tree branches. Piper loves Mr. Davis. She would never pursue a story that would hurt him.

But the last place she was headed was his office.

PIPER

Two Weeks Before She Fell

"It's out of the question," Mr. James hisses, baring yellowed teeth. "I told you last year. It's not an appropriate topic for a school paper. A man's livelihood and reputation are on the line."

"That's why I want to do this," I argue. The stinging scent of chemicals wafts into the room from the classroom being cleaned next door, and I blink to keep from tearing up. I've been asking since last soccer season to cover this story, and Mr. James keeps shutting me down. "Mr. Davis is obviously innocent. But people are spreading these lies, and eventually, it could end him. Let me prove his innocence to everyone and blast all these rumors to hell."

Mr. James inhales slowly, his thin frame rising and falling in his cushioned rolling chair. "It is a *no*, Piper. The firmest possible *no*. I appreciate your loyalty to Mr. Davis, but the best thing you can do for him is to let this go." He is saying one thing, but I know he means another by the way the word "loyalty" drags on his tongue. "And if you ask me again, I will remove you from journalism altogether."

"You can't do that," I protest, pressing my fingertips into the desk like if I hold on tight enough, he'll give in.

"Watch me." His neck pulses, the skin sunburn red. "This isn't a debate tournament, Piper. You can't win this one. Now, if you would please see yourself out, I have grading to do, and I'd rather not be here all night." He flicks two fingers toward the door and then lowers his head, gaze fastened on the pile of papers in front of him.

I resist the urge to knock over one of the miniature potted plants adorning his desk. The things I used to find invigorating about this room now feel suffocating. "Fine," I spit, grabbing my notebook and spinning around. "But if he goes down for this, you're just as guilty as everyone spreading the rumors."

Flying out into the hall, I weave through the clumps of straggling students, passing Mr. Davis's chemistry classroom, the door now shut. It's also locked; I know this from the numerous times I've tried to get in there and dig around while he's been in the athletics office.

I'm not buying this *looking out for Mr. Davis's welfare* crap. Mr. James is jealous. Everyone loves Mr. Davis, and everyone is perfectly indifferent to Mr. James.

By the time I reach Mr. Davis's office, my jaw hurts from grinding my molars. The door is open, Mr. Davis at the desk, and I head straight to the table along the left side of the room. I smack my notebook down, the chair screeching as I drag it along the linoleum before plopping down into it.

In front of me, the computer screen is black, but I don't try to revive it. Instead, I stare at the wood veneer of the desk until my eyes fall shut in an attempt to block out thoughts of Mr. James.

"Everything okay?"

I startle, turning to see Mr. Davis peering over at me from the desk, brows slanted.

"Oh, yeah. Hi, Mr. Davis." I try to think up a reason for storming in here without greeting him, but an image fills my head: Mr. James's fingers waving me toward the door, nails as discolored as his teeth. "Just a rough class. But I'm here now. What do you need me to do?" A ripple of impatience runs through my chest. I should be trying to prove Mr. Davis's innocence, not spending an hour grading his papers. "Teacher's aide" will look great on college applications, but the main reason I agreed to it was to get closer to him so I could find some way to vindicate him. I owe him that. Being the only freshmen in his AP chemistry class full of seniors wasn't exactly easy. The older kids started calling me Dr. Piper and asking if I was lost. Mr. Davis turned everything around, though. Instead of making a huge show of my age, he treated me just like everyone else. And pretty soon, I felt like everyone else.

But I haven't found a thing to exonerate him, and whenever I try to question the guys on the team, they just joke about how they've been eating their Wheaties or how *when you're on fire, you're on fire.*

I had hoped any speculation regarding boys' soccer would fade away after time, like the scent of dryer sheets on your clothes. But this morning I overheard the athletics director asking Principal Winters if they could look for a new coach before soccer season starts. The administration had practically pinned a scarlet *c* for *cheater* on Mr. Davis's shirt without giving him a chance to prove he wasn't involved in any illegal activities. They're willing to sacrifice him to save their own skins. Like cowards.

The only person who cares about the truth is me. And plan A is failing me. There's nothing in this athletics office that will clear Mr. Davis's name. I had pictured working in his classroom at least some of the time, but so far, he's brought all of my TA assignments down here.

"If you could make copies of these pages, that'd be great," he says, pointing to a small stack at the edge of the desk.

"No problem." I stand and pick up the papers, forcing a smile.

After finishing the copies in the teachers' lounge, I meander back, taking my time. When I approach the office again, whispers trickle out into the hall. I halt, taking two steps back. I should turn around and give my teacher some privacy. But something pulls me forward like a magnet. I press my back against the wall beside the door frame and listen.

"You just need to keep quiet." Mr. Davis's voice is low and sharper than I've ever heard it. Numbness spreads down my spine. "My job is at stake here. You'll get into whatever college you want and live your charmed life, but you have to stop running your mouth."

"I didn't—"

"I'm going to have to redo everything," Mr. Davis cuts in, "because of you idiots. You knew this would be the new protocol after last season. And now my ass is on the line."

"Coach, it was only a couple of guys. Can't you just—"

"Get out," he says.

Before I can decide what to do, I hear footsteps coming toward me. I speed walk away as fast as my stiff legs will carry me, my heart thumping over the steps fading down the hall in the opposite direction.

My breathing is so ragged, I can barely see straight. I peek over my shoulder and catch a glimpse of goalkeeper Jaime Sanderson's enormous frame.

Shame heats my cheeks. I'm known around here as the smart kid. The only sophomore to have won the Peterson

Award. The girl who can't be accommodated by her own school, so she has to travel to Foothill for science classes.

But I'm a complete moron when it comes to some things. Like who to trust.

I take a deep breath, letting the oxygen fill my lungs until clarity floods my mind.

It's time to take this investigation up a level. Since plan A was an utter failure, it's time for plan B. Something that'll get me closer to dear Mr. Davis. Something that'll get me access to his classroom, the one I haven't been inside since freshman year.

I return to the athletics office, fresh photocopies in hand. "Here you go," I say to Mr. Davis, making my voice light as I set them down on the desk. Still clearly frazzled by his conversation with Jaime, he mumbles his thanks.

"Hey, Mr. Davis?"

He looks up, irritation in his pursed lips.

"I was thinking of joining Survival Club."

21

"So, you think Piper caught Mr. Davis doing something shady?" A whisper of terror passes over the back of my neck. He could've been outside the tent when Jacey and I were talking. He could've painted that message.

"I don't know," Alexandra says, brown skin blushing rose in the early-morning light. "But we have to consider the possibility. Someone wanted her out of the club. The last place she went was the school, looking for him."

"I still think this is ridiculous." Jacey looks to Noah for help. "Okay, so Piper was investigating the soccer team, but we don't know that she found anything."

I turn to Alexandra. "You never listened in while Piper was recording?"

"Believe me, I tried. But she was so careful. All I've got is this scrap of paper. There are a couple more initials, like the letter *C*." She points to some scribbles at the bottom of the page. "Looks like 'Where are the ROTs?' But the *O* could be a *D*. I don't know." She shrugs and stuffs the paper back into her pocket.

"Random drug tests," Tyler says suddenly. "RDTs. Maybe Piper figured out it was a drug thing."

"It wasn't drugs," I blurt, realizing too late how defensive I sound. But they're wrong. Grant would never do that.

"Let's think about this," Alexandra says, trying to calm me but only adding to my irritation. "If it was drugs, then the *C* could stand for—"

"Coach, obviously," I say. "The athletics director wasn't going to let Mr. Davis keep his coaching job if they had another losing streak. Mr. Davis might've panicked. If he's involved in some sort of cover-up for the boys' soccer team, maybe Piper found out. And he caught on."

"It could explain why that cop was so eager to send me on my way." Tyler picks up a branch and starts plucking the needles from it one by one. "Maybe Mr. Davis has the Grayling PD in his pocket."

"Then what are we supposed to do?" I ask. "We can't go to the cops—"

"Not *that* cop," Tyler says. "But we could head down the mountain right now and demand to speak to someone else. There are too many of us to ignore."

"It's not enough." I wind a section of hair around my finger so tightly some strands snap off. Their frazzled ends blow in the wind. "Piper's pack is gone. The only proof we have she even went to see Mr. Davis is your word."

"The recorder." Tyler stops plucking pine needles and looks up. "Piper always had that recorder on her."

"In her jacket pocket," Jacey adds, nodding.

"So, then," Tyler says, dropping the branch and trampling it, "where is it?" He looks at me, and I freeze.

"It could've been in the bag with the rest of her stuff at the hospital," I say, a tremor in my voice. Only I'm not sure. When I had that hospital bag, I was too busy searching for Piper's phone to register anything else.

"Maybe the recorder wasn't on her," Noah says with a shrug, wandering over to peer down the face of the cliff. "It could be down there somewhere."

"We should talk to Mr. Davis," Jacey offers. "If Piper spoke to him that day, maybe he can tell us something about her state of mind or where she was headed."

"But if they did meet, why is he keeping it a secret?" I ask. "If he saw Piper that afternoon and she was distraught enough to hurt herself, why not tell my parents? He never even bothered to mention it."

Alexandra hugs her notebook to her chest. "We should head down the mountain. We can tell the cops—good cops—everything we know, and they can question Mr. Davis."

"If we accuse our teacher of hurting Piper," Jacey says, getting worked up, "it will *ruin* him. Drug gossip is one thing, but you can't just shake off a rumor that you tried to kill a student. We need more proof."

"No," I say, shaking my head, even though a second ago I was on her side. I have no idea what to do. "I think Alexandra has a point."

"Of course you do, Savannah." Jacey's voice is low and caustic. "You didn't hesitate to sell out your own sister. So why would you stop to consider the life of your teacher?"

Whatever has been keeping me levelheaded suddenly breaks off with a crack. "Oh, and you're so much better?" I trample a clump of wildflowers on my way toward her, blond locks blowing in front of my face, sticking to my lips. I must look feral.

"Hey, let's talk this out like rational campers," Noah says with a forced, grating calm. He glances around, scratching his head. "We could tell Mr. Davis we need to take Savannah back down the mountain. We'll say she's not doing well with the Piper situation. He'll let us leave, as long as nobody tips him off about this drug cover-up theory."

"I don't know," Alexandra says, a panicked trill to her voice. "If Mr. Davis wrote that threat on the tent, he's more aware of how much Savannah knows than we're giving him credit for."

"That's why we should go now," I say, "before he makes

it back down and covers his tracks." Somewhere in the trees, a bird makes a high-pitched chirp like a wakeup call. The rest of camp—Mr. Davis included—will be up soon.

"The best thing we can do is split up," Noah says. "Two people can head down while the rest of us stay."

"And you think Mr. Davis is just going to ignore the fact that two students are missing?" Tyler throws his hands up. "Today is Sunday. We're all headed down in a few hours anyway. Let's play it cool. As soon as we get back, we'll go to the cops."

A few heads nod, followed by a low murmur of consent. Tyler and Alexandra walk toward the trail, a fervor in their steps. Noah and Jacey hesitate, then follow.

I stay where I am in the weeds, wanting to argue some more.

But there's no point. I trudge after them, spinning the useless chain link around my thumb.

I don't have to convince these people.

I just have to get away.

An hour later, my eyelids are heavy, and my limbs are sore. We near camp, and the smell of smoke trickles into the air. Tyler points ahead to where the treetops are bathed in a white haze.

My stomach sinks. *He's awake.* And now we have to explain why we were all up and out of camp at the crack of dawn.

We scrounge up small bundles of wood. My heart is ready to leap from my chest as we enter camp, but only one lone resident sits in the campfire circle.

Sam. He's crouched in the dirt, whittling a branch with his knife.

My gaze shoots from the tents to the trees, then back to the fire. "Where's Mr. Davis?"

"Not awake yet, I guess," says Sam.

Tyler lets his wood drop to the ground, and I shush him.

"Sorry," he mumbles.

"What's going on?" Sam asks. "I thought you were all still sleeping."

"Nothing's going on," Jacey spits too forcefully.

"Just collecting some wood to help you out, buddy." Noah nods to his meager stack and places it near the fire ring.

Sam watches him leerily. "Thanks." He goes back to whittling, pretending like we're not surrounding him. We each add our wood to the pile and plop down around the fire to wait out the morning.

After a minute, Alexandra pulls that scrap of paper hidden in her notebook, squinting at the scribbles again. Beside Jacey, Noah yawns and draws circles in the dirt with a stick.

I scoot closer to Tyler. "Now that the charade is over, you can tell me your true feelings about squirrel mix."

He ignores me, tossing a log onto the fire.

I take a deep breath. "Look, I know you think I'm horrible," I say, my voice low. "And you're right. But I'd do anything to be able to tell Piper how sorry I am. I would own up to the grade scam in a millisecond if it would wake her up. I would take back everything I said to her that day and tell her how amazing she is"—I try to swallow as the words catch in my parched throat—"and how much I love her. How much I want to be a better sister for her." Tears well up in my eyes, one blink away from spilling over.

"Good." He shifts to clear a rock from the dirt beneath him. "If she does wake up, she deserves all of that and more."

Embarrassment smolders in me. I'm an idiot. I can't believe I ever shared two words with that guy. That I drank it all up when he pretended to believe I was nothing more than a distraught sister, while he knew every crooked turn of my soul the entire time.

He's only standing up for Piper. Still, it stings. I believed he wanted to be my friend.

I lean in closer. "You might think you're special because you were friends with Piper, but I'm her *sister*. I've been in her life since the day she was born."

"They should carve your name on a plaque," Tyler mutters, gaze still locked on the flames.

"I already told you, I made a mistake. I really thought"—I swallow—"you wanted to help me."

"Do you even want help, Savannah?" he snaps, his eyes

sparking fiercely as he finally looks at me. "Piper tried to help you, and look where it got you both."

"I'm sorry about everything I did to her. I was upset that she insulted Grant. And that she didn't care about my future." I shake my head. "It doesn't matter. All that matters is finding out who did this to her. Maybe if I can help, she'll—"

"Forgive you?"

My lips press together so tightly they hurt. "You don't think she will. You don't think I even deserve to make it back into her good graces. You think I'm a monster." My voice is raised, and Jacey springs to attention across the fire. I mouth that I'm fine, but I'm not. Because Tyler is right.

"I'm worse than a monster," I admit, dropping my voice. "I don't deserve her forgiveness. But I'm still going to try."

I get up and stride in the direction of my tent. I don't make it far, though, before Tyler brushes past me to block my path.

He sighs, running a hand through his black hair. "That's not what I was thinking." I look up at him. "Well, not in those words." That fire edges back into my limbs. I try to stomp away, but I seem to be fighting through a patch of tall, soundless weeds.

"Not even close to those words," he continues, reaching for the edge of my jacket and tugging lightly. I stop, my eyes fixed on the weeds. "I was going to say that I see you, Savannah Sullivan." He dips his head forward, in front of mine, fingers resting lightly on my arm. My sneaker pushes aside the tall grass in lazy circles as our eyes meet. "The real you. I think you're better than all of this. And I hope Piper wakes up so you two can have another chance."

My fist curls, sending a jolt of pain through my injured finger. "You're so full of crap. Even your name is fake."

He gives a curt head shake. "I meant every word." His voice is steady, and I can't read that glint in his brown eyes. That glint is kindness and cruelty. Love and hate. It's everything and nothing, and I can't look at it for another second.

I try to respond, choking instead as the tears I've been holding back finally wet my cheeks. This is what I deserve for sending Piper back to the school that day, straight into the arms of danger. I sniffle and wipe my eyes with the back of my hand.

Tyler reaches out, his fingertips grazing my still-damp cheeks, but something moves in my peripheral vision. Grant ducks out of his tent, kneeling to tie his boots. I back up, throwing one quick glance at Tyler before leaving him standing alone in the weeds.

Running a hand through his hair, Grant stretches, then catches my eye. "Hey. You're up." His eyes narrow in concern as he shuffles over. "Are you okay?"

"Just couldn't sleep. I'm anxious to visit Piper in the hospital."

Grant's head draws back. "Really?" He glances in the

direction of Mr. Davis's tent. "Maybe you and I can get an early start back. Mr. Davis might let us if we go together."

I smile weakly. "That would be great."

His lips touch my hair. "When he wakes up, I'll ask him."

He heads back to his tent for his thermos, and I move to the now-abandoned fire. I squat down to warm my hands, this morning's events tumbling through my brain. Events that Grant knows nothing about. Should I head down the mountain with him? He'd be a comfort at the police station. But then I'd have to confess the real reason I came up here to begin with. I'd have to convince him that his beloved coach can't be trusted.

Zip. "Hey, guys," Mr. Davis's sleepy voice says behind me, turning every inch of my body to stone. "Can't believe you're all up before me."

"Well, the early bird catches the worm, Mr. Davis," says Noah. A horsey, clunky laugh follows.

"Does that mean you caught something, Mr. Crawford?"

"Uh, no. I left my bow and arrows back home, sir." Dark circles rim Noah's eyes, reminding me how tired I am. Jacey yawns, causing me to yawn.

Off to one side of the camp, the bright green tent begins to rustle. The door unzips, and Abby pokes her head out, rubbing her eyes and rolling her neck sleepily. She pulls a beanie over her tousled hair and meanders over to the fire.

Mr. Davis starts assembling his Jetboil, and Grant tosses me a reassuring smile before joining him. Smoke burns my throat and distorts the scene as I watch them, my hands fidgeting in my lap.

A minute later, Grant returns, frowning. "He says we can't split up the group. I would've thought he'd be more understanding."

"When are we heading back down?"

He shrugs. "He wants us to enjoy the morning up here in the fresh air."

Great. I take a breath, but my senses no longer register pine or smoke or the vast glory of the mountains.

The only thing I sense right now is my purpose. And that's to get down this mountain, with or without the buddy system.

PIPER

The Day She Fell

As soon as Savannah's door creaks open, my ears perk up. Something rustles in the kitchen. Of course—minutes after shattering my world, she's grabbing a snack. I tiptoe down the hall, lift the keys to her car slowly from the hook, and ease open the front door. Then I slip out into the afternoon sunlight.

Tears blur my vision as I drive the short distance to Grayling High. I left at the beginning of sixth period, so school has only been out for half an hour. Mr. Davis will be in the athletics office. Alex called after my fight with Savannah, asking if I wanted to study for our AP physics quiz. I had to talk to someone, so I answered. Maybe I shouldn't have, because he didn't like my plan, and he sounded like he might try to stop me.

I pull the chain link from my pocket, tumbling it around in my hand. I ended the call with Alex before he managed to talk sense into me. The truth is, I know that what I'm about to do doesn't look good on paper. My big sister should be solving my problems, not causing them. Yet I'm the one sitting here in tear-streaked desperation, waiting for Mr. Davis to escort me to the gallows.

I still have to do it.

Before homecoming, I really thought Savannah and I had turned a corner. I'd forgiven her, shown her that being sisters trumps everything. And she'd sacrificed all the pre-dance pomp and circumstance that goes with being queen to help me. For the first time in forever, I'd felt like we were close.

And then when Noah and Jacey betrayed me, she was nowhere to be found.

I remember her words from earlier today with a stab. *We're done, Piper. As far as I'm concerned, you don't exist.*

As far as my sister's concerned, maybe I've never existed at all.

But after today—after I save her from her own mistakes and probably ruin my entire future in the process—she's going to remember me.

And maybe even love me.

I wipe my tears, dry my hand on my jeans, and knock on the athletics office door. Mr. Davis doesn't answer, but the door is cracked, so I give it a nudge. The small room is empty. Some papers are scattered over the desk, and his laptop is here, screen saver flashing. He must've gone to make copies or grab coffee in the teachers' lounge. The last of the students has long since shuffled out of the hallway, leaving only the distant rumble of voices on the outdoor fields. I pull out my phone—four p.m.

Then, with a pinch of disappointment, I remember. Survival Club is meeting up on the trail this afternoon.

I start to leave, but something on the desk catches my eye. Something Mr. Davis has never left out before. The thing I've searched this office, his classroom desk, and the equipment locker for countless times since I heard him whispering with Jaime Sanderson two weeks ago.

His soccer binder.

It's finally here, right in front of me, after all these hours of playing TA and survival girl. Of course it's here, now that I'm in so much trouble the story no longer matters.

Or maybe it does.

I don't know exactly what I heard that day with Jaime. Maybe Mr. Davis has simply been helping some troubled students and that threat I found in my Survival Club backpack was someone messing with me. Maybe there's no deeper meaning, and if I close this case once and for all—if I can clear Mr. Davis's name and get the school board off his back—he'll overlook Savannah's and my crimes.

At this point, I certainly don't have much to lose. If he's hiking all the way to the Point, I should have plenty of time before he returns to lock up. I cast a quick glance over my shoulder into the hall and then stride to the desk.

The binder is thick, filled with dividers labeled things like PLAYER CONTACT INFO and HEALTH RELEASE FORMS. But on the first try, it opens to the subsection I'm looking for.

RANDOM DRUG TESTS.

I've done enough snooping over the last month to know that the league is looking into whether performance-enhancing drugs are the reason for the team's sudden spike in wins. I flip through the forms, all of which are marked "normal" in the results space in the upper right corner. Each is signed and stamped by a company called Phelps Lab, and there's a large manila envelope, already addressed to the athletics association. But for whatever reason, Mr. Davis never sent the forms.

It's a rather thin stack. I count them, and there are only eight forms, not even enough to field a team. It's still preseason; maybe these are the only returning players. But something gnaws at me as I flip through the pages. Ben Walters is a returning senior. His test isn't in here. And another player's form is missing too.

Jaime Sanderson's.

I shut the notebook and pull out my audio recorder. "Found Mr. Davis's random drug tests. Some are missing, including Jaime Sanderson's. Mr. Davis never sent the forms to the athletics association." I press stop, slide the device back into my jacket pocket, and stoop to check the trash. But there's nothing besides a browned apple core and a few crumpled sticky notes.

I spin around, the vein in my temple pulsating faster than it ever has before. Mr. Davis could return any second. There's a paper shredder in the corner. I kneel down clumsily and tug at the lid until it pops off, then sift through the slivers. It's impossible to tell if any of them came from a drug test without piecing them together, fragment by fragment.

I hold up one sliver to the light that filters through the small window, squinting to make out a word. I might have the beginning of a name. *Ja*—this could be it. My heart lifts, but then a deep voice hits me like an ice-cold wind.

"What are you doing in here?"

Keys jangle in the doorway as I turn to face him.

22

I'm engaged in a stare-down with the tent poles.

"What are you doing?" Jacey is eyeing me from a safe distance.

"Trying to speed this show along. Mr. Davis has no intention of leaving, ever."

She checks over her shoulder before inching closer. "You haven't said anything to Grant, have you?"

"He had nothing to do with Piper," I say, words dosed with anger.

"We don't know that. He's on the soccer team."

I sling her a withering look. "You'd love for this to get pinned on Grant, wouldn't you? A little retribution?"

She glowers at me, and I feel the progress we've made this weekend start to slip away.

"Any idea how to take this thing down?" I ask, changing the subject.

"You weren't able to coax it into breaking itself down with menacing glares?"

I huff and start beating the nylon thing into submission.

"Or you could try that." She sidesteps to avoid losing an eye to a pole.

A few minutes later, Jacey has the last pieces of our tent secured within her backpack.

"What do you guys say we practice some hunting methods?" Mr. Davis asks while tidying up the breakfast area. "Just technique," he clarifies when Alexandra's mouth drops open. "No animals will be harmed in the making of this educational moment, I assure you."

"We already did that," I say. "We woke up early while the woods were quiet."

Mr. Davis's eyes widen. "Unsupervised?"

"Tyler was teaching us," I say, sacrificing Tyler—Alex— whoever the hell he is. "It wasn't dangerous."

Tyler's mouth twists as he turns to hide the bruise blooming over his jaw. "Yeah, just showing them your basic atlatl throw. Stuff my dad taught me." Brilliant dead dad diversion tactic.

"Well, I'd like to try," Sam says, earning a big smile from

Mr. Davis. Abby stops humming to join them, and Grant soon wanders after them too.

"I'll keep an eye on things," Noah whispers to me before jogging to catch up.

I bite back a growl. We are seriously going to be here all day.

"Do you guys really think Mr. Davis did something to Piper?" Jacey asks as Tyler sidles up next to us. "He's my favorite teacher. Piper's too. I just can't see it. I need more proof before we talk to the cops."

"It's going to be tough to prove anything when we're stuck up here," I mutter.

Tyler glances at where the others have disappeared into the trees. "We could do some digging now." He makes a grand gesture toward Mr. Davis's tent.

"Now?" Jacey asks. "We don't know when he's coming back."

"I'll be the lookout," Tyler says, shrugging. "And I can try to move the group a little farther into the woods. If Mr. Davis ends the hunting expedition, I'll give you a signal."

"Gonna clank your chains in the wind?" I ask.

Tyler presses his lips flat, holding back a smile. "I'll yell, 'Hey, Mr. Davis,' and then make up a question he can't answer about primitive survival skills. That should buy you enough time to get out of his tent."

I let out a long sigh. The plan sounds risky, but reasonable. "What are we looking for?"

"Find his phone, if it's in there. It'll be locked, but I know a guy down in Foothill who deals with that sort of thing."

Jacey throws me a wary look.

"Just check his bag," Tyler says. "If he's guilty, he probably cleaned up after himself. But it's worth a look."

"Oh, sure," I say. "It's worth a look, as long as *we're* the ones breaking and entering."

"Exactly." Tyler grins and strides after the group, leaving Jacey and me staring at Mr. Davis's closed tent.

I check behind us. Alexandra must've joined the hunt, because the camp is empty. "Stand right outside the tent," I whisper, and Jacey nods, spinning to face the woods, back pressed up against the fabric. I unzip the flap and enter, closing it behind me.

The inside is clean apart from Mr. Davis's backpack in one corner, stuffed and ready to go. Immediately, this feels wrong. I'm violating my teacher's privacy. His *underwear* is in here somewhere, for good old Aunt Mildred's sake. Speaking of my crimp-faced great-aunt, what would she think of me if she knew everything I'd done to my sister? I cringe and dip my hand inside the smallest pocket on Mr. Davis's backpack, feeling a stab of disappointment. His phone isn't inside like I hoped it would be. Just some lint and a pack of breath mints.

The next pouch is slightly larger, but the only thing in there is a first aid box.

I'm elbow deep in my chemistry teacher's things, and so

far, I'm only finding items to keep kids alive, which is the opposite of tossing kids off cliffs.

I turn my attention to the main compartment and go for it, plunging my hand into the rolled clothing and used socks and whatever else a twenty-something-year-old man needs for a weekend away. I feel for anything out of place—a sharp edge, anything heavy. But there's nothing.

I slide my hand back out, tucking everything neatly away like it was before. I've got to get out of here. I put the pack down in the corner, then turn to make my way out the flap.

But my sneaker catches on the nylon floor, and the backpack tips over with a thump, startling me. I freeze. My heart is beating like a million little soccer spectators applauding in my chest. I peer through the little mesh window. The camp still looks empty, but I press my ear to the fabric wall. Just chirping birds and rustling trees. Good.

I right the pack and push it back into the corner, trying to balance it the way Mr. Davis had it. But something I didn't see before snags my eye. Beneath the straps is another compartment that runs from top to bottom. I unzip it, feeling around inside until my fingertips pass over something rough and fibrous. I tug on the object until a coiled rope emerges. Setting it down, I dig even deeper this time, removing a roll of duct tape.

Okay. *Just breathe.* This is perfectly normal. Hikers use ropes, right? For scaling cliffs and lassoing wildlife? Mr. Davis probably keeps a rope in his hiking pack all the time.

And the duct tape? As Grant would say, what can't you use duct tape for? There's always a reason for duct tape. But my brain is thumping now, in time with my heart.

I shake the worries away, shoving the rope back inside the compartment. Then I grab the tape. The edge is frayed and jagged. Torn in a hurry, maybe. The edge sticks to my hand as I lift the roll, and I reach to pull it off.

That's when I see it. Stuck to the side of the roll, curving to hide beneath the frayed edge. A strand of hair.

A wavy, blond strand of hair.

Don't panic. But my lungs don't receive the message, because they seem to be shutting down. I have to decide what to do with this tape. If it's Piper's hair, the cops will need to test it, right? For DNA? But if I steal it, they might think I planted the hair.

I grit my teeth and begin to stuff the tape back down into the pocket. But there's something else inside—rectangular, about the size of a phone. One side is hard and flat—maybe a screen—and ridges line the edge. A twisted mash-up of fear and excitement spikes in my chest. This could be his pay-as-you-go drug phone. I slide my hand inside and reach until I'm nearly shoulder deep, grasping for it. Then I yank, my knuckles rubbing against the fibers of the rope until the phone pops free.

Except it's not a phone; it's an audio recorder. It's silver, with a speaker in the front and buttons along the side.

And it belongs to my sister.

23

Piper's voice on the recorder goes silent. "Now do you believe me?" I brush past Jacey, who's standing by the tent flap, gaping at the audio recorder in my hand.

"Maybe there's an explanation for why some tests were missing," she finally whispers, raking both hands through her hair.

I sling her a look. "Oh, there's an explanation. Mr. Davis is not the amazing teacher everyone thinks he is. He's shady as hell, and when Piper found that binder, he tried to shut her up for good." I stuff the recorder inside the zip pocket of my jacket.

"I can't believe this is happening."

"Well, believe it. We've got to get down the mountain."

"We're just going to leave everyone else up here with him?"

I secure my hair into a messy bun and let my head fall back. Sighing, I rub my temples. "I don't know, Jacey. I don't know what to do. For once in your life, *you* tell *me* what to do."

"Okay," she says, and then she just stands there, biting her lip. I'm about to lose it when she adds, "You go." She nods adamantly, like the idea just spun through the air and landed in a dive with perfectly pointed toes. "Yeah, you go, and I'll stay here and wait for the others. I'll keep an eye on Mr. Davis and fill the others in." She looks up at me. "You know the way?"

I inhale, slow and deep. "It's a trail, Jacey. As long as I keep heading down and avoid the bears, I think I'll be fine."

"It's not a joke," she says. "Hiking alone is extremely dangerous. If this weren't the only solution—"

"It's the only solution. You protect everyone, and I'll go to the cops."

She hesitates, clearly unsure whether she can break the laws of wilderness survival for something like regular old survival. Then she turns to face the forest, and I'm on my own.

I sweep through the trees at first, avoiding the exposure of the trail in case the others wandered this way. My water bottle is tucked beneath my arm. I left the rest of my stuff behind for Grant to carry. I plan to be halfway down the mountain before anyone notices I'm missing. My neck and back are sticky, so I pause to tug off my jacket. I tie it around my waist and continue at a brisk pace.

But something's wrong—the absence of cold ceramic bouncing against my chest.

I reach up to my throat and find it bare, and a wave of panic throttles me. I look down the neck of my layers of clothing.

My necklace isn't here. I pull at the jacket around my hips frantically, shake out the fabric of my T-shirt, praying for that gleaming thing to fall to my feet. Nothing jingles out. I try to remember the last time I reached up and felt for it, but I'm too sleep-deprived. Every memory of my fingers brushing against the ceramic blends together. My vision darkens, the thought of that necklace slipping away as terrifying as losing Piper herself. It could be a mile back up the trail, or it could be two inches from me, caught in the dewy foliage at my feet.

I have to find it.

I pound my fist against my thigh and pivot back around to face a battalion of identical trees. Scowling at a fern, I trudge back.

When I reach a familiar moss-strewn trunk, my name echoes through the trees. Apparently, the rest of the club noticed I was MIA. I kick the dead leaves, willing the shiny thing to reveal itself. The calls continue as I dig and curse.

Behind me, something crackles, and I drop my bottle.

In one last-ditch effort, I plow farther into the woods to the next identical evergreen. I can't leave without my necklace. My mind can't even process the thought of never having it again.

"Savannah." Mr. Davis's voice curls my nerves like a blade against ribbon. Frantically, I comb the ground with my shoe. Then I spin around to fasten my eyes on my teacher. "We talked about this. You can't just run off."

"I had to pee," I lie. "And then I lost my necklace somewhere in the woods."

He shakes his head, murmuring, "Do you know how much trouble I'd be in if you got lost? Or hurt?"

I comb my hair out of my face and take a breath, trying to squelch this anger stewing deep inside me. With him. With Jacey, who had one damn job.

But I fail. "You're going to be in trouble either way."

Mr. Davis's eyes darken as he crosses his arms. Unease wraps around my spine. I have to get back to the trail, to the open, to the others. Mr. Davis won't be able to do anything to me if they're watching. I scramble to the next tree, kicking aside the twigs and brambles. Still no glimmer of silver.

He's closer now. His aggravation hangs in the air like a thundercloud. It seeps into my skin. "Savannah, what are you talking about?" He shakes his head but doesn't hurry me along. He takes another slow step closer.

I can't handle this innocent teacher routine. My mouth

flies open of its own accord. "You were the last person to see Piper that day."

Mr. Davis's brow furrows. He's close enough now that I see his chest rise and fall in a slow, deliberate breath.

"You've been keeping it a secret."

He frowns, his boot crunching unnervingly on the forest floor as he steps closer.

"Because you did something to her," I add, shuffling backward.

One more long exhale. "Did something to her?"

"Piper was investigating the doping scandal. She found the random drug tests. The ones you didn't send. Was that why you tried to silence her for good?" I back up some more, and the clouds move with me, shrouding us in darkness.

Mr. Davis brushes aside some leaves with his boot, but his gaze remains on me. "Savannah, just let me help you find your necklace."

He's being too nice. I spin around, my gaze zipping around in one last desperate search.

Silver glints from within a tangle of vines, and my heart soars. I bend over to retrieve it, relieved to find the charm still clinging to the end of the chain. I clasp it in my fist just as Mr. Davis's heavy hand falls onto my shoulder.

Panic reels through my chest. His fingers press down, digging into my skin, and I scream with everything in me. Wrenching myself away, I make a mad dash for the trail.

Mr. Davis's footsteps pound after me, underbrush snapping beneath his boots. "Savannah!" he calls, deep voice slicing through the vegetation. I don't stop. He tried to kill Piper. If he catches me, he'll do whatever it takes to silence me. Clinging to my necklace so hard my knuckles ache, I run faster than I've ever chased a soccer ball.

I push aside brambles and dodge thick tree trunks, paying no mind to the talons of the branches as they claw at my flesh and hook my clothing.

Mr. Davis is close enough that I can hear his labored breathing behind me, over the birds, over the cacophony of our footsteps. He's not giving up, even though I'm about to reach the trail. Everyone will see him pursuing me, hunting me down like prey.

I near the edge of the woods, where the sunlight finally stipples through the pines. My foot catches on a rock, and I stumble, crashing through the trees.

But I'm free.

I pick myself up, Mr. Davis still close on my heels as I survey the trail. I open my mouth to scream for the others. But my heart catches in my throat, pushing the scream back down.

This isn't the trail.

I've simply breached one line in an endless page of trees. I must have gotten turned around while I was looking for my necklace. I curse under my breath. Ahead and behind and on either side of me, there's nothing but dark forest.

I battle the urge to hyperventilate. I have to press on; I just don't know which way to go. Even with a compass, I'd be lost out here.

"Grant!" I scream. But my breathing is so shallow, I barely make a sound. I'm not in soccer-season shape. "Somebody, help!"

Mr. Davis's steps are close now. I have to try and outrun him. I'll worry about being lost later.

I wipe my sweaty palms against my jeans and stash the necklace in my pocket. Then I sprint downhill, still listening to the sound of Mr. Davis barreling through the trees. Branches snag on the jacket flapping at my waist as I run, the recorder still bobbling in my zipped pocket. I step on a rock hidden in the foliage, and my ankle wobbles the way it did when I sprained it in that game against Lincoln High. But I recover, ducking beneath a branch and continuing at a dead run.

My lungs burn, and my legs become rubber. Just when I'm certain my heartbeat is the only thing I'll hear for the rest of my life, another sound surfaces.

Water.

The river must flow down through this part of the mountain. If I cross it, maybe Mr. Davis will give up and head back to the others.

I push through the thick layers of leaves, feeling my way toward the sound of rushing water. Gnarled boughs snag my hair and scratch my face and hands. I reach the edge of the forest, where the leafy undergrowth borders a steep ravine. Grabbing hold of a branch, I steady myself and scope out the river. It's not wide, but the current is fast, the water white and foamy. I can't tell how deep it is. It would be ludicrous to try and wade through.

I spot a fallen tree not too far downstream and immediately start clambering my way over the slippery rocks toward it. But as I get closer, my heart sinks. The makeshift bridge sits high on the ravine. A series of falls roil and lap over sharp rocks some ten feet below the log. I keep moving, trying to work up the courage to cross it.

"Savannah!" Mr. Davis breaks through the trees lining the bank. I toss a look back at him; it's a mistake. His royal-blue jacket pierces through the greenery, and my fear catches up with me. I can't do this.

The log is secured between two boulders on one side. I mow through thorny shrubs to get up to it. Then I heft myself on top of the slick log, ignoring the long prickers piercing through my jeans. Blood begins to seep through the denim. My hands are shredded. I wince and wrap my legs around the wood. Mr. Davis is still calling me, getting closer as he weaves along the path I just cleared. The log is thick—a good two feet in diameter—but I don't trust myself to walk on it. Instead, I shinny as fast as I can. He's gaining on me, though. If I don't adjust my position, he'll be here in seconds.

I try, but my stubborn limbs refuse to move. I was so stupid to end up alone with him, even stupider to blab those accusations. Why can't I ever keep my mouth shut?

"Grant!" I scream again. I take a deep breath, trying to envision the quickest way across—one that doesn't involve toppling down into the washing machine below. The churning water echoes my clashing thoughts. I shut my eyes, wanting to give up. But I push myself up onto my hands and knees.

Focus. I take in an even breath, allowing the whooshing sound of the falls to drown out Mr. Davis's cries behind me. Allowing it to deafen me completely. I stand up, but my body does one large, swooping wobble.

My arms spring out to my sides. I shuffle to regain my balance, heart firing in my chest. I should've agreed to take those gymnastics classes my parents offered in an attempt to keep me away from contact sports.

I lower the other foot, legs quivering, arms struggling to compensate. My gaze lights on my foot's next target. The farther out I get, the more moss covers the bark. My already shaky feet slip.

Risking a peek back at my starting point, I feel a stab of disappointment; I've only made it halfway. My foot lifts and settles on the moss-covered death trap again, and a crack sends me flying. My arms fling over the side as my sneaker crashes through a rotten section of the log.

I shriek. My hip hits the log, and I bounce. My hand grasps for purchase as I drop down, fingernails digging into the mushy bark. Nothing else is preventing me from falling. I can't hold on long.

A flash of royal blue passes above me. I'm a goner. Mr. Davis will simply flick the delicate, jagged fingernails that tether me to this log. In a few days, rangers will find my body downriver.

I shut my eyes and wait for him to reach me.

24

The world is a dull hum, vibrating in my head. My arms burn. Pain shoots through my nail beds as my fingernails tear. Cold spray from the angry rapids hits my bare ankles where my jeans have inched up.

I don't have enough strength left to pull my head back and check on Mr. Davis.

But he's up there.

All I can do is listen to the water, feel my heart beating in my throat.

I picture myself falling like a sliver of bark, breaking off and dropping into the gushing current. The image plays in my head on a loop. One of these times, it'll be for real.

"Savannah!" The voice bursts through the white noise.

Grant. He heard me. He came.

"Help!" I squeal, my weak voice drowned by the roaring river.

An ounce of resilience that wasn't there a second ago courses into my muscles. I swing my head back to find Mr. Davis above me, teetering on the log.

"I'm coming!" Grant yells, gliding from rock to rock on the bank like a web-footed creature. He scrambles onto the log, but my vision blackens from the effort of craning my neck.

I let my head sink back down, gaze catching the sharp rocks covering the riverbed below. Still feeling spittle on my ankles. My eyes fall shut, but the panic has already taken over. I wait, hoping with every fiery wave of pain that Grant will get to me first.

Then a voice drifts down. "Just hold on. I've got you." Not Grant.

Mr. Davis.

No. He's not going to help. He's going to—but a hand presses down on mine. Unsteady. Fingers slip over my skin. My body sways like a pendant beneath the log. Even the smallest gust of wind could knock me free.

I want to yell for Grant to hurry. But the effort could loosen my precarious grasp. Legs drop down, dangling on either side of the log. Grant's shoes. A second later, another hand—this one firm—grabs my hand from the other side.

My fingers are pried from the log. I don't know whether to scream or try to help.

But Grant grabs my forearm. My body is lifted until I'm secure, sitting on the log. He helps me up, ushering me back along the fallen tree. My limbs shake, but I reach the ravine. Grant's arms hold me up as he guides me down the slope. When we reach the bank, he lowers me onto a rock.

I try to catch my breath, but Mr. Davis comes into focus. He climbs down from the log, and that dark haze covers my vision again.

"He..." I gasp, but the leaves in my periphery flutter. I turn, taking in the orange pop of Noah's jacket, the vibrant red of Sam's flannel shirt. The rest of the group trickles through the brush above, some already scattered nearby on the bank.

Jacey moves to sit down on the rock beside me. Twigs and pine needles are embedded in her disheveled hair and clinging to her sweatshirt. Taking a few ragged breaths, she leans in, placing a water bottle in my hand. "What happened?"

I flick open the cap with bleeding fingertips. "You're asking me?" I hiss. "How did all of you manage to let him out of your sight?"

"I never even found him. By the time I caught up with the guys, they'd already lost track of Mr. Davis. I didn't get a chance to say anything. Just keep quiet."

"It's too late," I mumble. "He knows."

Her eyes grow wide as Mr. Davis collapses to the ground

in front of us, head bent over his knees. His breathing is labored and husky.

I fasten my eyes on him, watching his every move until a rattling sound breaks my focus. Tyler crouches down next to me. "Are you okay?"

I nod, my gaze skipping back to my target, but Grant steps in front of me, blocking my view. He wipes his forehead with the back of his hand, eyes wide as they skim over my torn, filthy clothes and bleeding fingers. "What were you doing, Savannah?"

"I'd like to know the same thing." Abby's boots crunch over the rocks as she moves to stand beside Sam. Noah and Alexandra hover behind us on the slope.

"Let her catch her breath," Tyler says, like he's some kind of saint. He promised he would keep an eye on Mr. Davis, and he broke that promise.

"I was running for my life," I mutter. "The only reason I'm still here is that you guys showed up. Otherwise, I would've ended up just like my sister."

"What do you mean?" Grant asks.

"Just keep Mr. Davis away from me."

Sam eyes me leerily. "It looked like he was helping you, Savannah."

"That's because you didn't see him chasing me through the forest!"

Mr. Davis lifts his head slowly. "Savannah, I had to make sure you didn't get lost. You're my responsibility this

weekend. You all are. I'm so sorry about your sister. I really
am. But you're mistaken. You said Piper came to see me after
school the day she fell, but I never saw her."

A bitter laugh escapes my lips. "Right." I glance at the
others, my tangled blond hair whipping into my face. "He's
not the *responsible teacher* you all think he is. He's dangerous! And he did something to Piper!"

Mr. Davis runs his fingers through his hair. "We have
surveillance cameras in the school halls, Savannah. All the
police have to do is watch the footage from that day."

"Footage that you probably already doctored," I snap.
But my stomach splits, both halves sliding around. If I'm
right and he did edit the footage, he might get away with this.

"You guys," Abby says, looking at us with a mixture of
terror and concern, "I'm sure Mr. Davis didn't *do* something
to Piper. I'm sure he can explain."

She doesn't get it. No one does. I have to make them
understand that our club advisor is dangerous. I unzip my
jacket pocket, dig my mangled fingertips inside. "Then why
was her recorder in his bag?" I tug it out, letting it rest on my
scraped, raw palm for all to see.

Mr. Davis squints at the silver object, and then darkness
shifts into his eyes. "You were in my bag?" There's an unset-
tling edge to his voice.

"You're avoiding the question."

"I know everyone's been under a significant amount of

stress," Mr. Davis says, wiping sweat off his neck with his plaid shirtsleeve. "But you kids can't resort to anarchy. There will be consequences when we get back."

"Yeah, there will be consequences," I retort, raising the recorder. "Because you did something to Piper. And this proves it. She went to see you before she fell, and somehow, you have the recorder that's always in her pocket. The recorder you obviously want hidden."

His lip curls, and he tugs at his collar. "Piper left it in my office. I only listened long enough to figure out it was hers."

"Then why do you still have it?"

He's silent for a too-long beat. "I was going to give it to her the next day, but then"—his eyes lower—"she didn't come back to school, obviously. I meant to pass it off to you, but I kept forgetting to grab it from my office. Right before the hike, I finally remembered and stuffed it in my bag, knowing I'd see you on this trip."

My heart drops another level. Is that all it's going to take for Mr. Davis to weasel his way out of this? Maybe I should've kept that roll of tape. I'll never be able to get to it now.

Mr. Davis kneels down beside the river to splash some water on his face. When he picks himself up, he looks like he's aged several years. "I think I can safely say this weekend's excursion has come to an end. Let's head back to camp and clean up."

Tyler glances at me, and anger needles back into my veins. Why did he abandon me?

We climb the ravine, pushing back through the trees until we reach the camp, where the fire has long since sizzled out. My stuff is already packed, so I rack my brain for a way to escape.

But Mr. Davis is keeping a close eye on us as he disassembles his tent. He's not about to let anyone else wander off.

The others are tearing things down and stuffing their backpacks, and Grant leads me behind his tent by the hand. "Wait a sec," he says before ducking inside to remove his sleeping bag. He folds it once, and then lays it in the dirt for me. "Sit down while I finish packing." He gestures to the cushion he's created and begins dislodging the stakes around the front of the tent.

Once he's finished, he comes around to the back again and kneels at one corner, tugging a stake from the ground. Two other pointed metal pieces lay nearby in the dirt. "Need any help?" I ask, though I'm too fatigued to budge.

He glances over one shoulder. "You have to rest."

I should. I feel like I could collapse and sleep for a thousand years. But something stirs beneath the fatigue. "Grant, do you know anything about Mr. Davis?"

He frowns and moves on to the final corner, still clutching the stake in one hand. "Savannah, come on."

I lick my lips. Forcing myself to my feet, I peer around the tent. "I think Piper caught him helping guys on the soccer team cover up drug stuff."

He smiles subtly but stops working. "That's ridiculous."

"He was the last person to see her that day. She was investigating the boys' soccer scandal, and then, what do you know? Piper falls off a cliff." Grant's hazel eyes, the ones that always mesmerize me, narrow. "And as soon as we can prove it—"

Grant moves so quickly I don't see him coming. I don't even manage a yelp as I'm backed into the tent panel. At his side, the sharp stake in his grip flashes. He looks down at me, the lips I love to kiss pressed tight, the glimmering gold gone from his irises.

Leaving only a storm.

PIPER

The Day She Fell

"What are you doing in here?"

I spin around to see Grant, car keys in hand.

"I-I was waiting for Mr. Davis," I stammer. "I'm allowed to be in here. I'm his TA." But I replace the lid on the paper shredder and back out of the room. Then I brush past Grant to wait on a cement planter in the hallway. He pokes his head into the office and turns back to me, lips tight.

"Aren't you supposed to be at that Survival Club meeting?" I ask.

Grant's brows furrow. "What meeting?"

"Didn't you get a note from Mr. Davis?"

He shakes his head.

"I guess it was only for those of us who need extra help," I say, shrugging. My phone rings in my pocket, and I startle. Grant eyes me carefully as I fumble the phone. It's Alex again, and I debate answering for a moment before picking up.

"Piper?" Alex sounds worried. "Are you at school?"

"Yes, and I'm fine. Please trust me." Then I hang up, guilt already pressing on my chest.

Grant takes a seat beside me, and I keep looking down at my phone, pretending to read text messages.

"Piper, are you okay?"

I almost laugh, the question is so absurd. I'm going to be expelled, and my teacher is covering up a drug scandal. These two thoughts keep spinning around my brain like atoms. I'm frozen to the rough cement. Nothing I've done up until this point will count for anything, all because I trusted my sister to "help" me. All anyone will ever see is the dripping red mark on my file. I'm over.

And my teacher is over.

Sadness wells up in my throat. I became Mr. Davis's TA and joined this club to exonerate him—to prove that he was doing everything by the book so the school board would leave him alone. I looked up to him.

And now? He's gone the way of Savannah and every other person I should've been able to trust. He's probably the one who wrote that threat in my pack.

"Can I give you a ride home?"

I tense. Grant could be involved in this. I never saw his form in that stack. I didn't have time to look for it. "I drove." I stand, but my legs are shaky. "I'll just check in with Mr. Davis in the morning."

"Piper, I don't think I should leave you like this."

"Like what?" I say, already walking away from him. But a new thought rushes into my mind, colliding with the others like a nuclear reaction.

Maybe Grant will help with the piece. Maybe if I can get information from an inside source, my story will hold more weight. Because what else do I really have now? I didn't find any solid evidence in Mr. Davis's office before Grant showed up.

I can't rely on my supposed role models anymore. All they do is prey on the innocent. They take your trust and hold it over a fire, then hammer until it's distorted and warped. Until it's unrecognizable. Leaving you changed for the worse.

If I can prove that Mr. Davis was involved in the soccer drug scandal, his class won't matter anymore. His grades won't matter.

If I can prove his involvement, maybe Savannah and I can get out of this unscathed. Maybe the school will overlook our crimes.

"Actually," I say, turning back, "there is something you can help with. But let's talk outside."

25

Grant hovers over me, his face centimeters from mine. My back presses into the nylon so hard I start to skid with it.

There's a sound—a sharp intake of breath—and I recover my footing in time to see Jacey cover her face, sneakers sliding in the dirt as she spins around.

Grant jerks away, rubbing a hand over the back of his neck.

"Wait!" I call, sliding out from between Grant and the tent while he's distracted. "We weren't—it isn't—"

But what was it? I don't even know.

Jacey looks from him to me, her face red. "What's going on?"

"Nothing." Grant stands there with slumped shoulders.

"Savannah?" she asks.

I'm too weak to think or move. "I don't know," I say, even though a moment ago, I was certain my boyfriend was about to go Van Helsing on me with a tent stake. A stake that's now hidden behind his back. "Grant, put it down," I plead, stepping toward Jacey, who gapes at him in confusion.

"Savannah, you're scaring me," Jacey says. "What's going on?"

"I don't know," I snap.

Grant straightens now, moving closer and pushing himself right between us. "Have you lost your mind?" His tan skin is flushed pink. With anger? "I wasn't going to hurt you," he hisses at me. "I was trying to get you to keep your voice down." But the stake is still at his side, his fingers curled around it.

"Okay," Jacey says, flashing me a warning look. "Message received." She tugs on my arm, but Grant blocks our path.

"Wait." He lets the stake fall in the dirt, a display of passivity. But he's tense. I glance down at his hands, empty now, but still balled so tightly the blue veins pop. My gaze moves to his shirt, to where he missed a button this morning.

I can't stop staring at that undone button. It's like a fly on a TV screen. Everything in me wants to button it, because that's what girlfriends do. But I don't dare reach out.

"You can't just blab about this stuff in front of the whole camp," Grant whispers. "You have to keep quiet until we can get down the hill to safety."

The words should sound protective. He's trying to keep us safe.

Still. The way my boyfriend says *keep quiet* makes every hair on the back of my neck stand up.

"Okay, Grant," Jacey says, attempting to push past him. "We'll keep quiet. Promise."

But he doesn't back up to let her pass.

"Did you—" I start to ask, even though it's a stupid question, maybe even a deadly question. But I have to know. "Do you know something about what happened to Piper? Did you see her that day?"

The letter *c*. Maybe it didn't stand for *coach* after all.

Maybe it stood for *captain*.

Grant sighs loudly through his clenched teeth. He rubs at the back of his neck again, hard enough to leave a mark. "I'm sorry," he says, looking straight at me.

And my heart stops beating.

PIPER

The Day She Fell

"I don't know anything about it," Grant says. I've led him around the main building, following the chain-link fence that borders the athletic fields. The football players must be at weight training, because there's no one around. At least, no one Grant cares about. An occasional cross-country runner jogs by, and color guard flags twirl in the shade of the trees at the far side of the fields.

"Please," I beg, shutting my eyes, racking my brain for how to make him see. But instead, the tears finally come, and Grant stares at me like I've lost my mind. "You don't understand how much I need this. How everything will be ruined if I can't write this story."

"Maybe I should call your sister." He glances at his phone.

"No!" I say, too fast.

"Then talk to me. Don't go snooping around Mr. Davis's office, though." Grant's tone is stern, but his hazel eyes soften as I sniffle pathetically. "He's not covering up some drug scandal. You of all people should know that."

"If you tell me what you know, I'll leave your name out of the story. I promise."

"You'll leave my name out of the story because there is no story."

He turns to leave, but a spark alights in my brain, pushing me to go after him.

"That's not what I gathered from Mr. Davis's office. Some random drug tests were missing. Including yours." This is a complete gamble; I never had the chance to look for Grant's test. "Any idea why that would be?"

He only frowns, so I press on. "Because I have a guess. I think it's because you and those other guys tested positive for anabolic steroids, and now Mr. Davis is scrambling for a way to fake the tests before he sends them to the athletics association."

Grant peeks over his shoulder, then leans in close. "You don't know what you're talking about." His breath is hot on my face.

But I see it in his jaw—a nervous twitch, like a worm beneath the skin, trying to bust its way out. He knows something.

"I'm going—"

"You'll talk, Grant," I interrupt, flinging a strand of hair out of my eye. "Or I will." He licks his lips, and he's still so close to me that my insides bunch up. But I force my shoulders down, force my face to relax. "Now, tell me why some of the drug tests are missing."

He glances around one more time, and then exhales slowly. "Mr. Davis called a handful of us into his office. He said we had to retest because our results had been compromised."

"What does that mean?"

Grant crosses his arms. "If my name comes up—and I mean *ever*—you're going to pay." He bares a flash of teeth like an animal, and I want to back up.

Instead, I force out, "It won't." Despite his threats, Grant knows I have the upper hand. Even if he's not worried about his athletic future, he's still worried about what my sister thinks of him. He can't walk away now. "You can tell me."

He flushes, fingers twisting the sports watch on his wrist. "I let those other guys use my"—his eyes drop down to my sneakers—"*sample* to pass the test. And I guess it was a mistake. The lab must've known we'd all used the same sample."

"You cheated."

"To help out some friends."

"Right," I say, trying to sound indifferent. Trying hard

not to make a comment about how he and Savannah really are a match made in heaven.

A perfect pair of cheaters.

"Mr. Davis made us retest right then," Grant says, "only this time, we went into the bathroom individually, and the door was guarded. Our new test results aren't in his office because it takes a few weeks." He stretches to look out at the lot over my shoulder. "We shouldn't talk about this here."

"Okay, then." I spin around and head down the steps toward the parking lot. "Anywhere you want to talk about it is good with me. Who's driving?" I dig my keys from my pocket, but when I look up, I spot Abby. My steps halt.

Her curly red hair is unmistakable across the parking lot. "Ab—" I start to call out before thinking better of it. Her back is pressed against the driver's side door of a black truck, and she's looking at her phone.

She's supposed to be up on the trail with the rest of the club. Something definitely isn't right. She spins around and says something through the window to a person sitting in the driver's seat. Probably Sam. Which means only half the club was invited to this extra meeting.

Or was it only me?

I want to go over there and ask why she handed me a fishy invitation to a meeting that no one's attending, but Grant is still standing behind me, shoe tapping anxiously on the asphalt.

"Sorry," I say. "So? Where to?"

"I can't be seen with you," Grant hisses. "Not by them. Not if you're going to write this story."

"Not by who?"

Grant scratches his head, then tips it subtly toward Sam's truck.

"Other Survival Club members?"

"They aren't just Survival Club members," he mumbles. "Look, like I said, I never took stuff. Never even bought anything. But I've seen the other guys—the ones who had to be retested—buy stuff. And that scruffy kid..."

"Sam," I say. Grant shoots me a *be quiet* look.

"He's their supplier," he says through barely cracked lips.

"No way."

"I've got to go." He starts fumbling for his keys. "Don't try to contact me about this again."

"Wait a minute," I say, but he's already past the first row of cars. And I'm not sure I care. Because across the lot, Sam gets out of the driver's side of his truck and walks off toward the football bleachers, maybe to have a smoke. I wait for Abby to follow, but she climbs into the passenger side of the truck, and the door clunks shut behind her.

Too many bizarre things are going on, like that invitation to a club meeting that doesn't seem to be happening. And Abby's part of it all. I'm not sure how, but after bending Grant to my will like I have telekinetic powers, I feel like I just might be able to get a few more answers. Abby's dating the dealer, so she might have some.

And she's right over there.

26

"What do you mean you're sorry?" But I ask the question like I'd rather not know the answer.

Jacey tugs on my arm again.

Grant's hands go to his temples, and he backs away from us. "I found Piper in Mr. Davis's office after school. She was in bad shape. Honestly, I thought she was out of her mind. She was mumbling and panicky. Talking about the soccer drug scandal."

So, Piper *was* working on the story. I'm an idiot. Deep down, I knew she hadn't joined Survival Club out of some sudden urge to become more adventurous. But after laughing at her, I never pressed her on it.

Even before the chemistry tests, I was a terrible sister.

"Mr. Davis wasn't there," Grant continues. "I guess she was snooping around, looking through the soccer files. She found the random drug tests, and some were missing, including mine. So she went all journalist on me, trying to get more info." He shrugs like that's all there is to it, and I want to take one of these tent stakes and bludgeon the rest out of him.

"What did you tell her?" I grip the tent pole nearest me like I might collapse without it.

"That Mr. Davis was having some of us retested because we...cheated."

"Cheated?"

"I wasn't using, Savannah, I swear. But I did help some of the other guys pass. It didn't work, though. So Mr. Davis didn't send the tests to the athletics association." He presses a knuckle to his jawline. "Maybe it was shady—I don't know. I just saw it as our coach being there for us. It definitely doesn't mean he had anything to do with Piper's accident."

"It does," I manage to get out, my mind on the audio recorder zipped inside my jacket pocket. On the tape and the rope. "I found Piper's hair matted in Mr. Davis's roll of duct tape."

"What?" Grant shakes his head.

"It was a long, wavy blond hair."

"Mr. Davis has a blond wife," Grant says, forcing my next argument back down my throat. "They go camping together all the time. He told us that at the first meeting."

A wife. Of course Mr. Davis has a wife. He mentioned her the first day of chemistry. I've never seen her photo, though. Never even tried to picture her. I guess with the way the girls at school admire Mr. Davis, it's easy to forget that his heart is at home with the woman he married.

"So, what happened after you told Piper about the drug tests?"

"She sort of...blackmailed me into giving her more information." Grant's gaze shifts to the mountaintops in the distance. "So I told her the only thing I knew: the name of the dealer the guys on the team were buying from." His voice drops even lower, forcing me closer, though every nerve in my body resists. "I had no choice. She was going to write the story either way. She said she was backed into a corner and this was the only thing that could save her."

"And did she try to track down the dealer?" Jacey asks timidly.

"I don't know," Grant says, lifting his hands in surrender. "But, I mean, if Piper wanted to talk to him, she wouldn't have had to go very far. He was right there in the parking lot when I left her."

"Why didn't you tell me any of this?" I ask.

"Because, Savannah! I knew it was my fault for leaving her! I knew she was all messed up. What was I going to do? Tell you I saw her right before she threw herself off a cliff but didn't call anyone or do anything to prevent it?"

"Yes! Then maybe we'd have known she didn't try to kill herself! She said the wrong thing to the wrong drug dealer and nearly got killed for it."

"Savannah," Grant says, reaching forward like he might grab me. "I told you to keep your voice down."

"We're in the middle of nowhere. This drug dealer's not going to hear us all the way down the mountain, I can assure you."

Grant scratches his head, moves his hand down over the stubble on his chin, and breathes steadily, in and out. "The dealer's not down the mountain," he says so quietly I can barely hear him. He lowers his hands and checks behind the tent before he says, "The dealer is Sam."

I take a second, letting that settle. Jacey's jaw drops, and she stares at Grant. But I'm so tired, it's like my face won't work properly. So I smile.

Jacey catches it. "What's wrong with you, Savannah?"

"I'm sorry," I say, still fighting a grin. "It's just—Sam? He's so...*flannel*."

Grant blinks, confused. Even though he got sleep last night, unlike the rest of us.

"He's not *flannel*," Jacey snaps. "He's a knife-wielding psychopath. I don't know why we didn't consider him earlier. He's got 'killer' written all over him."

"So, what do we do?" I ask. "We don't even know if Piper spoke to him that day, since Grant abandoned her at school."

"I'm sorry, Savannah," he says, voice worn. "I wish I'd said something."

Then a thought lashes me like a whip. My stomach curls up on itself. "Did you write the threat in Piper's pack? To keep her from finding out about the drugs?"

Grant's feet shift in the dirt, and I can't even look at him. I'm not sure I'll ever be able to trust him again. Not after the way he backed me into the tent. Not after I looked into his eyes and saw that darkness, something more sinister than I ever imagined, lurking beneath the bewitching surface.

"No wonder you didn't want me investigating that threat. You knew it would lead back to you, so you took the pack from the athletics locker."

"I only wrote it to protect her," Grant whispers. "Jaime Sanderson saw Piper spying on him and Coach. When she showed up in Survival Club a few days later, I knew why she was there. I had to send her a message before someone else on the team decided to handle her."

A cold wind whips through the trees, riffling the tent along with my jacket. I tug my hood up over my head to warm my ears. "And what about the note on our tent, Grant? I suppose that was to protect us too?"

Grant reddens, and pain pierces my chest. I don't want to be here anymore. "Savannah," he pleads. His fingers run through his hair, leaving it standing on end.

"Hey, guys."

I startle, my sneaker sending a rock skidding toward Grant's foot. Alexandra skirts the corner of the tent, her pink notebook tucked beneath one arm. She smiles brightly until she takes in the tableau: Jacey, Grant, and me. Not the prettiest picture any way you try to paint it.

Jacey smiles back, extra wide, and tugs at the neck of her pullover. "Hey, Alexandra. What's up?"

"Mr. Davis is wondering why this tent is still standing. He's antsy to head back down."

"I'm on it," Grant says, looking relieved to get off the topic of Piper.

I watch him as he bends over, yanking the last stake from the earth. Alexandra mouths, *What's going on?* I tip my head toward the woods and motion for her and Jacey to follow me.

I proceed to fill Alexandra in on Grant's version of events as she jots things down in her notebook. When I finish, she looks up at me, biting her lip. "It fits. Piper was following the story, and it led her to Sam."

"One thing doesn't fit," I counter. "In what universe would Piper approach a drug dealer, expecting him to spill?"

Alexandra shrugs, shutting the notebook. "She was desperate after what happened with the chemistry tests. She decided to throw herself into this story despite the risks. Maybe she thought getting a statement from Sam on the record would seal everything."

"I don't know." I run my tongue along my gums, feeling the grit on my teeth. "I can't picture it."

"Maybe it wasn't Sam she spoke to," Jacey offers. "Maybe she tried to get info from Abby. They were close, remember? And Abby didn't hesitate to throw me under the bus when Savannah questioned her. Maybe she was trying to get everyone to look at me instead of at her and her boyfriend."

Ah, Abby the walking musical. She certainly seems like the more approachable of the pair.

"So, they could've done something to Piper together," Alexandra says. She scribbles away in her notebook, teeth clamped on to her lower lip.

"It's a possibility," Jacey says.

I scratch at my hairline, scalp itchy now beneath the hood. "What do we do?"

Alexandra caps her pen. "We should try to find his phone so we can prove there's a connection between him and some of the soccer guys. And maybe we can track his activity if we see his texts from the day Piper fell."

"What if he wiped his texts from that day?" I ask.

"Then I would find that extremely suspicious, and I think the cops would too."

"How do we get his phone?" It won't be lying around. Pretty much everyone's wearing their packs, ready to hike back down.

"We should create a situation," Jacey says. "Something to distract Sam and Abby."

"Hmm, and what would distract our friendly neighborhood drug-dealing murderers?" I attempt to finger comb my hair, wincing when it snags on a broken nail.

A tangle of mischief and pride lights Jacey's eyes. "I think I have an idea."

After the way she totally screwed me over with her last plan, I naturally say, "Fine."

27

We all get into position. I'm by the fire ring, resting the way I should've been this entire time.

I know I've kept secrets—especially where Piper is concerned—but I never imagined Grant was hiding things from me about the day she fell. I was so worried he'd find out about the grading scam; turns out he's just as duplicitous as I am. He helped his team cheat, and he lied about the day of Piper's accident.

And then there's whatever happened when he backed me into the tent. That look in his eyes—everything familiar and gentle leeched from them, replaced by something unknown. Something savage. A shiver racks my body despite the warming weather. Whoever Grant really is, I sacrificed everything to be with him at Mount Liberty next year.

And now I'm not sure I can ever feel safe in his arms again.

I dig my fingers into my pocket, checking that the necklace is still coiled inside. Then I glance down at the ash in the fire ring, not knowing what to hope for but feeling like if I don't find something, I'll collapse into the dirt and never get up again. I'm on my way back to parents who will always resent me for being the one still here, with a boyfriend I no longer trust.

So I stare at the ashes, wishing for answers. Wishing for a home that doesn't exist. Wishing for Piper.

Our plan is a rush job. Mr. Davis is nearly ready to move, just taking care of divvying up the bear-resistant food bags. Sam's and Abby's packs are nestled by a tree a few feet from me. Noah is fake tying his boot, waiting for the signal. Alexandra wanders the camp, pretending to look for trash and any other remnants of our time here. In reality, she's checking out Sam's jeans, making sure he has his phone on him. She glances at me, nods slightly, and something like electricity buzzes through me.

Jacey returns from her "bathroom trip," and the buzz becomes a current. I sit up straighter.

Game time.

"You guys!" Jacey yells. "Come quick! There's a cat, and I swear it's a *Lynx canadensis*!"

"That's impossible," Sam mutters, but he's already on his feet, following Jacey toward the trees.

The rest of the group—Mr. Davis included—drop whatever they're doing to scurry after them, while Alexandra stops at the edge of camp. She'll remain there as a lookout, warning me as soon as everyone realizes the lynx, astonishingly, must've run off to be with his lynx friends.

"I know they're not indigenous, but it's there," Jacey says, running up to Sam. "Here, give me your phone so I can get a photo."

Sam's head rears back. "Can't you just—"

"Hurry! Mine's dead, and this guy's going to get away." She waves her hand in his face. "This could be our only opportunity to document a cat like this around here!"

Sam blinks, clearly overwhelmed by Jacey's high-pitched demands. Somewhere in the woods, Noah whoops like we planned, heightening the frenzied atmosphere. Jacey tosses Sam a panicked look. "Are you really going to stand here and let him scare off the lynx?"

He shrugs, handing her the phone, and Jacey shakes it at him until he unlocks it. Then he grumbles in his rugged voice about bobcats and misidentification as Jacey turns. She crashes into Alexandra, who exchanges her phone for Sam's just before Jacey disappears into the pines, the others chasing after.

I make my way over to Alexandra, who hands Sam's

phone off to me. After one quick nod of encouragement, she pushes the curls out of her eyes and heads into the woods.

Once she disappears, I sprint behind a large tree on the other side of camp and slide down into the dirt, already going through Sam's text messages. Abby's name is at the top, and I scroll through the other names, finding nothing from Mr. Davis or any of the soccer players. The taste of bile stings the back of my throat; a drug dealer isn't going to use his primary phone to make deals or chat about getting rid of someone.

But I've come this far. So for the hell of it, I open the messages from Abby and scroll back to Wednesday, September sixteenth.

And there it is.

[4:05] Abby: Piper's asking questions

[4:06] Sam: I'll take care of it

Cold trickles in like frost filling my veins. My phone is off. There might not be enough time to power it on and snap a photo before Sam realizes there is no lynx and finds me snooping. I take a screen shot and open up a new message to send it to myself. I start to type my phone number when footsteps thud against the earth behind me. The scent of dirt wafts through the air. I open my mouth to say Alexandra's name, and I can taste it.

Then there's a crack. Sharp pain. Light. Dark. Shattering glass.

And I'm falling over.

PIPER

The Day She Fell

Abby's still sitting in the truck, and I walk past, feigning surprise when our eyes meet through the rolled-down window.

"Abby?"

She straightens, pulls her black Vans down from the dash, and shuts her paperback copy of *The Great Gatsby*. "Oh, hey, Piper. What's up?"

"I know I'm a little late, but I was headed up the trail to the Survival Club meeting."

She stares back at me blankly. "It's Wednesday, Piper."

"Right, but the note you gave me from Mr. Davis?" She's

either not following or pretending not to follow. "It said to meet up the trail for an extra session."

Her lips purse as she takes in a slow breath. "Oh, that." She leans against the elbow rest of the door. "Listen, Piper, you should probably know..."

"Know what?" I ask, relieved that someone finally seems to have heard about today's meeting.

Abby twirls a red curl around her finger, and her gaze shifts away from me. "It was canceled, the extra meeting. Mr. Davis couldn't fit it in. Sorry you didn't get the updated memo."

It's a lie, though. Grant didn't get the first memo or the second.

"No problem," I say, already pulling up my text chain with Noah to ask if he got a note.

But then I remember. We're not speaking.

"It's not your fault," I add, lowering my phone. "If Mr. Davis is going to cancel meetings, he should probably stick to holding them on school grounds."

"Right?" She lets out a nervous chuckle.

"I'm a little worried that Crawford is lost and alone up there somewhere." I never call Noah by his last name, and it sounds strange floating through the air.

Abby gives me a knowing smile. "I'm sure he's fine. Mr. Davis's note to you probably just got lost in the office's stacks of memos." She pulls out a pack of gum and offers me a stick. "Is everything still...rough with you two?"

Rough. That would require the two of us to be anything at all. But Noah and I are nothing. Today's conversation at lunch is proof. "Still rough," I admit, moving close enough to smell the truck's cigarette-infused interior. I unwrap the gum and pop it into my mouth. The spicy taste of peppermint coats my tongue. I reach into my jacket pocket for my recorder, but it isn't there. I must've left it back in Mr. Davis's office.

My brain splits and scatters in a thousand directions as Abby stares at me. I turn my phone in my hand and search for the voice memo app I never use, pretending like I'm scrolling through texts. I press record and let my eyes begin to well. I don't have to try very hard; I've been on the verge of tears for hours. "You know," I say, "it's one of the hardest things I've ever been through, and I was thinking..." Abby nods, her head poised in a compassionate tilt. "I've heard that Sam has"—I stop chewing the gum and try desperately to sound like I've done this before—"stuff. To, like, *help* with things. To make me sleep and make things not so hard?"

Abby's mouth drops open, and fear surges in my chest. I've made a horrible mistake by listening to Grant. He must've used Sam as an excuse to get away from me.

But then Abby's lip hitches back up, and she smiles. "Sure, Piper. We can help you out."

And just like that, I've got them.

28

When my eyelids flutter open, light slices through my eyeballs like a blade.

I try to sit up, but pain tears my head in half.

"Help!" shrieks a voice much too close to my ear. The world spins. "Help!" it yells again. There's an arm behind my back now, cradling me. Helping me to sit upright. I bring a hand gingerly up to my head and wince. My fingertips come away painted red.

"Savannah, oh my god, I thought…" I turn to the person helping me, blinking until Alexandra's face comes into focus. "What happened?"

I don't know what happened. But I don't get the chance to tell her this before more voices punch through the trees, followed by footsteps pounding the earth. Every step, every shout feels like it's ripping my already-cracked skull apart.

"What's wrong?" Jacey's voice. I look up to find the others stumbling into camp behind her.

"I found her sprawled out in the dirt," Alexandra says, out of breath from the screaming. "She's bleeding."

Jacey crouches down beside us, and I squint against the blaring sun. The others press closer, and I'm suffocating. My head is pounding. My stomach swirls; I might vomit. Jacey swats a hand behind her. "Stay back," she commands with sudden authority. "I mean it."

Leaning in, she whispers, "Who did this to you?"

"I-I don't know," I stutter. "Someone came up behind me. I thought it was Alexandra, coming to warn me." I swallow, tasting the dirt on my tongue. The dirt I tasted moments ago. Before someone...

I bristle, my eyes snapping to Alexandra. I wrench myself away from her, immediately overcome with another bout of nausea.

"You were supposed to be watching," Jacey hisses at Alexandra. "How did you not see anything?"

"I was looking the other way." Her hands press together. "At the woods, the way you guys headed. Whoever did this came from the opposite direction."

Jacey huffs. "Savannah, did you hear a voice? Try to remember."

I can't. My head hurts too much. I was looking for something. No—I *found* something. Those texts between Sam and Abby.

My gaze darts to Sam, to the pocket of his jeans, which was flat when he headed into the woods.

But it isn't now.

I was hit in the head. When I was digging through Sam's phone. I got too close, and I was caught.

Sam was supposed to be with Jacey, though. Searching for the elusive lynx. I look at him, examining his face for a trace of guilt. "Did you have your eyes on Sam?" I whisper to her.

Her features freeze. "We all scattered to search for that cat," she finally says. "One second, his bright red flannel shirt was in front of me. And the next..." She casts a glance over her shoulder. "He could've gone around the back of the camp."

"Savannah!" Grant barrels through the others, brushing past Jacey and kneeling to take me in his arms. "What happened?"

I look up at him, unable to speak. This is the boy I love. The one who was there for me after Piper's accident. The one who wants to spend his future with me. But snippets of another Grant—the one I saw earlier today—trickle in. When he lifts me, I don't resist, but my insides squirm as he walks me over to a fallen log on the outskirts of camp.

Mr. Davis, the last of the group to make it back, pushes through the small crowd that has shifted to continue gawking at me. "What's going on?" he asks, huffing.

"She hit her head on a branch," Jacey says before I can answer. "When she was looking for the lynx." Nice—no need to let things get any further out of control. If the person who did this knows we're onto him, he may try to finish me off. Or he could beat us down the mountain and start wiping any evidence that's left.

"Not my finest moment," I say, trying for a smile that's probably more of a grimace.

Mr. Davis, too exasperated to move, simply stares at the ground. A moment later, he snaps out of his daze, blinking and rushing off to dig an instant ice pack from his bag.

Grant takes it, pressing it delicately to my head. I let him fuss over me, and I ignore Tyler, who keeps slinging me inquisitive looks. I have to think.

"How's the pain?" Grant asks, hovering over me.

"Not too bad," I lie.

"My girl is too brave for her own good." He shakes his head, the pride in his eyes sending a pang through my chest.

"More like too uncoordinated."

He smiles gently. "I'll find you some painkillers. Be right back." He guides my hand to replace his over the ice pack before trudging over to the others. I adjust my position and concentrate on breathing, the fresh pine aroma all but blotted out by the coppery scent of my own blood.

Noah moves closer to me. "Are you okay?" He bends down to examine me, face rough with worry.

"I'm fine. You know, other than the whole getting-knocked-in-the-head-by-whoever-tried-to-kill-Piper thing."

His eyes widen, and he crouches lower. "Wait a minute. You didn't hit your head on a branch?"

"Of course not," I say, adjusting the ice pack, so cold it burns my scalp. "Hey, you had eyes on Sam the whole time, right?"

Noah reddens. "We sort of got separated, not too long after he lectured me for scaring off the cat."

The ice slides in my grip, grating against my wound. "You had one job, Noah."

He looks momentarily hurt, and I feel a pinch of guilt. I didn't mean to snap at him. I approved this disaster plan. But he recovers, turning to scan the camp. "You really think Sam would do all this?"

I shrug. "His phone is conveniently back in his pocket, the same phone I had in my hands before I was knocked out. And Grant can place Piper a few yards away from Sam and Abby that afternoon, right before she fell."

"Abby?" Noah asks, brow furrowing.

Oh. There's that. The other possibility.

Maybe Sam didn't do this...but his girlfriend did.

I glance at Abby, who's out of breath, her pale, freckled complexion pink. Hood pulled over her head, red curls falling loose to frame her face.

Did anyone have eyes on *her* the whole time? If the mountain cult couple suspected something was up, maybe Abby headed around the back way and took care of things. To keep her boyfriend's secrets safe.

To keep her own secrets safe.

All I know is that we have to get down the mountain. Those texts on Sam's phone—and whatever else he's hiding—are about to be destroyed before the cops ever get the chance to see them.

"All right," Mr. Davis says, taking a seat on a large, shady rock. "We'll rest for a few minutes, until Savannah's in good enough shape to walk. If it's really bad, I have my radio."

"I'm fine," I say. "Can we just go already?"

"Savannah," Mr. Davis says, tugging his floppy hat down, "you could have a concussion."

"I'm a soccer player. I know what a concussion feels like. Trust me, I'll be fine."

I've never actually had a concussion from soccer, but the hard line of Mr. Davis's mouth softens. Like he's considering what I've said.

"All right, but if you need to stop, let me know. I'll use the radio, and we'll have the med team meet us."

"Deal," I say, even though I'm in more pain than the time

I broke my wrist trying to make a two-story blanket fort out of folding chairs with Piper and Jacey.

When he turns to gather his gear, Jacey sidles up next to the log, shaking a travel-size bottle in front of me. "Grant said you were looking for painkillers. Do you remember anything else yet?" she whispers, dropping a couple of pills into my palm and sitting down beside me.

"My back was to whoever hit me." I throw the pills back, washing them down with a swig of water. "But I found a text. A very bad text. One of them—Sam or Abby—hurt Piper that day. And they're onto us." We glance back at the others, and a tingle runs from my toes all the way up to the back of my neck.

"So, then," she says, gnawing on her dirty fingernails, "what are we going to do?"

———

When everyone's standing, backpacks strapped on, we begin our descent. Jacey walks on my left, Grant on my right, both making sure I don't keel over. The pills are starting to dull the pain, but it's still there. Blurring my vision, my hearing, my thoughts.

We keep Sam and Abby ahead of us, where we can see them. Mr. Davis's khaki hat leads the way like before, but he moves more slowly after this morning's fiasco at the river.

I don't know if the cops will listen to us. Not without

Sam's phone. But I have to try. If Piper wakes up, I want her to know that I tried. That I did everything I could to find the person who did this to her. Maybe it'll mean something.

A shadow falls over me, and I flinch. But it's only the rock formations bordering the trail.

I try to focus on our footsteps thudding against the ground like a drum, to let Grant's tall and steady figure at my side ease my fears like it always has. But it doesn't work. I can't relax or feel anything but this knot in my stomach that won't unravel until I get to the police station. I'm impatient. Sam already tried to hurt me once; he could try again.

We reach the fork in the trail, and my thoughts start to climb up the narrow, winding path on the right. I tug my focus back down to the path we're on, locking my neck so that I can't even glimpse that trail. I never want to see the Point again.

Let it find me in my nightmares.

I stop, shrugging my backpack off. "You guys keep going. I'll try my phone. We might have reception here."

"Good idea," Jacey says, but she drags her feet. Grant hesitates, lips twisted as he turns to watch me. But I wave him on. With one last long look, he concedes.

I find my phone, which has been off a record number of hours, and hold the power button until the screen lights up.

A spike of adrenaline runs through me. The phone still has some juice. Just enough.

I catch an unwanted glimpse of my reflection in the screen and cringe. I haven't seen a mirror in days—another record. My lips aren't glossed in Roses Are Pink. My face is more than just tired; it's feral. Leaves and twigs are trapped in my hair, Friday's mascara dried and crusted on the skin beneath my eyes.

The sun casts a glare onto the screen, blotting out my reflection. When I unlock the phone, my stomach pushes up into my throat. There are text messages—tons of them.

The space between me and the others has grown, so I heft my backpack on again and force myself to move forward. But my nerves are frayed, open and raw. Jacey slows her pace to fall in step with me. I catch her glancing at me in my periphery, but my gaze is on the phone, on the text messages.

"Savannah?" Jacey asks. "Are you okay? Is it your head?"

It's not my head. The thrashing pain is the least of my worries now.

I'm focused on my phone. Or maybe not really even on my phone anymore, but rather something just above it. Or maybe nothing, because I'm shaking so much I can barely see at all. My eyes don't even feel like they belong to me.

"Savannah, you're really pale," Jacey says. In front of us, Tyler turns around to look at me.

I try to speak, but my mouth is parched, cottony. I shove my phone at Jacey.

Hesitantly, she takes it, but she doesn't react, only squints at it. She presses the home button, then hands it back to me. "I think your battery died, Savannah. Just tell me what's going on."

"It's Piper." My voice is nothing but an echo. Like my eyes, it's detached. Not my own.

"What is it?" Jacey breathes.

I can't hear my own steps as I walk, trance-like, along the path. I don't hear the others ahead of us or the birds. Only a low, steady hum playing in my head, drowning out everything around me.

Then my voice—the one I no longer recognize—punctures the buzzing, as two words slip out and freeze time.

"She's awake."

29

"She's *awake?*" Jacey asks, her voice grating against my already-throbbing head.

The pain is causing my vision to crack. I try to push the phone back into her hands. "Keep your voice down," I snap. "Did Sam and Abby hear you?"

Ahead, Sam turns around. How much did he hear?

"Sorry," Jacey whispers.

I inhale, letting the breath out slowly, like a leaking tire. "My mom texted me twenty-four times. She called me seventeen times." My hands shake, sweat making the pink case slick between my fingers.

Jacey touches me on the shoulder. "This is incredible news." But neither her face nor her tone matches the words.

I know exactly how she feels. "Yeah."

Tyler falls back into step with us, his eyes wide. "She's really awake?"

Way to go, Jacey.

"We should head straight to the hospital." Jacey's footsteps quicken, and dust rises around the hems of our jeans.

"Someone should go to the cops," Tyler says. "Tell them as much as we know so they can protect Piper. Even if Sam didn't hear what Jacey said, he's going to find out soon enough. Pretty sure *girl wakes up from coma* will make the local news today."

"Do you want to go to the hospital or the police station?" Jacey asks, touching me lightly on the arm.

"I have to go to the hospital. My parents probably already sent out a search party for me."

"Okay, you handle the cops," Jacey tells Tyler. "I'll drive Savannah to the hospital."

He nods, and Jacey treks ahead to join the others. Somehow, my tired, heavy feet have managed to gain some buoyancy. We haven't stopped to rest once, but I get a second wind as we swoop around the mountainside, pushing along the final stretch down the rock-lined trail.

I crane my neck and see the trees thinning out ahead. Catching up with Grant, I stand on my tiptoes to whisper into his ear. "When we reach the school, drive to the police station. Or find someone with a working phone. Tell the cops about Sam. Tell them Piper needs protection." I lick my dry lips. "Don't say anything to anyone, but she's awake."

Grant's mouth falls open. "What? Th-that's amazing. How are you getting to the hospital?"

"Jacey's going to drive me."

"And the others?"

I shrug. "I'll tell them to head to the police station too. Strength in numbers."

"I'm so glad she's awake, Savannah."

I force a swallow. "Yeah."

His fingers wrap around my sleeve. "There's something I need to say." I look up to find a sheen in his hazel eyes.

Immediately, my heart speeds up. I'm not sure I can handle another revelation. Not from him.

Grant's teeth clamp on to his lower lip. "I'm sorry I didn't tell you about seeing Piper that day." His feet shuffle in the dirt. "Or about any of it. I thought I was the last person to see her before she did it and that I didn't do enough to help. To stop her."

My stomach bunches. I understand his fear all too well. I can't fault him for holding out on me. But I can't be swept up by his charm either. This year, I've focused so hard on shiny things—on Grant, being prom queen, and getting into MLC—that I stopped seeing what really mattered. It's like this massive pain in my head has me thinking clearly for the first time. I'm not ignoring what's in front of me. Right now, that's my sister. "Just handle the cops for me, okay?"

He nods, and I speed ahead, the thought of what will happen between Grant and me fading to black as I reach the others.

"Is it true?" Noah asks, his voice low and faltering.

"Head to the cops with Tyler and Grant," I say without slowing.

The trail swerves ahead, and my heart thumps in time with my steps. I break into a run, leaving Mr. Davis and the others behind. He shouts after me, but I ignore him, pumping my arms, backpack bouncing behind me, moving my short legs as fast as they'll go. Mr. Davis is still calling out about debriefing but none of us are listening.

I make it to the small paved lot at the base of the mountain, Jacey and the others right behind me. But as we cross the shady road and head toward the school parking lot, I glance back, catching a flash of red flannel at the base of the mountain.

We aren't alone.

I hurry the others along, and we make the ten-minute walk to the school in half that. Only a few cars speckle the school lot on a Sunday afternoon. We're all racing, Jacey and me to her Honda, the boys to Grant's truck.

I'm almost at Jacey's car. When I move to hop a concrete divider, there's a hard tug on my jacket, and I nearly topple backward. "What?" I snap, turning around to see Tyler, whose face is sickly pale.

He points across the lot. "Does Mr. Davis drive that blue Chevy?"

I blink and follow his gaze to where the beat-up Chevy sits in a shade-strewn patch at the back of the lot. "No, he drives that black sedan." I flick my chin toward the only car in the designated faculty spots closest to the school entrance.

"That Chevy was here when I came looking for Piper on the day she fell. I figured it belonged to one of the teachers. But they wouldn't be here now, on a Sunday." He takes a shallow breath. "Whose truck is that?"

"I don't know. Let's just go." I continue to Jacey's car, and Tyler rushes off to follow Grant.

Suddenly, the Chevy rumbles to life, but I can't see its owner through the tinted windshield.

It throttles into reverse, and the smell of burnt rubber fills the air as it screeches out of the parking lot.

Another scent slinks into its place. Sharp, acrid.

Panic.

I pull open the passenger door of Jacey's car and dive inside. "We have to get to the hospital."

30

"Who drives that blue truck?" I ask as we screech to a stop at yet another red light. "Sam?" It's too hot in here. I wrestle my jacket off, discarding it at my feet.

"I don't know," Jacey says, her eyes fixed on the road. She nibbles the nails on her left hand, right hand on the steering wheel. When the light turns green, she guns it again, turning onto the road that leads to the hospital.

The sun is already low and hidden behind the medical buildings when we arrive. As we park, I scan the lot for the blue Chevy, but there are too many cars.

When we finally reach the fourth floor, a nurse asks, "Can I help you?"

"My cousin and I are here to see my sister, Piper." I point

toward Piper's room, not slowing as I jerk Jacey along by the crook of her arm.

"Go right ahead," the nurse says, smiling and scribbling something down on her clipboard. "Your other cousin is already in there."

My *other* cousin? A new wave of fear laps over me, pushing me down the hall.

I approach the closed door, a cramp of terror seizing my hand as I reach for the handle.

"Wait," Jacey says, grabbing the back of my shirt.

"What is it?" I spin around to find her white as a sheet.

Her eyes fall shut. "I just think..." She goes back to chewing her fingernails, then looks down at the swirl pattern on the laminate floor. I don't have time for this.

I push open the door and step into the room, its white walls muted in the dim light, and my heart slithers down to my feet.

At the center of the room lies my comatose sister, head turned away from the door, blond hair spilling over the pillow.

Still, and anything but awake.

And the person responsible for everything stands over her.

PIPER

The Day She Fell

Now I just have to get Abby on the record saying that Sam dealt to the guys' soccer team. I chew the gum, a gush of peppermint flooding my mouth. Carefully, I plan my next words.

But Abby starts shaking her head, red curls flopping around. "It was Jacey," she blurts. "The note. It was from Jacey, not Mr. Davis. I didn't know what it said when I gave it to you. But she wanted me to help her arrange a meeting up there between the two of you."

"She did?" Anger lances through me. Jacey's lies just keep piling up.

Abby chomps her gum. "She said she wanted to apologize, and she wanted to do it there. I told her I wouldn't lie to you, but I guess I was an idiot to pass along that note without reading it."

Jacey wants to apologize? My rage, sharp and rigid, starts to bend. "Do you think she's still up there?"

"She might be. Maybe"—Abby shrugs—"maybe you don't need pills, Piper. Maybe you just need your friend back in your life. What she did was super messed up, and I doubt anyone has ever tried to apologize this awkwardly before. Like, ever. But she's trying."

She's trying. I think about the drug story, about the segue ready on my tongue. The app on my phone that's already recording.

But *this*.

Finding a way to forgive my best friend. Finding a way to get past this. Wouldn't that be better than some story? I'd finally have someone on my side again. Someone who knows me, inside and out.

Alex is great, he really is. But he's not Jacey. Maybe Jacey can help me get out of this mess. Maybe she'll listen the way no one else will.

I look up at Abby and see the hope flickering in her eyes, and I get a strange twinge of guilt for trying to entrap the only person who's attempted to comfort me about Noah and Jacey.

"Thanks for telling me, Abby." I turn away from the truck, pull my keys from my back pocket, and trek out to my car at the edge of the lot. Normally, I'd walk to the trail, but it's four; Jacey may have given up on me already. I buckle my seat belt like a good girl. Like a girl who's not about to get expelled.

The car is hot, so I roll my window down. A gust of wind ruffles my hair, and beneath the whistling, it sounds like someone is calling my name.

An unfamiliar blue truck rumbles by on the street that borders the lot, and Noah's head sticks out the window. The truck does a U-turn and then enters the lot, parking in the space beside mine.

Noah gets out and ambles toward me. "What are you doing here?"

"Nice truck," I say, avoiding the question.

He shrugs. "It's my brother's. Mine broke down over the weekend, and Nate is taking the semester off. But it doesn't have air, and the seat belt sticks, and—hey, can we talk?"

"Now's not a good time," I say, my voice cracking. My nose is still running from when I conjured up those fake/not-fake tears. "I'm sort of in a hurry." I turn the key in the ignition and reach for the button to roll up the window.

"Piper, please." He reaches out, placing his hand over the window so I'd have to smash his fingers to shut him out. I consider it. "I'm so sorry."

"It doesn't matter, Noah." It doesn't matter that Jacey and Noah both knew the way I felt about him, and they did it anyway. "It was just a date. We went as friends. I was stupid to get so upset. I'm headed up to the Point to tell Jacey the same thing."

"You are?" He keeps his hand on the window, running the other one through his ash-brown hair. The hair I've spent countless hours daydreaming about, hoping that one day, I'd be able to lazily run my fingers through it. Even back when Noah was skinny and awkward—before time carved so many changes on his body—I'd wanted to be held by him. I thought we were there.

"If she's still waiting."

"Well, let me come."

I let out a dry laugh. "You want to come with me to talk to Jacey? How's that going to work?"

"I don't know," he says, shaking his head. "Let me walk you up there. Let me say what I've been trying to say since Saturday. Please. I'll leave as soon as we get there."

"What makes you think I want to hear what you have to say?"

"You don't. I know you don't. But you're my friend, Piper, and I don't want things to be like this. Everything had just gotten back to normal with Jacey, and then I went and screwed it all up. I just want things to be the way they were between the three of us."

Oh. *The three of us.* My chest twinges. This isn't the *I'm sorry I kissed Jacey and now I know I want to be with you, Piper* speech. This is the *let's forget any of this ever happened* speech. Let's forget my hand on your waist, Piper. Let's forget the way my lips brushed your ear when I whispered to you, sending chills through your body. Let's forget the way I said you looked pretty in your homecoming dress and you believed me.

This is *that* speech. The twinge is distinct. It pushes through the aching pain brought on by the rest of the day.

Best friend: gone.

Sister: gone.

What I thought this was with Noah, what I'd hoped for the past seven years: gone.

"At the very least," he says, lips quirking into a half smile, "let me protect you from whatever lurks in the woods on the way up."

And there it is. That little bubble of hope is back.

"You're hardly a match for whatever lurks in the woods," I say, remembering the tales we spun as he, Jacey, and I hiked up to the Point over the years. "But get in. I can always sacrifice you to buy myself time to escape."

His smile widens. "Thank you." He swoops around the front of the car and gets in, the scent of library books and citrus shampoo wafting in with the breeze.

Noah is quiet as we make the short drive to the tiny lot

at the base of Mount Liberty, his hands twitchy in his lap. So much for this apology he's been planning.

I park, and my phone rings again as I turn off the car.

"Who's calling you?" he asks, coming around to meet me.

"No one," I say, pushing back the guilt rising in my throat and slamming the door. I click decline and slide the phone into my back pocket. Noah presses a hand to my back as we start up the rock-strewn slope, and I flinch.

He grabs his hair in a panic. "I'm so sorry. I don't—"

"It's fine," I say quickly, even though it's *not* fine. But I say it because I wish I hadn't flinched. I wish he'd left his hand on my back.

"Do you really think she's still up there?" Noah asks, trying to change the subject.

"Not sure. Have you two...spoken?"

"No, it—look, it was a mistake," he says, eyes on the dirt path in front of us. "What you saw at the dance was a mistake. We'd been joking around, and then Jacey—I don't even know what happened."

So, it was Jacey? She kissed Noah? But why? Jacey has never mentioned liking Noah. She knows how I feel about him.

That little bubble, delicate as it is, grows slightly.

I don't know what will happen with Savannah or the tests, but this moment blurs everything. Noah peers down at me, features ragged with worry. And I keep hoping, even though it will make things more difficult with Jacey.

Jacey, who I'm about to meet face-to-face in the place we've shared all of our fears and secrets and desires. She knew my biggest desire.

Did she really use it to hurt me?

Noah turns to face me, rubbing his hands together nervously. "Look, Piper, there's something I've been meaning to tell you for a long time. Since before the dance. This isn't easy for me."

My heart quickens. This is it. I reach out to take his hand, to calm him.

But Noah's body stiffens. I can feel how delicate my bubble of hope is now. Bubbles are just air trapped inside soap molecules separated only by the thinnest layer of water. The slightest prick can pop the film, leaving nothing but a tiny soapy puddle. Noah smiles, but it's uneasy, so I release his hand. He kicks a rock, which goes skipping off the mountainside. "Go on," I say, turning to walk ahead.

"Wait up!" he calls. "Aren't you going to try and outkick me?"

I force a grin. "I'm not much of a kicker." That was always Noah and Jacey's game. "But sure, I'll give it a shot."

I set my sights on a small stone and wind up my leg. When I make contact, it goes spinning through the air, plummeting into the shrubs that grow along the cliffside.

"Nice one," Noah says with a laugh. That sound makes my heart do a little dance. I could listen to that laugh every second of every day for the rest of time.

When we reach the Point, I shiver. The air up here is so cold compared to below. The place looks empty. It's quiet too. No sound of Jacey chomping licorice.

No Jacey, period.

"Guess I missed her," I say, relief and disappointment tangling inside me. I step forward, leaning against the guardrail so I can peer deeper into the chasm below, and Noah inches closer.

Something about today's events—about being here with him alone for the first time—emboldens me. I pull myself up onto the guardrail like I did that day with Jacey a couple years back.

The memory plays out before me. I was standing with my sneakers threaded through the bars, resting on the lower rail, shins leaning against the top one. My arms were spread wide, like Rose from *Titanic*. "I could be a bird," I said, my body barely tipping out over the canyon. "I could be a bird and fly from here." I leaned farther, testing the rails, tempting fate. So unlike me.

Or maybe just like me. The Piper that could become something else up here, empowered and free. "My wings would take me up there."

I pointed skyward, smiling into the blazing sun, turning to face Jacey with a laugh.

She laughed back. Her shoe carved mindless swirls into the dirt. "How about you stay a girl for today?"

"Fine," I huffed, stepping down onto the gravel. "But they're having all the fun." I nodded toward the chirping creatures that swooped between the boughs of a nearby tree.

This time, I don't stop with my feet on the bottom rail. I don't let Jacey's voice talk me out of it. Instead, I wrap my legs around the top bar, flipping myself up into a sitting position, legs dangling over the cliff.

"Careful." Noah slings an arm around my stomach.

I place my fingers over his, a demure smile tugging at my lips. "What, are you scared? Get up here." I pat the cold metal beside me.

Noah squints through his glasses, considering it. Then he grins, and I'm liquid, dripping down the bars.

He pulls himself up and scoots close to me. "Feeling better?"

"I think I am now, thanks to you."

"Not a problem, m'lady." He tips a hand toward me.

I shiver again, perhaps a little dramatically, and Noah doesn't miss a beat. He shrugs off his orange jacket, draping it over my shoulders.

He leaves his arm slung loosely behind me, and I snuggle back into his chest. His breath is warm on my neck. Tingles course through my body, lighting up every inch of me. I'm more alive than I've ever been. My mind made up, I take a breath and turn, slinging my arms around his neck and pressing my lips to his.

Noah jerks back, eyes wide. "Whoa, whoa, Piper—"

My arms slide from his neck. Nausea kicks me in the gut hard. "I'm going to be sick," I mumble. My breaths are short. Too short. My vision tunnels.

"No, no, you're okay. It's just—you were upset. You got confused, that's all."

"I wasn't confused!" I snap. "I'm in love with you! Don't you know that? I thought…"

Noah gapes at me in horror. "Piper, I'm really sorry. I was trying to tell you. I—I'm in love with someone else."

"Someone else," I say flatly, pulling one knee up and over the bar until I'm straddling it.

It all makes sense. And it all makes the sickness rise in my throat again.

"Someone else who's my best friend."

"I'm sorry," he repeats. But the words are empty and meaningless. It's all so meaningless right now. He's in love with Jacey. She might've been trying to bring me here to tell me the same thing, but right now I don't care.

I just want to stop his empty words. I just want him to hurt the way I hurt.

"You're sorry." I laugh softly, bitterly, and blink away the darkness. "Well, you know what? I'm sorry too," I say, nodding maniacally. "Sorry to be the one to break it to you that no one cares, Noah." I let the words crawl out, punctuating each one with a generous helping of scorn. "When are you going to wake up and realize that Jacey only cares about herself? She just kissed you to punish me. I doubt she spared you another thought after she succeeded."

The gum in my mouth is stale and hard, so I spit it out, watching it disappear into the foliage below. I swing my other leg over the bar, my back to the cliff now. "She used you. Now you're about as useful to her as chewed gum. As far as I'm concerned—and as far as Jacey is concerned—you don't exist."

Yeah, I used Savannah's words. I used them against one of my closest friends. They'd been hanging there at the forefront of my mind ever since I stormed out of Savannah's bedroom.

I want to take them back, to apologize, but then Noah's face contorts, and he grabs my wrist. His fingers clamp down tighter as his eyes narrow. A vein on his forehead bulges, and his hand squeezes harder. I gasp in shock and pain, but he doesn't let go.

Finally, I yank my wrist away, and he releases me. But my momentum takes me back.

Too far.

I topple backward, and Noah scrambles to grab me. But his hand closes around the jacket, which slips free of my body. The orange jacket flaps before me in the late-afternoon air. Like a fiery ball, it flickers, extinguishes, and blazes brighter again.

Then it recedes as my legs fly skyward.

31

"You knew it was him," I say to Jacey, staggering until my hand finds the armrest of the chair in the corner. I sink onto the cushion, my tunneling vision taking a slow-motion, jagged course around the room, finding the machine that blinks and beeps beside the bed. On the opposite side, white curtains hang immobile, no breeze to breathe life into them, only sifted sunlight trickling through.

Noah's back is still to us, shoulders sagging.

"No," Jacey says, crying now. "I mean, not until we saw the truck in the school parking lot. Then I remembered Noah sometimes borrows Nate's truck when his is in the shop. But even then, I hoped I was wrong."

Noah said the last time he spoke to Piper the day she fell

was during sixth period. He said he sat around at home after school.

But he lied. He was parked at the school even after Piper's car was gone.

"I don't understand." I clutch my head in both hands, wincing as my fingertips brush the crust on my scalp where blood has started to dry.

"It was an accident," Noah says, his voice breaking. He turns around, bloodshot eyes rimmed dark blue with exhaustion. "You two played me. You lied to draw me here." He tugs on the neck of his shirt. "She was never awake, was she?"

Jacey only sobs harder. Frankly, I'm surprised she didn't crack earlier. After I was hit and it was clear that someone was onto us, we needed to act fast. We thought we could draw Sam or Abby out by pretending Piper had woken up. Jacey played her part up on the mountain, saying my sister was awake loud enough for all to hear. Loud enough to lure the guilty party to the hospital so they could tie up their last loose string.

"And if she had been awake?" I ask. "What would you have done then?"

"I would've tried to talk to her." He rips at his collar until the fabric frays and lies misshapen. "To apologize."

"Get out of here, Noah," I say, using the armrests to push myself up.

"Just listen."

I shake my head. My eyes flood, and I feel just how drained I am—from the hike, from learning that the boy who was once like my brother may have taken my sister away from me forever.

Beside me, Jacey's crying so uncontrollably that my head feels like it's going to split in half. "Go outside and call Grant," I say, nudging her arm. "Tell him we made a mistake."

She nods, glancing at Noah, her face streaked with tears. Who knows if she'll actually tell the truth about him, but at least she'll keep Sam and Abby from getting dragged into the police station.

Once she's out the door, I turn on Noah. "You left her there." My voice is calm, like a windless sea. But a tremor racks my body, and it takes every ounce of strength to stay on my feet. "She could've died." An even darker truth hangs between us like a barrier as I struggle for air. *The doctors have given up on her. She's already gone.*

Noah is slouching so much that his head is at my level, but his gaze doesn't meet mine. "It's the worst mistake I've ever made, Savannah."

I try to step back, but my leg bumps the chair. "You let everyone—my parents, me—think she tried to kill herself. How could you do that? I thought..." I rub my hand over my wet eyes. "She was your closest friend."

"I know, and I was a coward! I wasn't sure what she'd say when she woke up and I...I freaked."

I look down at my fingertips, stained with the blood from my head wound. "Did you hit me today?"

Noah winces and then grabs at a chunk of his hair, his hand covering half his face. "I panicked." His voice drops. "I knew it was only a matter of time before you guys figured out I was the last person to see Piper."

"So you tried to sacrifice Sam?" The memories are sharp shafts of light, mottled by black tar. Sam's phone in my hand. Splitting pain. Darkness. Alexandra helping me up. Sam coming back to camp with his phone back in his pocket. "You hit me and then passed the phone back to Sam so we'd think he did it."

"He's a drug dealer," Noah spits.

"And you? Who are you, Noah?" In the dim afternoon light filtering through the hospital blinds, I can barely make out the green in his eyes. But I see his face, angular and taut with worry. And the most gut-wrenching part isn't that I never really knew him these past ten years.

It isn't that he broke my sister's heart.

It's that I knew him all along.

I recognized him then, and I recognize him now, even with the familiar green leached from his eyes.

Because we're the same.

We understand each other. We both reach for things that will cost too much. Things that will cost everything.

We both reach anyway, until finally, we grasp a great big handful of nothing.

"This was never what I wanted," Noah says. "I just wanted everyone to..." His head drops into his hands.

"You just wanted everyone to forget about her." With a quivering hand, I twist the doorknob, my own words—my last text message to Piper—smothering every thought. *You don't exist.* Then I push open the door.

Noah watches in silence, eyes shimmering jade again in the fluorescent glow of the hallway lights. And he walks out.

I watch him go, wiping the tears from my cheeks. I shut the door and turn to face the room, the necklace charm pressed between two fingers. Then I pad to my sister's bedside.

"Piper?" I whisper. But she's silent, her body still. Even weeks after her fall, the sight of her twists my insides. A bandage covers her forehead. Every inch of her body is healing from cuts and bruises. "Piper, I'm sorry."

Her chest rises and falls, thanks to the machines. But in every other respect, my sister looks like a corpse.

I move to the other side of the bed, lowering into the chair my mom usually occupies. I take Piper's cold, thin hand in my dirty, bleeding one and squeeze it. "Thank you for what you tried to do at school. I know I didn't deserve it. And I'm sorry I wasn't there for you that day."

I sniffle. "I wish it hadn't been a lie." I wish she'd really woken up. I wish it with everything in me.

A tear falls into her hair. Then another. I let go of her hand to wipe at them and to straighten the once-pristine bedsheet, now marred by tears and dirt. With each drop, something in me starts to yield. Some part that was steely and invincible, but somehow anything but strong. It wears and fractures until I give in. When I do, the tears come harder. I let them.

For once, I'm not trying to be tough in front of Piper. I'm just trying to be her sister.

32

Six Weeks Later

"Go fish," I say, using my splayed cards as a fan even though it's freezing in this hospital room.

Jacey growls and reaches for the draw pile.

I pretend to study my hand another moment. "Chains, give me all your queens."

Alex's head tilts as he squints at me. "Did you peek at my hand?"

I grin deviously over my cards, and he turns to Jacey with his mouth open.

She shrugs. "Just give her the cards."

Begrudgingly, he plucks out one queen and flings it at

me. Then he picks out another, and I throw up an elbow as a shield. "Such a sore loser."

Slamming what's left of his hand down on the tiny table, he stands and stretches. "Break time. Who wants one of those frozen coffee things they sell downstairs?"

Jacey and I raise our hands. "The cookies with the sprinkles too," I add. "Pretty please?"

I bat my lashes dramatically, and his eyes narrow at me in a way that makes my stomach do a little flip. He shakes his head. "Don't you dare look at my cards," he says before slipping out the door.

"He likes you," Jacey says, wandering over to Piper's bedside. "It's *so* obvious."

"Shut up." But I bite my lip to contain my smile.

Sometimes I think Alex could be more than a friend. Sometimes I remember the way he looked at me on the mountain, his brown eyes searing through me, seeing every blackened corner of my soul. *I see you, Savannah Sullivan.* He said it like he could witness those tarnished edges being filed away to something clean, something new.

I get up, yawning and dragging my chair over to join her. "You know I'm not thinking about boys."

She rolls her eyes, but she gets it. Neither of us is thinking about boys. While Piper is here, she's our focus. Jacey's trying to be a best friend in whatever capacity she can. And I'm trying to be a big sister. A good one. Right now, that means coming to the hospital every Saturday to be with her. She might not be able to beat us at Go Fish, but I like to think she hears us. That she understands she's part of every game and conversation.

It didn't start off this way with Jacey and Alex. The first Saturday visiting hours after the hike, we all just showed up here at the same time. Things progressed from there. An awkward conversation. A game of Scrabble.

Piper's prognosis remains the same. The doctors don't believe she'll wake up, but my parents refuse to let go.

"How are applications coming?" Jacey asks, straightening Piper's linens.

"Ugh, don't remind me." Trying to fill out community college applications without Piper's guidance has been a nightmare.

After the hike, I got home to find my parents livid. When I turned on my phone that day on the mountain, I really did find a ton of missed calls from them. Only they weren't about Piper; they were about me. Mom had called Jessica's parents after I didn't come home Saturday and discovered I was MIA.

Apparently, Jessica caved and told them about the hike to keep them from reporting me missing. But for a few hours, they really thought I was gone. After everything with Piper, they had to worry about losing another daughter. I felt horrible, so I told them about the chemistry tests, about how I couldn't face them.

It wasn't comfortable, and it didn't solve my problems with my parents overnight. But they listened. They cried with me—for my mistakes, for Piper. They also grounded me from doing anything but going to school and the hospital for eternity.

On Monday morning, I went to Principal Winters and confessed to stealing Mr. Davis's password and changing the grades. Then I handed over Piper's audio recorder so the administration could decide how to handle all of us. And boy, did they handle all of us.

Mr. Davis was fired for trying to cover up the fact that some of his players had tested positive for performance-enhancing drugs. Not even Detective Breslow, who we learned went to college with Mr. Davis, could ignore the facts this time. The team's championship from last year was revoked, and they were banned from the preseason tournament. This season, they have a new coach, and the players are being tested regularly.

They're also back to losing almost every game.

I've been punished for my crimes as well. Not only did I have to miss the soccer tournament that had me resorting to despicable behavior in the first place, I was kicked off the team. I was also suspended from school for two weeks; I was lucky I wasn't expelled. Due to my family's circumstances, the administration chose to be lenient regarding its cheating policy.

Still, my chance of getting into MLC was obliterated. I

barely cared. I'd only wanted to go there to be with Grant, and after everything in Survival Club, I broke up with him. It's still raw. When I see him in the halls, my first instinct is to rush over and slide my hand into his like before.

But things will never be like they were before—not after the way we deceived each other. The only way to build myself back up was to get rid of the rot. And Grant, despite his blindingly gorgeous veneer, was part of the decay that consumed my life.

We haven't told anyone about what Noah did. Jacey begged me to keep it a secret, and I didn't have it in me to crush her any further. More than that, I think Piper would've wanted me to show grace. She would've given Noah the life he nearly stole from her. He still calls me sometimes; I don't answer. He tries to snag my gaze in the halls, in the parking lot. In my heart, I've forgiven him. His conscience is punishing him far more than the law ever could.

And then there's Jacey. She and Noah were in love—at least, their twisted, selfish version of love. Now, he can't get her to look at him.

Two months ago, I never would've imagined spending time with Jacey like this. I never would've believed we could get past our differences. Yet here we are again, side by side in this sterile room, strung together by our darkness.

Or maybe it isn't darkness anymore. The darkness was reaching past what was right in front of me for something I never needed. This—whatever *this* is, with my sister in front of me and my former archnemesis at my side—feels different. Painful, but new. Uncomfortable, but full of possibility. Like the first day of preseason training, when your muscles hurt so bad you just want to soak in a hot tub all day, but somehow, you welcome the pain. Because it's making you stronger.

"Hey, did you bring a brush?" Jacey asks, running her fingers through the ends of Piper's knotted hair.

"Piper never cared about her hair when she was awake." But I turn around and rifle through my purse, which is slung over the back of my chair. "Remember when she gave her award-winning speech in seventh grade? My mom forced her into that fancy velvet dress, but when Piper got on stage, half of her hair was all gnarled and matted with twigs?"

"Literal *twigs*," Jacey says, laughing. "Like, what had she been doing?"

"Who knows." I pull out my brush and spin around, standing over the bed, looking down at Piper's hands. Her fingers are spread out over the sheet. Two months ago, they were battered, the pale skin marbled with bruises. They've all but healed now. It's so strange to think that my sister, whose body can heal, may never regain consciousness.

Reaching down, I start to brush out the dry ends of her hair. "Maybe the stick crown was a fashion statement. Definitely better than her fedora phase."

"She probably found some new species of plant behind the school and fell into it." Jacey rubs her eyes. "Where is Alex with our coffees?"

"Must've gotten his chains caught in the elevator."

"Whatever. You think those chains are hot."

I twist my lips, focusing on working out another knot. "We should definitely check his cards before he gets back, though, right?"

Jacey waggles a finger at me, and I tuck the brush back into my purse. When I turn around again, something grabs my attention.

Piper's hand—the one I was staring at a minute ago. The fingers that were spread flat—they're curled now. Did Jacey move Piper's hand? No, Jacey's been sitting there, whining about coffee and teasing me.

My pulse pounds in my ears until I'm certain I imagined it. Piper's fingers must've been curled to begin with.

My heart sinks, and I sit down. Voices from the hall seep through the door—probably Alex chatting up one of the nurses. He takes his mom's advice about making friends very seriously.

I lean back in my chair, and that's when I spot it again.

My gaze whips to Jacey. "Did you just—" But I see it in her eyes, too, wide as open windows.

My sister's fingers.

They just moved.

ACKNOWLEDGMENTS

It's no less astonishing when an idea transforms into a real book the second time around, and I have so many people to thank for making this happen. To my fantastic editor, Eliza Swift, thanks for your enthusiasm, brilliance, and for always being such a joy to work with. My thanks go out to the entire Sourcebooks team, especially Cassie Gutman, Ashlyn Keil, and Wendy McClure. Thank you to Erin Fitzsimmons and Nicole Hower for the perfectly chilling cover.

My endless gratitude to Julie Abe and Laura Kadner. You two are there for everything, and I don't know why you put up with any of it. May your lives be forever filled with cupcakes and unicorns. Thanks to Laura, Emily Kazmierski, Monica Lewis, Rebecca Kienzle, Karis Rogerson, and Katlyn

Duncan for your early feedback. Thanks to Madeline Dyer and WritersFightClub for your friendship. To Suzanne Park, Alexa Donne, and Dana Mele—thank you for telling me how to do all the publishing things. I would be lost without your guidance.

I'm forever grateful to Kristy Hunter for your help and support with this book. Thank you to my AMM fam—it's been such fun traveling this road with you.

Much love and gratitude to my parents, George and Rebecca Kienzle, for supporting my dreams since the day I was born. Thank you to my Ichaso family and to my Lewis family for your encouragement. To my church family, thank you for your prayers and for always asking how the book stuff is going.

Matias, thank you for being the most supportive husband a girl could ask for. Thank you for all the hours you've spent brainstorming with me, for all the drafts you've read, and all the millions of little things that mean everything. Kaylie, Jude, and Camryn—thanks and hugs for all of your love, encouragement, and patience with me. I consider this book a family accomplishment, especially since we were all stuck at home during a pandemic while I worked on it. Kids, keep writing your amazing stories.

Finally, all gratitude and praise to my Lord and Savior.

Read on for an excerpt of

LITTLE CREEPING THINGS,

another pulse-pounding thriller by Chelsea Ichaso

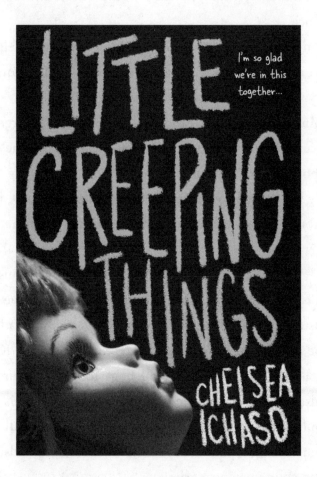

1

"Kill it, Cass!" Tina Robbins yells over the pulsing music. My tank top–clad teammates scramble into position, shoes squeaking across the gym floor.

The ball is a high lob. I take three running steps to the net, inhaling the scent of sweat and deodorant. Adrenaline hums in my ears as I swing my arms, jumping. My palm slices through the air, pounding the ball.

Straight into the net.

I grind my teeth, biting back a curse.

Ever since Coach started trying out new girls in my spot, I've been training day and night. But I'm jittery; this practice is my only shot at tomorrow's starting lineup. Coach's hand is plastered over her forehead. I'm one screwup away from my new friend, the bench.

Laura Gellman, our setter, crouches in the back row, ready for the next serve. She sneers and murmurs, "You can't say the *K* word around Cass. It's like a trigger. It'll give her ideas."

As I find my position, a memory coats my thoughts in a smoky haze. I turn to glare at Laura, but her eyes aren't small and hazel anymore.

They are massive, like a doll's. And bluer than the sky.

Not now.

I blink hard, trying to clear my vision.

Stephanie Reed squats beside Laura, up at the net. But her eyes have gone impossibly cerulean too. Long, spidery lashes line her unblinking lids. The smell of smoke tickles my nose, and a swell of heat crawls up my skin.

"Cassidy, pay attention!" shouts Coach. I pivot, wrenching my mind from the hallucination to focus on the ball spinning over the net. Stephanie dives for it and sends a crisp pass to Laura, who sets it up my way again. I skitter into place, my steps timed to the beat of this über-inspirational '80s song from our practice playlist.

Three, two, one. I jump again.

But the phantom smoke swirls around me, filling my eyes, my lungs. Its tendrils expand into a thick black curtain as I soar through the air. Every voice drowns beneath crackling fire and the groan of the buckling gym ceiling. I search for the ball in the thick darkness, but my face collides with something real, and I fall backward. All around me, flames dance and leap and ash rains down.

I land flat on my back, face stinging. Gasps trickle through the buzzing white noise. I rub my eyes to find everyone hovering over me. Laura is in the middle, pink lips tugging at the corners like she's holding back a smile.

But her irises are back to small and hazel. The smoke has cleared. Not a single flake of white ash clings to my T-shirt or sprinkles the wooden floor.

I get up—much too fast—and shove my way through the swarm of volleyball players. I spot Gideon at the back of the gymnasium, clothed in football practice gear, and rush toward him. The panic starts to fade with each step closer.

Laura scurries ahead of me, flinging her chestnut-colored ponytail and impeding my path. "Cass, are you okay? Do you want me to call the nurse?" Her sugary voice brings on a wave of nausea.

I brush past her, my legs wobbly. *Do not lose it.* "I'm great." Other than the total-humiliation thing. In front of the whole team and the boy of my dreams.

When I reach Gideon, my voice barely emerges over the lump in my throat. "Can we get out of here?"

He studies me for a moment, his olive skin flushed, dark eyes concerned. Then he nods and slings an arm around me.

We exit the gym, the chatter behind us fading, and stop

at our lockers to grab our backpacks. "What were you doing in there?" I whisper.

"I knew today's practice was important, so I skipped warm-ups to watch."

My face ignites. "Pretty impressive, wasn't I? You know, I'm the only volleyball player to nail the triple-axel double backflip mid-spike." I tilt my head. "Minus the spike part."

Gideon squints down at me. "Cass, what happened back there? You can hit that ball with your eyes closed."

"Nothing. Let's just go." Technically, this counts as skipping school because we both have sports for the last period of the day. We sneak down the hall and out the double doors to our bikes. We don't need to exchange a single word about where we're going—we're headed to the underground hideout we built as kids, our one escape.

Any trip to the hideout includes a quick stop at my house for snacks; Gideon is always hungry. My mom's car isn't in the driveway, but we park our bikes against the back gate just in case. The fact that my brother Asher's car is out front doesn't worry me. Before he graduated last year, Asher would have ditched school with us. He was an accomplice in all of our shenanigans.

Asher was accepted to UCLA and NYU but turned them down to start a property management company. My parents were skeptical. *Everyone* was skeptical. It's difficult to imagine someone with only a high school diploma telling grown-ups how to run their investments. But Asher's not most people. My parents said he could live and work from home until he got his company up and running.

We reach the kitchen, where the burnt-toast smell of breakfast lingers. My eyes still sting. How did I let that shiny-haired attention fiend get to me again? I browse the contents of the pantry, tossing bags of chips into my backpack.

"Are we ever going to talk about this?" Gideon's voice is low and gentle. "I couldn't hear what Laura said, but I can imagine." He reaches for my shoulder, and I spin into him, a few tears leaking onto his green hoodie. I look up, and his deep brown eyes wear me down.

I can tell him. He's the one person I can trust with anything. I just don't exactly know *how* to tell him. *Gideon, I hallucinated flaming doll people.* Not quite right.

"Gideon, I think...I might be..." New tactic. "I think I have 'the shine.'" Gideon arches a brow. "You know how Jack in *The Shining* sees creepy stuff around every corner, and he's not sure if it's really there or if he's hallucinating?" I take a deep breath and spit it out. "I had a similar premonition in the gym."

Gideon shoots me a wry look. "You saw demonic twins in the school gymnasium."

"More like I saw the gym go up in flames," I say somberly.

"Wait a minute," he starts, leaning toward me, but the wooden hallway floor creaks and we jerk apart.

Asher saunters in, wearing dark jeans and a crisp gray polo. He stops when he sees us, eyebrows cocked, and gives a curt wave. "I thought I heard voices." His gaze travels to the wall clock above the counter. "Shouldn't you two criminals be somewhere?"

"Uh," I stammer, "yeah. We were—"

"Cass had a rough day," Gideon cuts in.

"What happened?" Asher's skin is paler than Gideon's, but their furrowed brows match.

My face burns as I draw in a slow breath. "Fire stuff."

Both boys bristle, and Asher's fingers graze the jagged pink scars on his left hand. He steps closer. "Who was it? Laura?"

"Calm down. I'm fine."

Asher's shoulders slacken. He steps closer, peering down at me with those crystal blue eyes we share. "I know what you need. A movie night. Tonight?"

I force a smile. "That sounds good." As long as it's not *Firestarter*.

"Great. Maybe Brandon will stop by."

A week ago, the thought of sharing a sofa with Brandon Alvarez would've sent me deeper into depression. Asher's former best friend hasn't been around much since he decided to date Laura Gellman freshman year. Out of loyalty to me, Asher stopped hanging out with him. Then last spring, Brandon and Laura broke up, and Asher got the deluded notion that I'd magically forgive and forget.

It doesn't help that Asher spied Brandon and me getting on swimmingly together at a party last week. I told my brother the truth about my moment with Brandon: we'd discovered we had something in common.

I'll never tell a soul exactly what it was. When the buzz wore off, I tried to go back to despising everything about Brandon, down to that stupid dimple. But I couldn't. Everything's weird now.

Asher's head tilts toward Gideon. "Cass, give us a sec, okay?" I nod. They duck into the hall, and I can't make out a word over the hum of the air-conditioning.

I stand alone in the cold kitchen, backpack heavy in my hands. The whispers floating through the air send pangs into my gut. I hate their guy talk.

Moments later, they slink back in, smiling.

"Okay." Asher checks his back pocket for his wallet. "I ran out of printer ink, so I'm off to see if Carver's has anything remotely compatible. If not, I'll be back in three hours." He's exaggerating, but not by much. Maribel, Oregon, is a tiny former lumber town in the rural depths of the state. We have one drugstore, one diner, one dive bar, and one ice cream parlor. If that doesn't cut it, the nearest shopping center is an hour drive. Though Maribel boasts breathtaking scenery, boredom is the leading cause of death. I don't plan on sticking around long enough to challenge that statistic.

Asher grabs his keys from the hook by the door. "See you tonight." He tosses me one last concerned look before the door clanks behind him.

I turn to Gideon. "What was that about?"

He sighs. "What do you think? He tried to pump me for more information. I honored your wishes and kept quiet. He just told me to watch out for you."

My heart surges and falls. Of course. My brother, the hero. He has a way of making me immensely grateful and astoundingly irritated all at once. "You always watch out for me, Giddy."

Gideon zips my backpack and takes it from me, shoulders rolling as he hefts it on. "Tell your brother that. And tell me we're going to exact some sort of vengeance on Laura."

I follow him out the back door. "Why is she such a terrible person?"

"Please remember she's not really a person. Laura—demon spawn, alien, whatever she is—is jealous of you."

"Sure," I mutter dryly. But we both know why Laura really targets me.

We begin walking through the forested area behind my house. The fragrance of my mom's perfectly pruned jasmines fades, replaced by fresh pine and earth. A cool wind whips through the trees, and I wrap my arms around myself. Gideon stops suddenly, and grumbles, "I forgot about Dave's thing tonight."

Right. Dave Halper's big party. Gideon and the rest of the football players are supposed to go, which means he wants

me to go and keep him company while our schoolmates grope
one another until they puke.

I pick at a fingernail. "We already met our quota of *things*
for the year. Wouldn't you rather stay in tonight and watch
movies?"

"Of course. I just promised I'd stop by. But I can text
Dave that something came up."

He starts walking again and I tag along after him. "Gid—"

"Cass, I'm supposed to be making *you* feel better. Forget
the party. Forget Laura. Let's talk about life's big questions.
Like…what are you going to study in college that combines
your academic prowess with your volleyball abilities?" Gideon
scratches his head as if in genuine, deep thought. "What sort
of profession entails working equations while cramming a
ball into someone's face?" His smile is contagious.

"I'm sure we can think of something," I joke.

"We'll have to make a list of those prerequisites and you
can give them to the guidance counselor, Whatshername, at
your next appointment."

"Whatshername was always my favorite counselor."

"Definitely beats out my counselor, Whatshisname,
a.k.a. Haymitch, when it comes to counsel." Gideon's steps
pause. "Though I'm starting to wonder if the Haymitch thing
applies to more than his uncanny resemblance to Woody
Harrelson."

"Ahhh, you think there's a flask behind the desk?"

"His cheeks are so gosh-darn rosy." He passes me a silly, knowing look, and I punch him in the arm.

We reach the small creek that runs through my family's property. At this hour in the afternoon, the creek becomes enchanted by the sunlight that bursts through the spaces in the trees, making the water shimmer. We carefully hop over a few stones blanketed in green moss to cross to the other side.

Gideon and I approach the barricade of trees that shelters our sanctuary. We crouch down like forest animals and push through the bases of the tree trunks where the leaves thin out. The grass and weeds itch all the way up to our faces.

Once inside the clearing, we kick aside the woven cover of twigs that camouflages the opening. We tug off the large blue tarp, setting it to one side, and use a wooden crate to step down into the roofless, bunker-style hideout. A crumpled math test and a few empty soda cans litter the floorboards. Gideon shoos a stowaway lizard up the wall and brushes aside some cobwebs while I pull out the snacks. Then, using my backpack as a cushion, I settle into a corner, breathing in the musty scent.

This place had been Gideon's idea. When we were ten years old, I read *The Lord of the Rings: Part 1*. Gideon, on the other hand, didn't have the attention span for it. But one day, he appeared before me beaming.

"I saw *The Fellowship of the Ring*," he said, his words dripping with excitement and mischief. "My parents were watching it last night. I snuck out of my room and sat behind them in the hallway."

"You watched a three-hour movie sitting on the hallway floor?" I struggled to imagine Gideon staying silent and still for anything for three hours.

"Mm-hmm." His eyes had a vacant look that let me know he was somewhere else—in this case, Middle-earth. "Gave me an idea."

I thought for sure we were in for an afternoon of sword fighting and arguing over who would get to be Aragorn when he simply said, "We're going to build a hobbit house."

"A hobbit house?"

"It'll be our *secret hideout*. No one will know about it except us."

It was our first secret.

Now, Gideon digs a hand into a chip bag. "And if Whatshername and Haymitch can't help—you know who'd *love* to help you find your true calling? Peter. He can't stop asking about you when he's supposed to be helping with my math homework. He's a smart guy. I'm sure he'll have some ideas about your *unique future*." Gideon is smiling, but his eyes aren't.

Peter McCallum is Gideon's tutor. "He's probably trying a lot harder on your math homework than you are," I mumble. It's an old argument, that Gideon could easily get out of the remedial class if he applied himself.

He munches noisily on a handful of chips, reclining against the wooden boards that make up the underground walls. We'd done a decent job for two ten-year-olds, but our hobbit house ended up more of a glorified six-by-six-foot hole. Dirt seeps through the cracks in places, and we have to be careful to avoid loose nails. Rain sometimes trickles beneath the tarp, leaving a perpetual smell of damp wood.

Leaves rustle above us, and the snap of a twig echoes through the woods. "Shh," I whisper, swatting my hand to silence his munching. "I heard something."

ABOUT THE AUTHOR

Chelsea Ichaso is the author of *Little Creeping Things* and *Dead Girls Can't Tell Secrets*. A former high school English teacher, she resides in Southern California with her husband and three children. When she isn't writing, she can be found on the soccer field. You can visit her online at chelseaichaso.com or on Twitter and Instagram @chelseaichaso.